LINDA HARRIS SITTIG

COUNTING CROWS

Freedom Forge Press, LLC

Counting Crows

by Linda Harris Sittig

Published by Freedom Forge Press, LLC

www.FreedomForgePress.com

Copyright © 2019 by Linda Harris Sittig

Cover art ©Val Fox

Cover photography by Brian Fox and Doug Graham

All Rights Reserved

ISBN: 978-1-940553-09-2

More praise for *Counting Crows*

"A captivating coming-of-age story set in 1918 Greenwich Village, New York City. *Counting Crows* deftly weaves together romance and the hard facts from a time in our country when women yearned for the vote, a flu pandemic raged, and the world was at war. Sittig once again shares a story of a woman of strength."

~Diane Helentjaris, MD, former National President
of the American Medical Women's Association

"When Maggie Canavan leaves her teaching job in rural Maryland behind, setting her sights on Greenwich Village in Manhattan, she discovers that life in New York City means re-inventing herself. Well researched and well written, Sittig has created another great story."

~Mary Younkin-Waldman, author of *To Hear the Birds Sing*

DEDICATION

This book is dedicated to the 146 victims of the Triangle Shirtwaist Fire who died on March 25, 1911, in valiant attempts to escape the raging inferno. The Triangle Factory was located in Greenwich Village, New York City, not far from the ubiquitous Washington Square Arch.

"We don't accomplish anything in this world alone…and whatever happens is the result of the whole tapestry of one's life and all the weavings of individual threads from one to another that creates something."

~ Sandra Day O'Connor
Associate Justice of the Supreme Court

CONTENTS

About the Threads of Courage series

In *Cut From Strong Cloth,* Book #1, we meet nineteen-year-old Ellen Canavan. A strong-minded, young Irish immigrant. Ellen is intent on becoming a businesswoman in the cut-throat Philadelphia textile empire. The year is 1861, right on the cusp of The Civil War.

Rebuffed on all fronts, she enlists the help of factory owner, James Nolan, and together they design a blended cloth of wool and cotton which they intend to sell to the U.S. Government for soldiers' uniforms.

But Ellen is completely unaware that a malicious arsonist is tracking her every move, determined to destroy her dream of becoming a successful textile merchant.

In *Last Curtain Call,* Book #2, we meet Ellen Canavan's adult nephew and niece, Jonathan and Josie. The Canavan siblings have left Philadelphia and come to Porters Glen, Maryland, a coal village. The year is 1894 and the beginning of the United Mine Workers Union.

They meet seventeen-year-old Annie Charbonneau, and Annie and Josie set up a night school for the immigrant miners' wives. As the women become more proficient, the coal company retaliates, and a scandal of sexual abuse becomes exposed.

Resolute to force the coal company to atone for its atrocities, Annie galvanizes the women of the village to fight back. This brings down the wrath of the coal company upon Annie and one official decides that she must be silenced, permanently.

This brings us to *Counting Crows,* Book #3, where we will meet Annie's daughter Maggie. Maggie teaches fourth grade in Porters Glen, but longs to become an artist. She decides to tempt fate and go to New York City for the summer to visit her aunt, and hopefully enroll in art school. The year is 1918 and the Great War (WWI) has changed everything.

Once in New York, the bohemian lifestyle of Greenwich Village beckons Maggie to stay. Torn between her allegiance to her parents and the promise of an adventuresome life in New York, Maggie inadvertently becomes involved with the budding feminist movement and falls in love with the city, the movement, and two men who will forge her destiny.

PORTERS GLEN, MARYLAND

SPRING 1918

ONE

Maggie Canavan glanced at the fashion sketch she had been working on all week. The folds in the skirt still did not fall quite the way she wanted.

Drawn like a moth to a flame, she picked up a pencil, pulled her sketch pad to her lap, and began adding subtle retouches. Lost in her art, she only became aware of the time when the downstairs clock chimed on the half hour.

Oh, Lord! Can't be late again. There's already a note in my file about tardiness.

She splashed water on her face from the china basin and jerked open the wardrobe. A quick decision led her to pull out the new ivory shirtwaist and full-length dove gray skirt. She could dress in the dark if need be, but she chastised herself once again for running late on a school morning.

After a quick peek in the wardrobe mirror, she smoothed down the V-neck collar of the shirtwaist. Its new lower cut design, dipping below the collar bone, would have scandalized conservative women, but it suited Maggie's taste. In her opinion, the sole positive aspect of the Great War was that fashions were finally less rigid. The ridiculous hobble skirt had even been retired.

She pushed her feet into a pair of sturdy oxfords. Sharp bits of coal studded every road, lane, and alley in Porters Glen and would tear soft leather to shreds. Once at school, she could slip on her gray Parisian pumps that had cost half a month's salary but were worth every penny.

With no time to pin the wild wisps of her soft brown hair, she combed the strands up into a quick French chignon. The comb sputtered out of her fingers and fell to the floor. She picked it up and tossed it over her left shoulder – the only way to thwart bad luck for the day.

Then Maggie dashed down the stairs and grabbed her black wool coat and matching hat. The last item was her father's old leather satchel that now belonged to her.

In ten weeks, the school year would be over. Seventy days, to be exact.

It wasn't the children; Maggie loved them. But the expectation of having to follow in her parents' footsteps shadowed every day. Rather than choose education as they did, she wanted to become a fashion artist. What she didn't want was to be stuck in Porters Glen for the rest of her life. She wanted to live where art and fashion peppered the air.

Maggie quickened her pace. Her watch showed the minutes ticking. There was barely enough time to reach her grandfather's bakery, grab the morning paper, and catch the trolley.

When she arrived on Store Hill, Charbonneau's Bakery had already opened. The yeasty smell of freshly baked bread, rolls, and muffins wafted out into the street. Her stomach grumbled.

Maggie darted into the building and made a beeline for the front display. "Morning, Mama."

Annie Canavan stopped fussing with a tray of fresh rolls, wiped her hands on her flour-dusted apron, and came over to give her daughter a light kiss on the cheek. "Maggie, your hat. It's crooked."

"It is? I'm running late."

"Again?"

"No time to chat. Got to catch the trolley." Maggie blew her mother a kiss. Then she grabbed a sweet-potato muffin and stuffed the morning paper in her satchel.

Hastening down the street, she passed a group of miners dressed in heavy overalls and sturdy canvas jackets. Their steel-toed boots clopped on the hard-packed dirt as they jostled with one another waiting for the mantrip to take them down into Mine Number Four.

Thank you, God, that Papa's not a miner. She crossed the middle finger over her forefinger for extra protection.

The distinctive clang of the trolley rang as it approached the village. Maggie held her hat and sprinted.

Moments later she climbed inside the dark-green car and stepped forward to pay the nickel fare to Mt. Pleasant. "Morning, Mr. Lancaster."

"Good morning, Maggie."

As her nickel dropped with a C-L-I-N-K into the receptacle box, the trolley lurched forward. Passengers scrambled to claim seats. Maggie sat down and flipped up the collar of her coat, reminding herself not to sit near the window with a crack in it on the way home.

The tram pulled westward up the Pike, and the crackling overhead wires sang with the ascent. Passengers began to chat with one another.

Now that she had made the trolley, Maggie let out a sigh of relief. Her shoulders relaxed. She noticed that Mrs. Jennings, sitting across from her, was wearing a new coat. It was a navy double warp wool style.

It would look even better with a matching hat.

She unwrapped the sweet-potato muffin. The dense consistency spoke of her grandfather's patriotism. Louis Charbonneau practiced Wheatless Wednesdays even on Mondays. Maggie missed the days of strawberry tarts when sugar and wheat flowed freely at the bakery.

Maggie bit into the muffin, and as the train climbed the incline, she pulled out the newspaper. The headlines alerted readers to the new Daylight Savings Time, set to start on March 31st. This innovation was supposed to save on fuel needed for the military.

Another effort to support the war. How much longer could the war keep going?

She lowered her gaze to the frontpage story and stopped.

A photo depicted a long row of bodies draped with blankets, shoulder to shoulder like fallen comrades along a bleak city sidewalk. Maggie peered at the caption and then clamped her hand across her mouth. The victims were all young women.

Oh, dear God. Instinctively, she made the sign of the cross.

The muffin now tasted like sawdust in her mouth. She swallowed and read the full article.

Seven years ago, this day, over a hundred-eighty young women of the Lower East Side of New York City squeezed out of their crowded tenements and walked together toward the garment factories of Greenwich Village.

When they reached the tall corner building on Greene Street and Washington Place, they dutifully waited for the freight elevator to transport them in small groups up to the eighth and ninth floors. They worked for the Triangle Shirtwaist Factory, producing ten thousand garments per week.

The girls ranged in age from sixteen to twenty-five, with a few older women mixed in. All of them were immigrants, mostly from Italy and eastern Europe and glad for the employment of earning four dollars for a sixty-hour work week.

Unbeknownst to the women, The Triangle Factory had been cited on numerous occasions for unsafe working conditions.

As the girls entered their workspace, flammable tissue paper patterns hung directly over their tables and finished garments dangled above them on thin wires. Every inch of space in the workroom was occupied with rows of crowded sewing machines, large cutting tables, bolts of cloth, and overflowing scrap bins. Only one or two narrow aisles allowed the women to walk from one side of the room to the other.

Close to quitting time -

TO BE CONTINUED: *For the remainder of the story, please wait for the Evening Edition.*

What? Maggie wanted to read the rest of the story. Now.

She wrapped the remains of the muffin and jammed the newspaper back in the satchel.

A moment later, the conductor rang the bell, and Maggie climbed out onto a well-trodden path. She set out across the road, down a lane, and across several more streets until Hillside Elementary came into view.

Pulling open the heavy back door, she walked to the office and signed the time report. Then she went straight to her fourth-grade room, no longer having any desire to chit chat with the other teachers over a cup of coffee.

Within fifteen minutes, a noisy gaggle of thirty students spilled through her door like they had been poured from the wind.

Maggie's classroom, papered with student artwork, was her attempt to encourage budding artists. Although art wasn't part of the established curriculum, Maggie had woven art opportunities into cleverly presented literature and social studies lessons.

She had purchased the supplies with her own money, which annoyed her, but she had decided that incorporating art was the only way she could get through the school year.

Today she had decided on teaching part of the local history of western Maryland. After explaining to the students about the topography of the George's Creek coal area, she gave instructions on how to draw and illustrate a map depicting the different villages scattered throughout the valley.

At lunchtime, Maggie walked with her class to the cafeteria. Usually, she brought her meal and ate with the other teachers in the small faculty lounge. Today the purchase line offered macaroni and cheese with mushy peas.

Ugh, not my favorite. I have to plan better for Mondays.

Balancing her food tray, and leaving the din of the students' lunchroom behind, she headed to the faculty lounge. Her noon break consisted of thirty minutes for lunch and fifteen extra minutes while her class was at recess. The only perk to Mondays was that she did not pull playground duty.

She chatted half-heartedly with the other teachers while she ate the limp noodles and watery cheese sauce. The image of the dead girls from the morning paper stayed with her, and she remained more quiet than usual.

When school let out for the day, Maggie tidied up the room, flicked off the lights, changed her shoes, and grabbed her coat.

Retracing her path from the morning, she arrived on Union Street and purchased the evening paper. Then she walked to the trolley stop.

Close to quitting time - a scrap pile caught fire. No one knows for sure how this happened. With little room to maneuver, women were suddenly stranded at their workstations as the fire jumped from one bin to another and then to the bolts of fabric. Within moments the flames leaped upward to the tissue paper patterns. From there, the fire zig-zagged across the room, igniting everything in its path. The intense heat blew out the windows, and the wind fanned the flames.

Everyone panicked.

Many rushed to the one narrow exit door that was still unlocked. With over a hundred people desperate to escape, pandemonium set in. The few who managed to exit the room on the eighth floor found the elevators were already engaged. The owners, busy with their families on the tenth floor, had quickly shepherded their wives and children to the roof to depart the burning building.

The New York Fire Department promptly responded, but their ladders only reached the sixth floor.

In less than ten minutes, the entire eighth and ninth floors became one raging inferno.

The workers, almost all women, now had two choices: stay and burn to death, or jump from the windows to the concrete sidewalk, multiple stories below.

Sixty-two women leaped to their deaths. Eighty-four more died from burns, smoke inhalation, or being crushed in the darkened stairwell as they tried to escape. All the victims were from the same neighborhood.

In the clean-up the following day, nineteen different engagement rings were found in the ashes and debris.

The owners of the factory, Max Blanck and Isaac Harris survived the catastrophe, as did the manager, S. Steinberger. Both Blanck and Harris stood trial. However, neither man was convicted. It could not be proven that they knew the exit doors were locked.

Maggie shook her head.

Not know the exit doors were locked! How did that happen?

And how old was I? Fourteen? I would have been in my first year of high school, but I only vaguely remember a mention of this event.

Maggie thought of the new shirtwaist she was wearing.

I've always thought the best fashions in America came from New York. But I've never thought about the workers who sew them. The Triangle Factory sounds horrid. I wonder if all the garment factories are that bad.

As she waited for the trolley, a lone miner advanced up the hill, his right hand wrapped in a layer of bandages. His entire body appeared black, covered in coal dirt from his miners' hat to his boots, with only the whites of his eyes peering out on the world.

When he came alongside her, he stopped and took a few deep breaths.

"Do you need help?"

He shook his head. "I'm heading up to Miner's Hospital. Got injured mid-afternoon and the foreman wrapped my hand so I could finish my load. Pain got so bad; I had to quit. They'll dock me for leaving before the end of the shift, but..." he shrugged. Then he put his left forefinger to the brim of his grimy hat, winced, and moved on cradling his injured right hand.

Maggie's eyebrows furrowed.

Doesn't the world care that immigrant girls slave away in factory sweatshops and coal-crusted miners spend their days grubbing in underground tunnels?

The trolley arrived, and Maggie climbed on board. The vehicle rattled east down the main thoroughfare of Mt. Pleasant and headed for the flats outside of town.

Easter was next weekend. Maggie loved the Resurrection Mass and then Grand-papa's special ham dinner with fingerling potatoes. But even the thought of Easter and her new spring outfit could not overcome her present feeling of melancholy.

When the trolley stopped in front of Burnes' Store, Maggie disembarked. The car continued in a cloud of dust without her.

Arriving at the main intersection in the village, she turned toward her grandfather's shop.

Like all the other stores in the village, it needed a new coat of paint. Even paint, however, could not disguise the condition of the old weather-beaten boards.

A gust of wind blew a few dried leaves up against the wooden sidewalk. The breeze reminded her of the newspaper article.

The wind had fanned the flames.

Someone should still care about factory women. Maybe I can visit Aunt Marie this summer in New York and take some lessons on fashion design. Then I could sketch working clothes for the garment girls; perhaps even sell my sketches to a woman's magazine like Ladies Home Journal.

Who am I kidding? No one in Porters Glen cares about events that occur elsewhere. It's as if they're all insulated against the happenings of the outside world.

Or, perhaps, everyone is just too occupied with their own troubles.

That night Maggie wrote a letter to her aunt:

> March 25, 1918
>
> Dear Aunt Marie,
>
> It has been so long since I have written to you, and I still love the beautiful scarf you sent for Christmas. I have worn it all winter.
> How is business going at the hat shop? In spite of the war, we are doing well at the bakery, even though rationing has drastically changed the type of baked goods that Grand-papa offers.
> Winter weather here was beastly, as usual. Summer cannot come soon enough! What plans do you have for summer?
> Love,
> Maggie

TWO

By the third week in May, the weather graced western Maryland with warmth. A delightful breeze chased away the memory of harsh winter winds and brought a promise of longer days and gentler nights.

Saturday shoppers arrived early at Charbonneau's lured by the tantalizing aroma of French bread hot from the oven. For Maggie, mornings spent in the bakery were a welcomed change from the weekly pace of teaching.

"Hello, Maggie."

Maggie looked up from the tray of warm rolls she had in her hand. Two girls from the Berkowitz Shirt Factory greeted her. They had all gone to high school together. Maggie noticed their new Panama sailor-style hats. Plus, one of them had an engagement ring.

"Hello. Can I interest you in fresh rolls, right out of the oven?"

One of the girls leaned over to inspect the baked goods. She inhaled deeply. "Ooh, milk rolls?"

"Yes."

"We'll each take a dozen. How have you been, Maggie? Still teaching?"

Maggie nodded.

"You should come with us to the talkies down in Riverton," continued the first girl.

"Thanks, but I always help my grandfather on Saturdays." Maggie turned to the other girl. "Connie, you're engaged. Who to?"

"Danny O'Neal." Connie stretched out her hand, and Maggie

noticed the diamond was quite small.

"Didn't he enlist?"

"Yes, and I'm counting the days till he gets home and I become a bride." She practically squealed.

"Sure you don't want to come with us?" The other girl posed once again.

Maggie held onto the bakery tray as if it were a lifesaver. "Thanks, anyway."

"Well, you don't know what you're missing." The two girls paid for the rolls and continued chattering as they walked out the door.

Maggie watched them leave and wondered what type of safety precautions were installed at the Berkowitz Factory. If fire could destroy an entire New York garment factory, then, almost any workshop might be unsafe.

Once again, she crossed her middle finger over her index finger.

By two o'clock, all the customers had left, and Maggie helped her mother and grandfather close up the store. The rest of the afternoon would be hers.

The trio walked back to Coal Bank Lane past fields of pink and white wildflowers dotting the landscape. Off in the distance, a mockingbird trilled his mating song. Maggie winced. Connie Moore was a lucky one, even if her diamond was tiny.

Maggie missed getting dressed up and going to the talkies with a group of guys and girls, and she hated the war that had taken all the eligible boys from Porters Glen. She rubbed a tense spot on the back of her neck.

There's no use crying over spilled milk.

Minutes later, they crossed the creaky footbridge over Squirrel Creek and arrived at the white clapboard house that Grand-Papa Louis had built decades ago.

Once they were home, everyone lapsed into their own Saturday routine. Louis took a nap, Annie retired to the parlor with a new book, and Maggie retrieved her sketchbook. Her father, Jonathan, was spending the day browsing in the new library up in Mt. Pleasant.

Maggie liked to sit out on the front porch and sketch the dresses she had seen at Hennessey's Store. Last night, however, she had dreamed about the Triangle Fire again. Now she wanted to sketch a tribute to those girls.

"Mama, I'm going up Piney Mountain to sketch. Be back in an hour or so."

"Be mindful of what's around you."

She had heard that same refrain since childhood, but she knew the mountain trails like the back of her hand. Her favorite spot beckoned.

Grabbing her satchel, she walked to the path and climbed uphill.

After a while, the path forked. Off to the left, a trail led to a rocky ledge with enough space for Maggie to sit. From there, one could look down on an old hunting cabin. Maggie had often drawn its silhouette anchored in a small clearing with the sky for a backdrop.

Retrieving the newspaper clipping she had brought along, she stared at the photo of the girls. Her scrutiny riveted on the body laying closest to the sidewalk's edge. What would that girl have looked like on the last morning of her life? Picking up a pencil, Maggie started a sketch.

She gave the girl dark curly hair framing a round face, and a shy smile. Suspecting that the girl was careful with her money, Maggie penciled in a coat of plain dark wool.

The longer she sketched, the more her shoulders relaxed as the familiar motion of the charcoal pencil skating across the paper soothed Maggie's spirit. She barely even heard the raucous chatter of the three starlings perched in a nearby tree.

She had sketched for over an hour when she spied her grandfather climbing up the path. She put down her pad and walked to meet him.

"Grand-papa, I'm surprised to see you up here."

His face brightened. "Coming to join you. Your mother said you needed to get away from the house. I know that feeling, so I escaped too." He winked.

They walked back up the path until they came to the ledge.

"I suspected this is where you might be."

"You know this place?"

"I walked all over these mountains when I was a younger man. They hold many spots for solitude."

They sat down, and Louis picked up the art pad. "My, these drawings are good."

"Thanks, but I want to learn how to make them better." Maggie hesitated, then took a deep breath. "I'd really like to go to art school."

"I thought you loved teaching."

She shook her head. "I'm only teaching because Mama and Papa wanted me to."

Louis's face registered surprise.

"I planned to quit after my first year, but then Papa had the heart attack. I knew my salary would be an important safety net."

Her grandfather reached out and held her hand.

Maggie took a deep breath, then released it. "I feel trapped here, and my parents are completely unaware of my feelings."

"Maggie, I had no idea."

She chewed her lower lip. "Papa doesn't even see me when Mama's around."

Louis remained pensive. "Your father loves your mother, but he loves you, too."

Maggie shrugged, trying to ignore the silly tears gathering in the corners of her eyes.

"Tell me about this idea of art school."

"I'd learn how to be a fashion artist. Maybe draw for women's magazines."

"Where would this art school be?"

"New York City."

Louis whistled. "Maggie, leaving home is a big decision."

"But you said my sketches were good."

"They are." Louis peered off across the mountain path. "I think what you're really searching for is your north star—your direction in life."

"Why can't art be my north star?"

"*Peut-être*."

"I don't want to stay in Porters Glen forever."

Louis nodded. "Your Aunt Marie left to open a hat shop in New York. I left France to follow my dream of owning a bakery in America."

"Was it hard?"

"*Oui.* I would hate to see you leave, but I want to see you happy." Louis leaned over and squeezed her hand. "*Dieu aide ceux qui s'aident.*"

"Grand-papa, you'll have to say that in English."

"God helps those who help themselves. If art is your dream, then you need to find a way to make it happen."

"But Mama and Papa depend on my salary."

"Your father's health is stronger now. He's back to almost a full load at the college."

Maggie blew out a deep breath.

"And I think the afternoon is running away. We should head back before your mama sends out a search party."

As they wound their way back down the mountain, Maggie worried that her art might not be strong enough to take her to New York City.

***

The next day after attending Mass, Maggie sat in her room and composed another letter. She leaned back in her chair and thought how to craft words so she wouldn't sound desperate.

> May 20, 1918
> Dear Aunt Marie,
> I hope this letter finds you well and that you are enjoying the spring weather. We still had snow on the ground here in April.
> You said in your last letter that you would be working at the shop all summer. I am investigating an idea of how I could become a better artist. Can you tell me about art classes in New York, maybe even art schools?
> This would have to stay between you and me, no use making Mama worry. Please write back in the care of the Hillside School, where I teach in Mt. Pleasant.
> Your loving niece,
> Maggie

Maggie sealed the letter and tucked it in her satchel. She'd mail it tomorrow after school. Then she walked downstairs to the kitchen and saw her mother chopping vegetables for ratatouille.

"Mama, did you ever go to New York City to visit Aunt Marie?"

"Once or twice, but I don't care for big cities."

"Where in New York does Aunt Marie live?"

"Greenwich Village. Why this sudden interest in Marie?"

"A few months ago, I read an article about the Triangle Fire in New York. It piqued my interest in garment factories, and I wondered if Aunt Marie lived near them."

Annie stopped chopping the vegetables. "I don't know, and you certainly don't need to be concerned about garment factories."

"Do you remember the Triangle Fire?"

"Yes. It was a tragic event."

"Were the factory owners ever taken to court?"

Annie stiffened. "Owners of factories, like owners of coal mines, are rarely indicted." Her mother returned to chopping the vegetables. "Dear God, I hope you're not thinking of going to New York. Just be content here."

But I'm not content! And I don't intend to get stuck here, an old maid school teacher.

God helps those who help themselves. Maggie repeated the adage to herself.

The following week a letter arrived at school.

May 28, 1918

Dear Maggie,

How nice to hear from you again. I am sorry you've had such a long winter! We do get snow in New York, but nothing like Porters Glen. There are excellent schools here that offer an art curriculum, like Parsons, Pratt, and Cooper Union. All are quite competitive. Maybe you and your mother would like to visit? I have an extra room, and I live near the schools. You would be most welcome.

Love,
Aunt Marie

Maggie read the letter. She would have to be more forthright. Lord, there was no way she wanted to take her mother with her to New York.

May 29, 1918

Dear Aunt Marie,

Thank you for quickly responding to my letter. To be truthful, I am considering the possibility of enrolling in art school -- hopefully in New York City. My parents don't know about this ambition, so please do not mention it. If I came to visit, it would be without my mother. Would that still be acceptable?

Love, Maggie

Now she'd have to pray that her aunt would still issue an invitation. Maggie crossed her middle finger once again.

THREE

Although Americans practiced food rationing during The Great War, the housewives of Porters Glen faithfully patronized the Charbonneau bakery. Baked goods had changed with the limited amount of sugar, and pastries were only available on holidays. But the women still came to shop and mingle with each other.

This warm Saturday in early June, with the buzz of cicadas in the air, customers arrived early, the hems of their light-weight summer cotton skirts swishing against the floorboards. Maggie greeted the women and listened to their chatter as they roamed around the shop, baskets on their arms.

Later, Maggie breathed a sigh of relief as their number dwindled toward noon. Today had been doubly busy since Grand-papa had stayed home dealing with his arthritis.

She had hoped to hear back from her aunt with an invitation. But no other letter had arrived.

Her thoughts were rudely interrupted by the harsh B-R-I-N-G of the store phone. Maggie kept busy as her mother went to the wall and picked up the black receiver. By the expression on her mother's face, the call was disturbing.

"Who was that?"

"Your Aunt Marie."

Maggie's eyes opened wide. "What did she want?"

"We'll talk about it later after the store closes." Then her mother went back to waiting on the few customers still milling about with baskets of produce and bakery items.

Her aunt wouldn't call to talk about the letters. Would she? Maggie paced through the aisles, eyeing the clock as the last two hours dragged.

On the walk home, Maggie forced a calmness she did not feel. "So, why did Aunt Marie call? Everything okay?"

"Yes. Well, mostly. It seems she fell three days ago and broke her wrist."

Maggie let out an audible sigh.

"I'll explain everything at home, rather than repeat the story for your father."

Ten minutes later, Maggie and her mother climbed up the wooden steps of the front porch.

"We're home!"

Jonathan Canavan got up from his reading chair and kissed his wife. Any bystander would have seen his eyes light up at the sight of her.

"Busy day?"

"Like all Saturdays."

"Papa, Aunt Marie called."

"Marie called?" This came from Louis, who had been napping in his overstuffed chair.

Annie breathed out an exasperated sigh. "It seems she had an unfortunate accident and broke her wrist. I think she tripped over an errant hatbox on the floor."

"*Mon Dieu,* thank goodness it wasn't anything worse."

"And, she was asking if Maggie might come to New York when school lets out and help in the shop. At least until her wrist heals. She said finances are not a problem, and she can even afford to pay Maggie a modest salary."

Maggie swallowed the beginnings of a nervous cough. "Of course, I could go and help." She purposely avoided looking at her grandfather.

"Whoa, Maggie. Your mother and I would need to talk this over."

"If Aunt Marie needs my help, Papa, I should go."

Annie looked at her husband with anxious thoughts everyone could read. "Maggie, this isn't a lark. You have no idea what city life is like."

"But it would be a new experience for me."

Her father turned his gaze from his wife to his daughter. "You'd still have to return home in time for teaching."

"I know that."

"Oh Maggie, you're so young to be on your own in a big city."

Louis cleared his throat. "She would be with Marie. And it would be an adventure. She could even take an art class in the city."

"I still think she's too young."

"Mama, I'll be twenty-two next month!"

No one spoke. An uncomfortable tension settled on the room. Only the ticking of the hall clock broke the silence.

"How old was Aunt Marie when she left for New York?"

Louis answered, "Nineteen."

"See, Mama, I'd be three years older."

In a small voice, Annie whispered, "But Marie never came back. She stayed there."

"Oh, Mama, is that why you're worried? Of course, I'll come home."

"Can we talk instead about something more pleasant? Like your upcoming birthday. Is there a special gift you'd like?"

Maggie stared straight at her mother. "I'd like to go to New York. It's the only gift I want."

***

In the last ten days, Maggie had sailed about her classroom, packing up for summer. Still surprised her parents had agreed to let her spend the summer in New York, she couldn't wait to get on an eastbound train.

Her mother had suggested they go down the mountain to

Riverton to shop for a traveling outfit. They found the perfect dress at Rosenbaum's, a black and white shepherd-check. Black satin loop trimmings with matching buttons cascaded down the front, providing a contrast of fetching details. Her mother's sense of fashion was paired with practicality because the skirt afforded enough space for Maggie to climb gracefully on and off a train platform.

Now, June twenty-first had dawned with glorious swirls of a mauve and pink sunrise, a fitting salute to Maggie's upcoming departure.

Jonathan, Annie, and Maggie left Riverton on the early morning train to Washington D.C. and spent the ride talking about Marie and how city life differed from Porters Glen.

"One thing you need to know is that Marie doesn't usually tell people where she's from, and she goes by the name of Anne-Marie in New York."

"Why?"

"Probably embarrassed she grew up in a coal village. As for using Anne-Marie, I think she wanted to sound more French. You know, for the hat shop."

"Why hasn't she ever come home to visit?"

"I've invited her numerous times, but she's always too busy."

When her parents began talking to each other, Maggie rested against the back of her seat. Outside, the scenery rushed by with a blur of green foliage and wild pink blossoms.

Once they arrived in Washington, her father hailed a cab, and the three rode in comfort to the Hotel Washington, a block from the White House.

When they entered the hotel lobby, Maggie's eyes widened. Glistening chandeliers hung over the black and white patterned tile floor. Several people lounged on tufted beige velvet chairs while others sat on small burgundy-colored sofas. Everyone seemed to be reading a book or chitchatting with each other.

Maggie couldn't help but notice the number of couples she saw. So, not every guy was a soldier.

A young man dressed in a crisp hotel uniform picked up their suitcases and placed them on a cart. Then he disappeared. "He's the bell boy. He'll take the cases up to our room." Maggie marveled at her father's ease in a hotel. She guessed it was a result of his growing up in Philadelphia.

Their room was on the fourth floor. Two single beds, both draped in beautiful white cotton chenille, greeted them. Between the beds, a small but ornate mahogany chest held an electric lamp for reading and a small cut-glass vase filled with white daisies. Maggie sat down and spread her fingers out over the chenille cover.

Her mother came and sat next to her. "You can always tell the quality of fabric by feeling the threads."

Maggie looked around. "There are only two beds."

"Your father will sleep on a folding bed the hotel will provide."

"But I don't want Papa to have to do that."

"Nonsense, this is your birthday. We both want it to be memorable."

"Thank you."

Maggie walked over to the china pitcher and bowl on the washstand so she could clean her face. Picking up the linen cloth, she dipped it in the cooled water and wiped her forehead and cheeks. *Wow, not like the old chipped bowl in my room back home.*

After freshening up, the three travelers took the elevator down to the lobby, and her father steered them toward the hotel's restaurant. "Order whatever you want, Maggie." He smiled.

A man appeared, as if by magic, and asked, "A table for three?"

They walked to ivory damask-covered tables, also centered by vases of white daisies. The man pulled out her chair and waited for Maggie to sit down.

The menu offered many selections with French names. Maggie already knew that *Vichyssoise* meant a cold leek and potato soup, and *Filets de Soles Bonne Femme* would be a white fish cooked with mushrooms and wine. She silently thanked her grandfather for teaching her so many French translations through the years.

Maybe I will be able to handle myself in a big city, after all.

After the meal, they walked outside the hotel.

"Jonathan, let's walk down the street so we can see the stores."

Maggie saw her mother hang onto her father's arm the way a woman in love touches the arm of her sweetheart. *I hope I find their kind of love myself one day.*

As the trio sauntered east on F Street, Maggie stopped in front of a store called Garfinkels. The window display flaunted an aura of class and money with mannequins dressed in the latest fashions.

"I'd love to sketch those figures," Maggie said, pointing to the window. But her parents were whispering to one another. The familiar feeling of invisibility descended on her. She shrugged, telling herself that by tomorrow she would be in New York City and off to a fresh start.

***

When Maggie climbed aboard the eastbound Royal Blue the next morning, the excitement of going to New York erased the awkward feelings from the night before. Decked out in her new black and white checked dress, she looked the part of a confident young woman traveler.

She kissed her mother and tried not to acknowledge Annie's silent tears, but Maggie's voice came out thick with emotion as she said, "Good-bye."

Her father helped Maggie climb up into the vestibule while he carried her valise and suitcase. He found a Pullman porter and asked him to stow the luggage in the baggage compartment.

Then he turned to Maggie. "I see you're taking my old teaching satchel. Don't get any foolish ideas about teaching in New York."

"I promise."

He gave her a longer than usual hug. Maggie assured him she would be fine. As he turned back to look at her one last time, she blew him a kiss. He left, and Maggie sat down on a plush red leather seat and looked out the window. Her mother waved, tears now streaming down her cheeks. Maggie's father put his arm around his wife's shoulders.

Maggie waved to them both. Here was the freedom she had been craving, but the reality of leaving made her palms sweat.

Then she blew out a deep breath and busied herself by inspecting the train.

The Royal Blue cars had been painted a deep Saxony blue with gold leaf trim, and each one had a fully enclosed vestibule opening to a spacious leather seating area. The interior walls were of polished mahogany, and the lead glass windows were reminiscent of church windows. Victorian-styled gas lights now used electricity, so every seat had lighting capability.

With a chug and blast of steam, the train inched out from Union Station. Maggie strained to catch the last glimpse of her parents, still holding each other for support, then she settled back in her seat.

Dear God, please make this the right decision. What if she and her aunt did not get along? What if she couldn't find any art classes? What if she hated the big city life?

She bit her lower lip, then tucked the shoulder bag under her arm.

No turning back now. I'm on my way.

GREENWICH VILLAGE, NEW YORK CITY

SUMMER 1918

FOUR

"Is this seat taken?"

Maggie peered into the warm brown eyes of a stranger. He smiled and nodded to the empty seat next to her.

"No, go ahead and take it if you like."

He removed his bowler hat and placed his valise on the shelf over the seat.

Maggie calculated him to be slightly older than she and sporting the mannerisms of a person accustomed to railroad travel. He sat down, cradling a smaller travel bag on his lap.

She tried not to stare.

He's wearing the new two-tone spat boots. So, he cares about his appearance, and he can afford to dress well. It's hard not to notice how his clothes complement his trim figure. I wonder why he's not in uniform.

"I've made this trip many times, but never had the pleasure of sitting next to a girl as pretty as you."

Maggie blushed.

"I'm sure you've heard that before."

"I don't know whether to say thank you or call the conductor."

The stranger broke into spontaneous laughter. "Call the conductor because I paid you a compliment?"

"I'm not used to strangers being so...cheeky."

"Cheeky? I'm a photographer and believe me; I know a pretty face when I see one. Allow me to start again."

"How so?"

"May I introduce myself? I'm photographer Charles Finch, of New York City. There, is that better?"

Maggie smiled back. "All right then, I won't call the conductor." She turned her head to peer out the window.

Mr. Finch waited a few moments. "I assume you're going to either Philadelphia or New York?"

Was this common on trains? Did passengers talk so freely with one another?

"Yes, that's correct."

"Which one, the city of brotherly love or magical New York?"

Maggie hesitated. "My destination is New York."

"Good, then we will have the pleasure of each other's company for the rest of the trip. My friends call me Rees."

Maggie nodded politely. "Mr. Finch."

"Rees, please."

"But we're not friends, only train acquaintances."

Rees let out another hearty laugh. "Well, if you're going to New York, perhaps we'll become friends."

Maggie's safety intuition went on full alert, but she found herself drawn to flirt with him. He was quite good looking with his shock of brown hair, and dimpled smile. It had been such a long time since she had enjoyed any male company.

"Are all New Yorkers as outspoken as you?"

"I am a born Southerner and taught to be friendly with the ladies." His eyes danced with amusement.

"And what is a Southerner doing in New York?"

"I told you, I'm a photographer. Here, I'll show you my camera." Rees gently removed a camera from the bag on his lap. "A Graflex. Isn't she a beauty? It's what all the press photographers use."

"I'm afraid, Mr. Finch, I know nothing about cameras."

"We have a couple of hours before we pull into Penn Station, so let me take your picture, and I'll teach you about the camera."

"Take my picture, here? On the train?" Maggie laughed with the impromptu delight of serendipity.

"Why not? It will be my keepsake of how we met."

"Mr. Finch, your statements are bold with presumed familiarity." Maggie forced herself to turn away from his mischievous gaze.

"Smile!"

Maggie found herself turning and grinning, even though she was trying to retain her composure.

C-L-I-C-K.

"Now that I've taken your picture, we have to become friends. I have an idea. We can play the parlor game of Twenty Questions. That way we can get to know each other."

"But we are not in a parlor. And what if I don't want to play?" She teased.

"Ah, but you do, I can see it in the catch lights of your eyes."

"My catch lights?"

"Yes, the tiny point of light in your pupils that lights up the eye in photography."

"And these 'catch lights' let you know that I'm willing to play Twenty Questions?"

"Yes, indeed."

"Very well, Mr. Finch. I'll play. Who goes first?"

"Remember, we each get to ask ten questions of the other person, and both of us must answer truthfully. I do have one rule, though, that I insist upon."

She waited. "And that is?"

"You must call me Rees. After all, parlor games are played among friends."

"You are persistent, aren't you? Very well, Rees. I'll start. Where in the South were you born?"

"Savannah, Georgia. My turn. What is your name?"

Maggie smiled at his cleverness. "Magdalena Canavan, or… Maggie to my friends. Why are you not a soldier, Rees?"

"I'm colorblind and was rejected."

"Colorblind? How can you be a photographer?"

"That counts as question number three. I see black and white with shades of gray, but I cannot discern the difference between similar colors like black and dark blue. Why are you going to New York, Maggie?"

"We hardly know each other, and you are comfortable calling me Maggie?"

"Question number four! Do you live in New York or just visiting?"

Maggie waited a moment, calculating her answer. "I will be in New York for the summer, living with my aunt. How did you get a nickname like Rees?"

"It's a family name on my mother's side. How did you get the nickname of Maggie?"

"I'm named after my grandmother, Magdalena. What type of photography do you do?" *I think that's question six.*

"I freelance as a photographer wherever I can get hired. What do you do, Maggie, back home? I see you're not wearing a wedding ring."

"I teach grammar school, fourth grade. I'll ignore your comment about a ring. Where is your favorite spot in all of New York City to take photographs?"

"Washington Square. Do you like teaching?"

Maggie hesitated. "I like children. Do you miss the South?"

Rees now paused. "My parents died in a railroad accident when I was six, so I don't remember much about Savannah. An aunt and uncle took me in and raised me in Annapolis. Where did you grow up?"

"Porters Glen, Maryland. Why did you move to New York?"

"I wanted to become a newspaper photographer. What does your aunt do?"

"She's a milliner. My parents have cautioned me that city life can be dangerous. Would you agree?"

"Any place can be dangerous if you are not aware of your surroundings. I'm sure your aunt will point out the sections of New York to avoid. Where is her shop?"

"That's your final question. It's in Greenwich Village. Do you know that section of the city?"

"You can't ask me that. It would be the eleventh question." He cocked his left eyebrow and grinned. "I'll answer your last question if I get to ask one more of you."

"All right."

"Yes, I know Greenwich Village quite well. Do you plan to work in your aunt's shop?"

"At least for the summer. I'm hoping to take art classes, or maybe even get into art school."

"That sounds ambitious. You're too pretty not to succeed. What type of art?"

"Are we still playing the game? You've gone over your limit."

"Ooh, and you're smart as well." He grinned. "I'd still like to know about your art."

"I love to sketch and am hoping to become a fashion artist for a woman's magazine."

"New York is certainly the place for that. Just don't give up. The city is a hard task maker."

It sounded like an odd comment, but Maggie kept the thought to herself.

With still an hour left to travel, Rees demonstrated to Maggie how his camera worked.

Although she knew little about cameras, she found herself genuinely interested. Capturing a photo was similar to her attention in drawing an image. Maggie admired his devotion to his craft and his care of the equipment.

He's an artist, like me.

Then he leaned into her and pointed out the window. "There she is, Maggie, New York City."

Maggie peered out the window, but not before she had inhaled the scent of his shaving cologne. Not having any brothers, she wasn't used to the proximity of a male body. She found the sensation quite pleasing.

"So, what do you think, Maggie?"

Maggie turned back to him. "Oh, my. I knew it was big, but I didn't realize how far it stretched."

"I've made this train trip countless times, and I still get excited when the New York skyline comes into view. She's a city like no other." His eyes twinkled with enthusiasm.

As the train pulled into Penn Station and lurched to a stop, Maggie felt goosebumps on her arms. They had entered a cavern-like space filled with multiple rail tracks. Train whistles blew, and iron wheels screeched to a halt. She craned her head and momentarily forgot about Rees Finch as she stared at the countless passengers ascending and descending different platforms. In an attempt at the farewell, the train belched a cloud of steam.

To Maggie's ears, the sounds were magical.

"A lot of noise, huh? But you'll get used to it. The city has a pulse all its own. We've entered Penn Station, the busiest of all New York train depots."

Maggie nodded, lost in the wonderment of it all.

"I'll stay with you until you meet your aunt."

"That's not necessary. I'll be fine."

Rees threw his head back and laughed once more. "Well spoken, but a bit naïve. You don't exactly know where she's meeting you. Am I right?"

Maggie averted her gaze.

"All right, then. It's time to disembark. But I am going to stay with you."

Reese grabbed his travel bag and helped Maggie retrieve her suitcase from the porter. "I assume you sent a trunk ahead?"

"Yes, of course. I'm not a ninny."

Rees grinned. "I would never call you that." Leading the way, Rees climbed down first and took her suitcase, then reached for her hand.

Once they were on the platform, the exhilaration of arrival danced around her.

"Your aunt will most likely be waiting on the upper concourse.

Perhaps in the waiting room."

"I'm sure she'll be easy to find," Maggie answered with presumed confidence.

"Here, let me carry your suitcase."

"I'm fine, Rees. Really."

"Have it your way, then."

Rees pressed his way into the crowd. Maggie wobbled as her luggage thumped along the concourse. She held her satchel and valise in one hand and tried to pull the suitcase which now banged up against her leg. People jostled her as they passed.

They climbed the staircase together, and Maggie felt a burning in her calves. At the top, she heard a stirring of birds—pigeons flapping around a honeycombed ceiling amid the yellow glow of electric lights.

She tried to savor the moment. However, the sour smell of human travelers hit her full force. Hundreds of passengers laden with luggage soaked the inside air with their sweaty bodies.

"Maggie!"

Anne-Marie Charbonneau rushed over and gave Maggie a one-arm hug. The two women embraced. "I can't believe you're here!"

Maggie stood back for a moment. She did not remember when she had last seen her aunt. Anne-Marie did not look anything like Maggie's mother. Where Annie wore sensible clothes that gave a hint to fashion, Anne-Marie looked like she had stepped out of the pages of *The Ladies Home Journal*. No one in Porters Glen would wear silk to anything other than a fancy wedding, but here her aunt wore dark blue silk with a fashionable empire waist and stylish hat with matching silk taffeta bow.

No Gibson Girl hairstyle, either. Anne-Marie's coffee-colored curls peaked out from under her gorgeous hat and softly framed her face. It wasn't only the clothes and hair that set her aunt apart. Even with a war going on, Anne-Marie Charbonneau managed to be a glamorous woman. Maggie wondered if Anne-Marie had always been this stunning.

Rees cleared his throat.

"Oh, my goodness. Aunt Marie, I mean, Aunt Anne-Marie. I want you to meet Mr. Finch. We rode together on the train. Mr. Finch, this is my aunt, Anne-Marie Charbonneau."

"I am pleased to make your acquaintance, Ma'am."

"Thank you for helping my niece, Mr. Finch."

He nodded. "The trip became more enjoyable."

Anne-Marie's eyes scanned him from head to toe. "Are you in the city on business?"

"I live here. I'm a photographer."

"What type of photography?"

"I often take portraits."

Her shoulders eased a bit. "Well, if you are ever in need of renting hats for a photography session, please come to my shop. Anyone in the Village can point it out—Hats by Anne-Marie."

"Thank you. Good-bye, Miss Canavan. Good luck with your summer in New York. I'm sure we'll run into each other again."

Maggie lowered her lashes. "Good-bye, Mr. Finch."

He winked at her, picked up his bag, and disappeared into the crowd.

"Maggie, I didn't expect you to meet someone the same day you arrived."

Maggie giggled. "I'll probably never see him again."

"He seemed to be nice. But men here are not always as they appear. You'll need to be careful about the company you keep."

"Oh, Aunt Anne-Marie, I doubt he'll even remember me."

Anne-Marie arched her left eyebrow, a gesture Maggie's mother used as well.

"Let's go. We'll take a hansom cab home. I don't want to get elbowed on an omnibus. And I can't wait for you to see the shop. Do you need a porter?"

"No, I can manage. So, you *did* break your wrist?"

Anne-Marie laughed. "Yes, I did. The accident came at a good time, no? It lent the perfect opportunity for me to invite you for the summer."

Maggie picked up her bag and forced herself not to gawk at all the people as Anne-Marie launched herself into the crowd.

All at once, Anne-Marie stopped and pointed upward. "Isn't the ceiling marvelous?"

Maggie stretched her neck. "It's beautiful! I feel like I'm in an architectural art gallery!"

Maggie soaked up every detail. Graceful steel support beams held up the ceiling. Sunlight from the spider-webbed cantilevered windows danced in patterns on the station floor. Shops and restaurants nestled next to each other throughout the station.

Maggie stopped to look at a young boy.

"He's a shoeshine boy," Anne-Marie said. "He'll polish your shoes after a long train ride."

Would all of New York be this fantastic?

But once outside, Maggie recoiled at the onslaught of commotion. Police whistles shrieked, horses' hooves clopped, trolleys and omnibuses screeched to a halt outside the station. Loud conversations came from every direction.

Maggie had never seen or heard so many people in one place in her entire life.

Then the outside odors hit.

Maggie detected the lingering smells of garbage in the street, competing with the stench of urine and animal feces. She quickly covered her nose and mouth.

Anne-Marie hailed a cab. The vehicle looked strange. No horses pulled it, and the passengers sat inside with the driver on a level above them. The black contraption had an electric motor powering the hack and looked like it belonged in a children's fantasy, similar to Cinderella's coach.

The cab sputtered to life and pulled away from the station. Maggie found herself glued to the open window next to her. As the vehicle picked up speed, she spied a horse-drawn wagon ahead of them. Maggie assumed their driver would slow down, but he pulled around the cart instead. Maggie marveled that the animal took this occurrence in stride and did not get spooked by the faster vehicle. Even after they passed the horse, she could still hear the clip-clop of its hooves.

Maggie didn't want to miss a single detail, although it was impossible not to be a bit overwhelmed. A commotion of people was either crossing the streets, walking in the roadways, or hurrying along the sidewalks, and Maggie could hardly wait to join them.

She glanced up at the first street sign which indicated the cab was traveling along Eighth Avenue at W 31st Street. "What does the W stand for on the street sign?"

"It means the street is on the west side of the city," Anne-Marie answered.

"So, there would be an E 31st Street as well?"

"Yes. The city is divided east-west by Fifth Avenue."

"What about where you live, in Greenwich Village. Is that east or west?"

Anne-Marie laughed. "I live on West 13th Street, between Sixth and Seventh Avenue, which is considered the West Village."

"I thought you said Fifth Avenue marked the dividing line."

"Normally, it is. But many of the street sections have changed since the Dutch laid out the original grid. You'll get used to the quirky pattern."

As the cab whirled along, Maggie turned to take in everything. The tall loft buildings made the stores in Riverton appear small by comparison.

"Driver, please take us over to Sixth Avenue."

When the cab spun left and hurtled down a side street, Maggie clutched her seat. Did all New York cabs travel this fast?

Then the cab abruptly turned right and rumbled south.

"This area is called The Ladies Mile, the most *au courant* area of the New York garment business. It served the carriage trade."

"Carriage trade?"

"Where wealthy women arrived by private carriages and shopped, unescorted. Many stores have moved further uptown, but fashion history started here."

"Like the Triangle Shirtwaist Factory?"

Anne-Marie lowered her voice. "No, that tragedy occurred in the Village. How did you learn about the Triangle?"

"The story was reprinted in the Riverton Times. The photo of those girls' bodies on the sidewalk has bothered me ever since. I even sketched an idea of one of them on her way to work that morning."

"You sketched a Triangle Girl?"

Maggie nodded. "I'd like to use my art to sketch fashions for young working women."

The cab made another right turn and pulled onto West 13th Street.

"The middle of the block, driver. Thank you."

After Anne-Marie paid the cab fare and the driver helped them with their bags, she stood in front of a six-story brick apartment building and said, "Welcome to New York, Maggie; home for the next ten weeks…perhaps more."

Maggie looked up at the apartment building with its five stories and quaint gray-brown brick façade. No residence in even Riverton could compare to this genteel street and demure structure.

"Aunt Anne-Marie, can we wait a minute more? I want to make a quick sketch of my first impressions of where you live."

Not waiting for an answer, Maggie whipped out her sketchpad and drew the rudimentary lines that would allow her to go back and later compose a proper sketch.

"Are you ready now?" her aunt questioned.

Maggie took a further moment to breathe in the aroma of freedom and adventure. Then she picked up her suitcase and entered her new summer address.

FIVE

Maggie woke up feeling a bit tired. She had not anticipated all the late night and early morning city noises. Where at home she fell asleep to the hoots of an owl or cry of a fox, here, motorized vehicles were on the move throughout all the hours.

I'll have to get used to the difference here.

She wrapped a robe over her nightdress and trundled out into the living room, which curiously was only two steps from her bedroom. She peered out the front windows which faced West 13th Street and gazed down on the slender elms that dotted the sidewalk below. They had been a surprise. Their graceful branches gave the surrounding area a feeling of gentility and softened, she hoped, the harshness of the road traffic.

As excited as she was about living in the city, the tiny living space of the apartment, all 891 square feet, had surprised her.

At home, her family had all rambled about in a comfortable farm-style clapboard of two stories and four bedrooms. Why, the kitchen on Coal Bank Lane could swallow up Anne-Marie's kitchen, living room, and hallway combined!

The small space of the apartment was enhanced, however, by the elegant furniture in the living area. A Victorian love-seat with red, blue, and gold flowered upholstery hugged the main wall. Next to it sat a half round mahogany console table with three spindle legs holding a telephone. In the corner, Anne-Marie had showcased a wooden library chair with a moss-green velvet seat. Looking across the room, a small upholstered chair of the same fabric sat in the opposite corner.

The room doubled as a dining room with a walnut pedestal-style table surrounded by four art nouveau style chairs. A large pewter bowl filled with miniature roses made a striking centerpiece.

The last piece of furniture was a slender, carved oak side-by-side secretary desk with an attached vertical bookcase. An amber stained-glass lamp on top gave off illumination.

Maggie wondered if her mother might be a bit jealous of both Anne-Marie's lifestyle and the opulence of her furnishings. At home, the furniture was all serviceable, but nothing special. Here, Maggie felt the taste of luxury, even on a small scale.

She pulled her robe tighter and walked toward the kitchen. The lure of fresh coffee propelled her steps.

"Aunt Anne-Marie, your living room is beautiful."

"Thank you. It took years of attending auctions to acquire what I wanted."

"I see you even have two prints of Wallace Nutting. Are they originals?"

"Yes, his landscape drawings remind me of Porters Glen."

"So, you are a bit nostalgic about home."

"Home is always a part of you, never matter where you move."

The hat shop was closed on Sundays and Mondays, so Anne-Marie announced they could start exploring the Village today.

Maggie watched as her aunt dressed in a simple yet elegant shirtwaist of ivory Moiré silk. Belted over a camel-colored pleated skirt, and with a shapely reverse patterned collar, the blouse gave the slimming hint of a lithe bodice.

Pulling out her Easter dress of lavender and white striped linen, Maggie adjusted the square embroidered collar, so it tucked perfectly into the front yoke of the top. As pretty as it had been for Easter, it needed additional flair here in New York.

"Aunt Anne-Marie, do you have a sash I could add to my outfit?"

Anne-Marie smiled, disappeared into her bedroom and re-emerged with a violet sash. "This should do the trick."

"How are you closing your buttons with a cast on one arm?"

"Very slowly!" Her aunt winked.

Both women donned summer hats of light straw with trendy wide brims and white satin ribbon hat bands. Maggie stepped into the elevator, ready to take on New York.

Out on the sidewalk, Anne-Marie stopped a moment and turned to face Maggie. "The Village still adheres to the old grid plan, and streets often run off in nonsensical ways. Always remember that Washington Square anchors the center of the community. If you can get to the Arch, you can orient yourself."

"Are you afraid I'll get lost?"

Anne-Marie ignored the saucy comment. "We live north of the Square and west of Sixth Avenue. That will always get you back to our neighborhood. Let's start walking; I'm starved."

"Is the entire area called 'The Village'?"

"Yes, but divided into different sections: north, south, east, and west."

"How are they different?"

"Different populations."

"How?"

"The north part is the genteel section, where the wealthy Protestants built their brownstone homes."

"Where are the garment factories?"

"Over in the east, particularly down on lower Broadway."

"And the south and west?"

"South of Washington Square is the low rent tenements, and immigrants who work as day laborers and homeworkers."

"What's a homeworker?"

"Are you always this inquisitive, Maggie?"

Maggie's eyes sparkled. "Only when I get excited." She grinned.

Anne-Marie smiled. "Homeworkers are the women who work the needle trade out of their homes, sewing silk flowers and piecework clothing for the garment business."

"What about in the west?"

"That's filled with artists, writers, and free spirits. While you're living here, you can go north or west of the park, by that I mean Washington Square. But I don't want you to venture alone into the east or south. And especially not the lower East Side. You're still innocent to the ways of the city."

"Lord, Aunt Anne-Marie. You make me sound like a child!"

"You need to be careful. Remember, I came here at almost the same age, and I remember the taste of yearned-for freedom."

"And look how well you've done for yourself, owning a shop."

"Yes."

But Maggie detected a wistfulness in the answer.

"Stop here a minute. See that building beyond the El?"

Maggie had to move her head so she could see beyond the elevated train station.

"Yes. Do we cross here?"

"No. There's a policeman on a stand in the intersection. You cross when he blows his whistle and gives the go-ahead sign. Otherwise, you might get mowed down by a flying cabbie."

Maggie remembered the cab ride from yesterday.

"Over there," Anne-Marie pointed. "That was the original location of Macy's, the most famous department store in New York City. It's on 34th Street now."

The El train station looked far more interesting than the old Macy Building. Three tiers of stairs leading to the top track made it appear like a Swiss chalet straight out of the story of *Heidi*.

The policeman's whistle rang, and the crowd of people streamed into the street. Anne-Marie grabbed Maggie's hand and turned west instead, along 14th Street. After a few storefronts, Anne-Marie pulled Maggie into a small restaurant.

Maggie saw a large chalkboard with its listing of daily specials. But there did not appear to be any free tables, nor space at the counter. Maggie assumed they would leave, but her aunt marched up and stood behind two people who were finishing their meal. Then she turned back and motioned Maggie to join her.

"Isn't this a bit rude?" Maggie had to almost shout over the din of conversations around them.

"Of course not. If you don't move into position, you'll stand all day."

Maggie inhaled the mouth-watering smell of onions frying. The couple got up, turned to Anne-Marie, and smiled, and then vacated their seats. Anne-Marie immediately sat down and motioned Maggie to do the same.

Would other people soon be standing behind them?

"Tell me what you eat for breakfast back home."

"Usually café-au-lait and a treat from Grand-papa's shop. Mama insists on a piece of fruit, too."

"And on school days?"

"A quick cup of coffee and a muffin." Maggie laughed. "I'm usually running late."

"Well, today, I'll order for us both." A woman behind the counter came over, wiped the surface down with a wet rag, and asked Anne-Marie what she wanted.

"Two cups of coffee, both with cream, two small glasses of orange juice, and two plates with fried eggs, rye toast, and potatoes. And, also one order of a plain bagel lightly toasted with cream cheese."

Maggie showed surprise at so much food.

When the plates arrived, Maggie vowed to taste everything, although she wasn't keen on the fried eggs. And what was a bagel?

Maggie dutifully cut into her fried egg, dismayed to see the yolk run out of it.

"Take the toast and dip it in the egg."

Maggie did not rush but followed the directive.

"Well, what do you think of it?"

"A bit soggy. But I'm sure I'll get used to it." She pointed to the bagel sitting on a small plate. "How do you eat that?"

"We each get half. The waitress sliced it for us. Go ahead, take your half and smother it with cream cheese."

Maggie's eyebrows arched.

"It's good. I think you'll like it."

Anne-Marie waited until Maggie had taken two bites, dabbed her mouth on the napkin, and smiled.

"Well?"

"It's not sweet, like Grand-papa's pastries, and you have to chew it, but I like it. Better than the runny egg, anyway."

"Go ahead and finish it. Next time, order a poppy seed bagel. They're delicious, too."

Amid the clinking of cutlery, Maggie sipped the coffee, not nearly as delicious as the café-au-lait at her grandfather's bakery, but satisfying none-the-less. After two forkfuls of potatoes, she drank the orange juice and then placed her utensils across the top of the plate.

"Aunt Anne-Marie, how can you eat this much breakfast and still have such a girlish figure?"

"I don't eat this way except on Sundays. It is my treat to myself, and then I don't eat again until supper."

They finished the meal while two people stood behind their counter stools.

"You'll learn that I did not inherit the gift of cooking from Grand-papa, so I eat out a lot. To my good fortune, the Village has many good restaurants and delicatessens."

"Delicatessen?"

"Wonderful places that sell delicious foods ready to eat. I'm a frequent customer at Murray's Deli. Ready now? We're heading back down Sixth Avenue. I want to take you to Bigelow's. It's where I get my toiletries."

"You have a favorite shop for toiletries?"

"Yes, and once I take you there, you'll be a loyal customer as well."

"It's an entire shop, selling toiletries?"

"No, it's a pharmacy, selling medicines, remedies, and various household needs. Even Mark Twain was a frequent visitor." She held up her cast. "I had to buy some pain medication to help me with this."

"Is the store close by?"

"Yes, across from Christopher Street."

"So, that would be West Christopher Street!"

"No, plain Christopher Street." Anne-Marie smiled.

"I'll never get this right." Maggie let out a sigh.

"Oh, you will. Trust me."

They walked down Sixth Avenue, and the excitement of the hustle and bustle of the street enveloped them. Shops lined both sides of the avenue, and the crowded sidewalks held shoppers of every description. A giant elevated rail loomed above them with trains barreling along the track.

Maggie stopped and looked up; the screech of the rails sounded like a mechanical beast but did not frighten her.

Five city blocks later, they came to Bigelow's sign, O. Bigelow Pharmacy, Established 1838, Free Delivery.

"My goodness. It looks a lot bigger than Red's Drugs in Riverton."

Anne-Marie smiled. "Just you wait."

Maggie entered the store, and her eyes darted to the wooden display cabinets that reached from floor to ceiling. Clerks slid along on movable ladders that hugged the walls, reaching for the higher up, out-of-the-way goods. Display counters piled with alluring products, tempted Maggie to explore.

"We'll head straight to the back so you can meet Mr. Otis, the pharmacist."

They walked toward the rear, passing more enticing displays. At the back, a man dressed in a white laboratory coat wearing thin spectacles broke into a broad grin when he spied Anne-Marie.

"Miss Charbonneau. How nice to see you! Still being bothered by those headaches?"

"Yes, a bit. I'm rationing the aspirin after you told me Bayer would continue to be scarce until the end of the war."

Mr. Otis turned his attention to Maggie. "And who do we have here? Another potential customer, I hope."

"Mr. Otis, this is my niece, Maggie Canavan. She's staying with me for the summer."

"How do you do, Miss Canavan. It will be my pleasure to help you with any medical needs you might have."

"I'm hoping you might have a jar of your wonderful lemon cream for my niece."

"For, you, I always save a jar." He winked at Anne-Marie.

"Here, Maggie." Anne-Marie opened the sample jar. "Trust me; once you use this cream, you'll wonder how you ever lived without it."

Maggie inhaled the pleasant scent of fresh lemons.

"Thank you. I'll pay up front. I need one more item."

"It was a pleasure meeting you, Miss Canavan. Please stop in anytime you need medicine or cosmetics."

They made their way up the right aisle to the front of the store, and Anne-Marie stopped. "I need to buy a new smoother."

"A what?"

"A smoother." Seeing Maggie's confusion, she whispered. "It removes the hair from under your arms."

"It does what!"

"Removes the hair. Ah, Annie doesn't use one yet, does she?"

"I have no idea. My mother never talks about those private matters."

"Summer in New York is nothing like summer back home. Wait till mid-July when perspiration soaks through your clothes. We all use smoothers and Odo-ro-no to feel a bit fresh."

"Odo-ro-no?"

"You wipe it on your underarms, but not directly after using the smoother. I'll teach you how."

What else am I going to learn while I live here?

Leaving the shop, Anne-Marie asked Maggie, "Well, what did you think?"

"It was beautiful. I loved the large glass orbs in the front window."

"Those are apothecary globes. They serve an important function. Did you see they were filled with green liquid?"

"Yes."

"Green shows that no major disease is present in the Village."

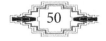

Seeing another confused look, Anne-Marie continued. "Back when most people were illiterate, all shops used a sign to let people know the nature of the business. Apothecaries used large glass orbs to signify a place where one could get medicine."

"But what about the colors?"

"They act as an early warning. Green means no disease. Yellow liquid might signify that Yellow Fever has returned. And if the liquid is red…well, let's hope you never see that. It means an epidemic, like typhoid.

Two blocks further Anne-Marie stopped. "Here is the most important part of the Village, Washington Square."

Maggie gazed up at a magnificent white marble arch. "Oh, my!"

"Mothers bring their children here, lovers stroll hand in hand, and you might see a small group of intellectuals sitting and debating the ills of America. That section over there used to be called 'Tramps' Retreat' with a lot of beggars. But the park is relatively safe, and I never tire of coming here."

Maggie stood mesmerized. The tall white arch anchored the north section of the park, and the main walking area fanned out in a semicircle with a stately fountain in the center. Elm trees lined the borders of the park. People sat on benches chatting, reading, and feeding pigeons.

They strolled inside, on the path.

"Why is there a flagpole so close to the fountain?"

"It commemorates the boys from the Village who are fighting in the Great War. Do you know anyone from back home who is serving?"

Maggie nodded. "Several families have sons in the war."

"I'm sorry to hear that."

"Aunt Anne-Marie, many people here are enjoying themselves. Back home, people rarely do anything for leisure."

"Don't the men still go to Beer Alley?"

"Yes, but none of the women do."

"Well, you'll find yourself coming to the park all summer long."

"Is the Triangle Factory near here?"

"It's over on Washington Place, past the east edge of the park. Do you want to see it now, or can we save that for another day?"

"If it's not too much trouble, I'd like to see it today."

Anne-Marie nodded.

They crossed Washington Park and emerged at Washington Place.

"It's up ahead on the intersection with Greene."

As they continued walking, Maggie sensed the air changing. She listened to her aunt's banter, but it sounded distant.

They stopped on the corner.

"We're here. This is the Asch Building, but after the fire, Mr. Asch restored the obliterated floors and renamed it the Greenwich Building. I think NYU rents the top two levels for classrooms now."

Maggie stood transfixed. The ten-story building of muted red brick had an Italian inspired façade. Tall and impressive with a top floor of arched windows and terra-cotta ornamentation, its beauty belied the tragedy the building had endured.

A man hurried passed them, his head down and his face obscured by his hat.

Anne-Marie stopped. "Mr. Steinberger? Is that you?"

He halted with surprised recognition. "Oh, hello, Miss Charbonneau. I didn't see you."

"This is my niece, Maggie Canavan. She'll be working with me this summer."

The man tipped his hat at Maggie without looking at her. "Must be going. I'm heading to an appointment."

"Certainly. Good-bye, Mr. Steinberger."

"Good day."

The man picked up his pace and headed east toward Broadway. His name sounded familiar, but Maggie couldn't quite place it.

Without warning, a solitary crow swooped down from the sky and perched on the corner street sign. It opened its mouth, and a loud CAW-CAW-CAW reverberated in the air.

"Well," Anne-Marie declared.

"Well, what?"

"Crows. One for sorrow, two for mirth. Three for a wedding, four for a birth. Our old housekeeper, Aunt Hulda, used to recite her superstitions to us when we were young. Counting Crows was one of her favorites."

"So, one crow means sorrow to come, or already happened?"

Anne-Marie turned her gaze back to the Asch Building. "In this case, I'd say already happened."

Maggie suddenly felt the sensation of smoke surrounding her. She tasted a clawing fear in her lungs.

"Maggie, are you all right? You look pale."

"Yes. But it's like I've been here before; during the fire."

"Oh, that's the Irish in you—a vivid imagination. I shouldn't have even mentioned Counting Crows."

Maggie bit her lower lip, but could not shake off the feeling.

The two women turned and walked back toward Washington Square, while the crow did not budge from the perch.

Its sentinel eyes followed their departure.

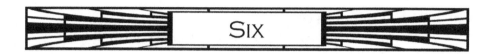

SIX

Yesterday had been a whirlwind exploration, but today, Maggie would finally visit the hat shop. She had imagined the space over and over, but her mother had only shared the barest of details.

"When the weather presents a cloudless sky, like this, I walk. If it's too cold or ungodly hot, then I take the Sixth Ave El. Ready?"

Maggie nodded. By walking, she would see more of the Village.

"One more thing. You'll notice that most of the women in New York dress in dark skirts with light colored shirtwaists for summer. The city is always dirty, shoes and hems both take a beating. Women splurge on buying nice hats instead."

"That helps you with business."

Anne-Marie smiled a Cheshire Cat grin. "We've already walked down Sixth Avenue, so let's go down Seventh today."

Proceeding west along 13th Street, they passed the Village Community Church with its Greek-inspired white columns.

Did Aunt Anne-Marie go to church anymore?

At Seventh, they turned south, passing less crowded stores. When they arrived at the corner of Seventh Avenue and W 11th Street Anne-Marie announced, "Here's our hospital, St. Vincent's."

Maggie gazed up at the towering brick hospital with the hospital name carved in stone over the front lintel. She tried to take in the enormity of the structure. The light-reddish brown bricks were the same as Anne-Marie's building, but Maggie imagined that these had an aura of compassion mixed into the mortar.

"Have you ever been inside?"

Anne-Marie appeared startled by the question. "Yes, many years ago. The Sisters of Charity opened it in the 1890s. It started with a soup kitchen located in the basement for hungry souls and the homeless."

Anne-Marie kept walking to the intersection, and Maggie hurried to catch up.

The street light changed. Anne-Marie turned left onto Greenwich Avenue. Another tower loomed up ahead.

"Aunt Anne-Marie, what's that?"

"The Jefferson Market, but it's been the Jefferson Courthouse since the late 1800s. It's where the famous Stanford White Murder Trial took place."

"Stanford White?"

"The architect who designed the Washington Arch. Unfortunately, he became involved with another man's wife."

"Oh, my. Who killed whom?"

"Stanford White was the victim; quite the scandal."

"The affair or the murder?"

Anne-Marie laughed. "The murder, of course. Anyway, the Jefferson Courthouse is another good landmark. You can always see its tall tower."

"Now, we turn here onto Christopher."

Maggie grabbed her aunt's arm. "Wait, isn't that Bigelow's, across the street?"

"Yes."

"You mean we were that close to the hat shop yesterday, and I didn't know it?"

"We were." Anne-Marie smiled.

Although the morning weather had promised gentle breezes, Maggie's linen blouse was now sticking to her skin. She would have to reassess what clothes to wear when out walking, and perhaps resort to using a smoother as well.

Two shops in from the corner, Anne-Marie gestured to the

front window display. A variety of hats all perched at different levels, but with an array of colors that made Maggie stop and gaze at the artful presentation.

"Let's go in."

Anne-Marie opened the door, and Maggie stepped inside, allowing her gaze to wander around the small shop. A sea of hats was displayed on various stands all around the room, giving the impression of good taste, yet also plausible affordability.

"Aunt Anne-Marie, it's lovely!"

"Thank you. Take your time and look around."

The newest style of low-crowned hats in faux silk and glacé flowers greeted customers as they entered the shop. Maggie waltzed toward the unique displays on the slender glass-top counters. Here, bonnets for fancy outings took center stage, and each one had an embellishment of a satin band, a long ostrich feather, or a nosegay of silk flowers.

Hats with large soft brims and hats with stiff circular rims sat on a side table, perched above turban hats. Poke bonnet mourning hats sat by themselves, while jaunty afternoon cloche straw hats rested at eye level.

Maggie peeked in the full-length mirror and playfully tried on a Panama.

Against the walls, upper shelves stood stocked with Anne-Marie's signature pink and white-striped hat boxes.

Aunt Anne-Marie has all the colors of the rainbow in here.

The range of hues throughout the store reminded Maggie of her grandfather's fruit displays. She experienced an unexpected tug of homesickness.

A few minutes after they arrived, the door opened, and an attractive young girl walked in and headed straight for the back counter. Her sassy demeanor and short-bobbed haircut announced the more outspoken trends of the times.

"Ah, good morning, Isabelle. Let me introduce you to my niece, Maggie Canavan, who is staying with me this summer. She'll work with us here in the shop. It will be helpful to have another pair of hands while I'm waiting for my wrist to heal."

Isabelle's eyes narrowed for a split second and then returned to normal.

"Hello, Maggie. It's nice to meet you."

"Hello."

"Isabelle has been working here a while and can help you get acclimated to how we operate. The most important idea is that we always want the customer to feel valued. Isn't that right, Isabelle?"

"Yes, ma'am, that's correct. Follow me, Maggie. I'll show you where to put your handbag. It's a small shop, so there's not a lot you'll have to memorize."

"Thank you."

The two of them ventured into the small back room while Anne-Marie tended to the front window display, rearranging a hat or two to attract attention.

Isabelle opened a drawer in a cabinet and laid her purse inside. She indicated that Maggie should do the same. Maggie only carried a handkerchief, coin purse, and a tube of lipstick in her small handbag, so she followed Isabelle's suggestion.

"So," Isabelle pointed upward, "that's where we keep all the spools of thread."

Maggie peered up at the large section of wooden shelves filled with cones of threads. The top shelves held the sewing colors of blue, black, red, white, brown, and green. The shelves below were each arranged by a color scheme ranging from the deep shades to lighter hues.

Who knew that yellow could have different variations?

Isabelle grinned. "Not expecting so many colors, huh?"

"Do we use them all?"

"No, but they're here if we need them. Your aunt usually buys the hat frames and then gets the accessories from the jobbers. We attach the ribbons or flowers ourselves. It saves money."

"Only ribbons and flowers?"

"Occasionally feathers or plumes. Those are kept over there, in boxes lined in tissue." Isabelle pointed to different shelves.

"What is that?" Maggie pointed to a small cloth bag hanging from a drawer pull.

"Can't you smell it? It's lavender," answered Isabelle. "Your aunt hangs them around the shop to make a pleasant scent."

"What else do I need to know?"

"Have you ever worked in a store before?"

"I helped in my grandfather's bakery."

"Did you handle the money?"

"No, my mother usually did that."

"Well, here, your aunt handles all the money." Isabelle shrugged as if there might be more to the story but did not elaborate.

***

An hour later, the shop bell tinkled, and Anne-Marie called out, "Maggie."

Maggie returned to the front of the shop where two ladies were talking to each other. Her aunt motioned to Maggie, indicating she should approach them.

Maggie took a deep breath and put on her best smile. "Good morning, may I help you?"

The two women nodded. One was a heavy-set woman and her companion rather slender; both were dressed conservatively and wore last summer's hat style.

"Yes. We will be marching next week in the Fourth of July Parade and need new hats. Designs that will make us appeal to the masses, yet also show that we are aware of modern trends."

"I think I can find the perfect solution."

Maggie steered them over to two of the newer styles she had seen when she entered the store — picking up the low-crowned picture hats designed from straw frames. Each hat carried different trimmings.

"You can see these are straw hats, but with the new style of a shorter crown. While this hat uses the colors of black and white straw with a medium black bow on the side, the other hat is done in natural straw and showcases a small nosegay of blue flowers."

The heavy-set woman spoke up. "The hats will do, but not the colors. Our outfits are white with broad sashes. We want hat bands in purple."

Maggie looked back at Anne-Marie, who nodded slightly.

"Of course we can do that. Which style do you prefer? The bow or the flowers?"

"We'll both take the natural straw with a side bow."

"You don't want any flowers, then?"

"Gracious, no!" The stout woman drew back. "We cannot wear a hat style encouraging the sweatshops! No artificial flowers! We support the VOTES FOR WOMEN campaign."

Maggie flinched and bit her lower lip. Does this woman think Aunt Anne-Marie supported places like the Triangle Factory? And what would sweatshops have to do with hat trimmings anyway?

Anne-Marie stepped forward. "I can assure you; we will only use ribbons for the trimmings. This current style will still keep the sun off your face and yet let the air breathe through. If you are walking in the parade, you'll want comfort in addition to fashion."

The two ladies agreed, and then Anne-Marie measured their heads for correct sizing.

"Thank you; we'll return next Tuesday for our hats. In the meantime, we invite you to attend the Margaret Sanger Lecture on July first at Cooper Union. She's speaking on Equality Healthcare for Women. We'll leave you a flyer."

"Thank you. Good-bye, ladies."

After the two women left, Anne-Marie, let out an audible sigh. "I'm glad we could appease them. Hopefully, they'll spread the news, and more of their associates will patronize our shop."

"Who were they, and what did the woman mean about flowers on hats encourage the sweatshops?"

"They were suffragists."

Maggie's eyebrows knit together.

"They campaign for a woman's right to vote."

"And the sweatshop comment?"

"She was referring to the immigrant women producing artificial flowers for hats. Remember you asked me about the South Village?"

"Yes."

"That's where the newly arrived Italian women are involved in the silk flower industry."

"What about being a sweatshop?"

"There are no enforced regulations. The women sew seven days, ten hours or more, and often have their young children working with them."

"If there aren't any regulations, why don't they work shorter hours?"

"They're paid by the finished piece, not by the number of hours they work."

"Aren't there laws against children working?"

"Yes. Children under the age of fourteen cannot work in a factory, but they can work in a home. And there are no regulations for the homemakers."

"Doesn't it bother you to buy artificial flowers? They may have come from a sweatshop."

"I run a business, Maggie, and I have to compete with all the other milliners. I buy flowers that customers demand."

"It seems to me there must be a middle ground."

"Well, when you find it, let me know." Anne-Marie tossed the Sanger flyer on the counter.

***

On Sunday, Maggie had been in the city for one entire week and had only had time to make a few preliminary sketches. She needed extended time to sit and draw renditions of her surroundings. Only then would she feel like she belonged in the Village.

"Aunt Anne-Marie, I'm going to Washington Square and sketch.

Would that be all right?"

"Of course. Will you be back for lunch?"

"I don't think so. I'll find a restaurant and hover behind a stool until I can get a seat." A mischievous grin spread across her face.

"Watch your money, then."

Maggie chose her ivory shirtwaist, and navy gored cotton skirt that would allow her to move unencumbered. She took one of last year's straw hats and swapped out the old ribbon and replaced it with a swath of navy satin.

Thank goodness Aunt Anne-Marie keeps a variety of ribbons and sashes at the apartment.

Out on the sidewalk, she took a moment to breathe in the New York air, so different from the gentle summer warmth back home. Maggie already missed the tang of honeysuckle and the taste of ripened sour cherries bursting with juice. But she was positive that New York would grant her other special treats.

Having already walked down both Seventh and Sixth Avenues, Maggie decided to try Fifth.

The cross street to Fifth was a mix of stores and apartments, but when she turned onto Fifth Avenue itself, everything changed. The residential section hosted lovely brownstone townhomes, and the genteel atmosphere bespoke the upper-middle class.

Looming up ahead stood the magnificent Washington Arch, the guardian of the park.

Maggie entered the path and walked around until she found a bench. She took the time to enjoy the scene in front of her.

An elderly woman feeding pigeons caught Maggie's attention. She picked up her pencil and started to draw with broad strokes. The rest of the world ceased to exist as Maggie inhaled the familiar scent of the carbon pencil and allowed her fingers to lightly stroke the texture of the drawing paper.

Later, a feeling of being watched made her stop. Looking up, she saw a policeman hovering nearby.

A bead of perspiration trickled down her face. Was this a

private bench?

She nodded as if to say, I see you there. To her dismay, the policeman walked over to her.

"Hello, are you drawing Gladys?"

"Who?"

"Gladys, the woman feeding the birds."

"It isn't against the rule to sketch her, is it?"

He laughed. "Of course not. You can sketch anyone you like. I saw you deep in concentration, and I wondered what you were drawing. Can I have a peek?"

Maggie hesitated, but then turned the picture toward him.

"Wow. You've certainly captured her likeness."

"Thank you."

"I'm Officer Murphy. I cover the park on weekends." He tipped his cap. "You should show Gladys your sketch."

"I don't usually show my art to anyone."

"That's a shame. It would brighten her day."

"Maybe, once I've finished it."

"Good-day, then." He whistled and continued his patrol.

Maggie smiled to herself at his compliment.

***

Later that evening as Maggie and Anne-Marie enjoyed a simple supper of *vichyssoise* soup and onion tart from Murray's Deli, Maggie asked about a local Catholic church.

"Aunt Anne-Marie, do you go to Mass?"

"I don't, but you can go to St. Joseph's if you like. Did you attend St. Bridget's back home?"

"Almost every Sunday with Mama. I like going to Mass. It gives me a sense of peace."

"Your grand-papa didn't go to church except on Christmas and Easter. And he never forced Annie or me to attend. I think Annie started going to church when she and your father were trying for a baby."

"Oh? I didn't know that."

"She and Jonathan were married a few years before you came along."

Maggie took a deep breath, digesting this news. "Have you ever wondered why I have gray-green eyes, and neither of my parents does?"

"What? No, I doubt anyone has thought about that. Your eyes are probably a throw-back to one of your father's Irish ancestors. Why are you asking about this?"

Maggie shrugged. "I often wonder why my father and I aren't closer. I don't know."

"Good Lord, Maggie. What are you suggesting? That Jonathan might not be your father? I can assure you that once Annie met Jonathan, she no longer looked at anyone else."

"Was there someone else? Before my father, I mean."

"She and Frankie Hennessey were sweet-hearts, but that ended when your father entered your mother's life."

"Hennessey, like the store in Mt. Pleasant?"

"Yes, it was Frankie's father's store. Trust me, Maggie. Your father is your father; and you have auburn streaks in your hair, another Canavan trait."

Maggie nodded but couldn't help a niggling in her brain. What color were Frankie Hennessey's eyes?

Over coffee the next morning Anne-Marie announced, "The Margaret Sanger Lecture is this afternoon. We could attend, and then you could also see the school. Next week, we can visit Parsons and Pratt, which are further uptown."

"Is Margaret Sanger a suffragist?"

"Probably. But she's most known for her bold statements on birth control. Mrs. Sanger has even been arrested because of the Comstock Act."

"What's that?"

"It forbids anyone from mailing out information about contraception."

"So, her lectures must be controversial."

"I think everything she says or does, is controversial. She and her sister run a clinic in Brooklyn that provides delicate information to women."

"What kind of information?"

"Maggie, this is a conversation you should be having with your mother, not me."

"But Mama isn't here, and you are."

"I think you'll gather a lot of information at the lecture. And I do agree with her views about healthcare. Women should be able to have control over becoming pregnant."

Maggie's eyebrows shot up. She never thought about that before.

A few hours later, Maggie and Anne-Marie walked down Sixth Avenue and caught a cross-town bus to Cooper Square.

Once again, Maggie stared up at an impressive multi-story building that took up most of a city block. Cooper Union featured a stately brownstone exterior with Romanesque columns and arches. The building dwarfed Maggie in its shadow, but she loved that she was standing on a piece of hallowed ground, artistically speaking.

Anne-Marie surged forward with Maggie at her side.

Following the crowd of mostly women, they walked down to the Great Hall of Cooper Union. It was a theater, like Ravenscroft's Opera House back home, except larger. This room held a thousand seats. The architecture of white interior columns supporting the ceiling gave an air of importance to the cavernous space.

They found seats near the front.

"Abraham Lincoln spoke here, as part of his campaign for President," Anne-Marie whispered.

"Really? I wouldn't have known that."

Within a few minutes, a woman marched across the stage and stood at the lectern. "Good afternoon," she said. "My name is Margaret Sanger, and today, I want to talk about women's health. I want to inform you how women, especially working-class women, should take measures to prevent unwanted pregnancies."

The crowd erupted with clapping.

For the next forty-five minutes, Maggie sat transfixed listening to Margaret Sanger give facts about how many women die prematurely from too many pregnancies and how simple solutions can be taken to prevent conception.

Margaret Sanger explained the process of douching immediately after having relations and how the man should use a rubber condom to prevent semen from entering the birth canal. Then she announced that both douche solutions and condoms were available over the counter at most pharmacies.

Maggie shifted in her seat and did not look at Anne-Marie.

Margaret Sanger went on to explain more expensive options, but also invited everyone in the crowd to visit her at her Brooklyn clinic. She would gladly pass out free contraceptives to any married woman.

When the lecture ended, Anne-Marie turned to Maggie. "I imagine you have questions. Let's wait till we're home to discuss them."

Maggie mulled over the information. She had never heard of a douche and had never seen a condom. And, she could not quite imagine having a conversation with her mother about any of this.

Once back at the apartment, Anne-Marie suggested they have a refreshing drink while they talked. She poured two glasses of iced tea.

"What questions do you have?"

"Um, I know how a woman gets pregnant. But what is a douche?"

"It is a means of cleansing your inner private parts with a special wash that flushes the man's semen out of the birth canal."

"Where do you get it?"

"Stores like Bigelow's sell the Bichloride tablets, and you make the wash yourself."

"Does it prevent pregnancy?"

"It's not completely effective, but it can help."

Maggie nodded, although she was a bit surprised at her aunt's cavalier manner. "I also want to know what a condom looks like."

"A small balloon-like sac of thin rubber that the husband pulls over his…penis, right before having relations with his wife."

Maggie nodded again while her ears reddened.

"You did hear Margaret Sanger talk about husbands and wives. She was not advocating for unmarried people to be having sexual relations."

"Yes. I understood that."

"Good. Was there anything else you wanted to ask?"

"Not about the lecture. Thank you for taking me. I doubt I would ever have had that opportunity back home. And I did love the Cooper Union building. I want to go back tomorrow and pick up an application for their art school."

"All right. I can close the shop an hour early and go with you. Then we can also talk about applying to Pratt and Parsons. If you want to, that is."

"Aunt Anne-Marie, I want to go tomorrow by myself. Going to school is a huge decision for me. I need to visit Cooper Union on my own."

Anne-Marie smiled. "Of course, you do."

SEVEN

Maggie left work early the following day and took the bus to Cooper Union. She entered the no-frills admissions office and asked for an application to the art school. The woman behind the desk handed it to her and was in the process of beginning a conversation when the phone rang.

The woman picked up the receiver and gave a deep sigh. "Yes, yes, I understand." By the wearied countenance on the woman's face, Maggie surmised this same phone conversation had occurred many times. Maggie pointed to her application, and the woman shoed her away, a gesture Maggie took for being permitted to leave.

Arriving back at the apartment, Maggie prepared a quick dinner of items from Murray's and set it aside to wait for Anne-Marie.

Then she tackled the application. The process was straight forward. She listed the apartment as her address and recorded where and when she had graduated from high school and college. She composed a short, but honest essay on why she wanted to pursue enrollment in the art school and how she hoped to become an illustrator for women's magazines.

The conclusion of the application stated that she would receive further instructions on how to submit artwork for the final part of the process.

Without any hesitation, Maggie licked the envelope closed. Tomorrow she would go to the post office and mail it, even though the application only had to travel a few blocks to its destination.

Anne-Marie peeked into the living room as she came home. "Dinner ready?"

"Yes. German potato salad with grilled cheese sandwiches."

"Sounds good. Won't we both be glad when meat rationing finally ends."

Maggie grabbed their plates and carried them to the dining table, moving the Cooper art envelope over to the side.

"Wait, did you finish the application already? Didn't you want me to go over it first?"

Maggie rolled her eyes. "Remember, I said I wanted to do this on my own."

"Yes, you did. So, let's eat, and you can mail it later."

***

The morning of the parade, the two suffragists came back early for their purchases.

Maggie walked over with their hats nestled in the pink and white striped hat boxes. "Hello, ladies. Here are your hats, decorated as per your requests. Please try them on, so we can see how attractive you'll look."

The stout woman frowned ever so slightly. "We are not wearing hats to look attractive. We are marching to attract attention to women's rights."

"Of course, I do realize that." Maggie's ears reddened. She looked back and saw Isabelle stifling a giggle.

Anne-Marie came forward. "I want to personally thank you for choosing our shop for your millinery needs and sincerely hope that you tell your associates about us. We support the campaign, and we'll be waving our flags for Women's Rights at the parade. Now, let's see the hats on you."

The two women took the hats, placed them on their heads, and did a small bit of preening. Maggie could tell that at least one of them needed to use O-do-ro-no. No wonder Aunt Anne-Marie hung lavender sachets around the shop.

Anne-Marie presented them with the bill, and the stout woman paid for both. When they glided out of the shop carrying the hat boxes, each woman wore a broad smile.

An hour later Anne-Marie announced they would close early to attend the parade. She retrieved her handbag, went to the cash register, and locked it.

Isabelle groused under her breath, "She doesn't trust anyone with the money."

"It's her shop, Isabelle."

Maggie turned away, but not before she saw Isabelle make a sour face.

The three of them split as Isabelle went to meet friends.

"I wish I didn't still have to wear this cast. Hopefully, it comes off next week, but I have appreciated your help."

"Will the parade last longer than half an hour?"

"Last year the parade went on for over two hours."

Thirty minutes later they joined throngs of people on the sidewalks of Fifth Avenue to cheer as the huge Fourth of July Parade passed. Marching bands played their instruments with gusto, and office workers lined up at the buildings' upper windows so that they could view the procession. Everyone was waving flags.

An hour in, Anne-Marie and Maggie spied the suffragists marching together. Dressed in white with sashes tied diagonally across their chests, they sported straw hats with purple ribbons and carried banners proclaiming VOTES FOR WOMEN.

Anne-Marie nudged Maggie. "Over there. See our two ladies? Wave at them."

***

The following day the memory of the parade and the fireworks over the New York harbor faded when the back-to-work routine took precedence.

During the afternoon, the shop bell rang, and Maggie looked up to see Rees Finch entering the store. He walked straight to her.

"Well, look who I found!"

Maggie's mouth fell open. "Mr. Finch! How did you find our shop?"

"I was in the neighborhood on assignment." He held up his camera. "I decided to take a short-cut up Christopher Street. The sign said, Hats by Anne-Marie, and I immediately thought of you and your aunt."

Maggie found herself at a momentary loss for words. Before she realized that Isabelle was on the move, Isabelle walked up and smiled at Rees.

"Why, Maggie, you didn't tell me you knew any men in New York."

"Isabelle, this is Mr. Charles Finch. Mr. Finch, this is Isabelle, who helps out in the shop."

In the next instant, Maggie came to two conclusions: one, she did not even know Isabelle's last name and two, Isabelle was a born flirt.

"Why, Mr. Finch, I am pleased to meet you. If I can help in any way, please let me know."

Like a lightning bolt, Anne-Marie emerged from the back.

"Mr. Finch, what a nice surprise. Are you here to buy a hat, or are you on a different mission?"

"My day started on a photography assignment, but now that I've discovered your shop, I'm changing my plans. Isabelle, thank you for your offer, but I owe Miss Canavan a stroll through the Village." He turned to Maggie with a smile. "It's late in the day, how would you like to go out for tea? Then I can show you around parts of the West Village."

"That is thoughtful of you, but I think Maggie knows her way around the West Village."

Undeterred, Rees addressed Anne-Marie. "Even the out-of-the-way hidden art gems? Please allow me to take her for tea and then on a short walk. I assure you, I am a gentleman at heart."

Anne-Marie tilted her head. "Mr. Finch, you are full of surprises, aren't you?"

"Customer traffic usually slows down by late Friday afternoon; am I right? I'll have her back here by closing time. And of course, you have Isabelle to help you." He smiled at Isabelle, but even Maggie could detect the insincerity of the gesture.

"I close at five-thirty. I'll expect you back by then."

With that, Rees offered his arm to Maggie, who took it and sashayed out of the shop like a veteran New Yorker, leaving Isabelle and her scowl behind.

"A teashop? I didn't know restaurants like that existed."

"It's an art gallery. The proprietor, Jessie, is a photographer who offers tea to the visitors. We often share ideas of possible subjects to shoot; as photographs, I mean." He laughed.

They turned south down Christopher Street and then branched off onto Grove Street. When they reached a three-way intersection, Rees announced, "Here we are, Sheridan Square."

He placed his hand under Maggie's elbow and guided her across the street.

"Jessie has built a solid reputation with the pictures she takes of the Village. She taught me to shoot any semi-interesting location if I had a potential buyer. I think you'll find her quite refreshing."

The building looked more like the entrance to one of Beer Alley's saloons, but the sign in the window read, *Tea Room*, so Maggie did not hesitate.

Inside, the small space showcased a display of photographs and paintings. Various artwork lined the walls, and black and white photos hung from thin wires, strategically placed at eye view.

A woman dressed in a flowing orange and yellow costume brightened by a mischievous smile emerged from behind a curtain. "Rees, how good to see you. You've brought a new friend." She kissed Rees on each cheek.

"Jessie, this is Maggie Canavan. She's new to the Village and hopes to become an artist."

"Hello."

"Maggie, Jessie is worth getting to know. She's famous for her hospitality."

"Welcome, Maggie who-wants-to-become-an-artist. It's a beautiful day, so why don't we sit outside where we can catch the breeze. I'll serve tea and strawberry shortcake."

They went back outside, and Jessie pointed to two tables fashioned from upside-down half barrels covered with oilcloths. Maggie looked at Rees, who smiled and pulled out a chair for her. Jessie came back out, carrying two plates in her left hand and a teapot in her right.

"Here is my famous shortcake." She put down the teapot and handed Maggie and Rees each a plate of the dessert. Disappearing once again inside, she soon came out with three teacups stacked inside each other, a sugar bowl, forks, and spoons.

None of the cups matched, and Jessie did not offer any saucers.

If I didn't know better, I'd think I had fallen down the rabbit hole and landed in Wonderland, mused Maggie.

Jessie sat down at the barrel table and poured the tea, not asking if they wanted one lump of sugar or two.

"Now, my dear, tell me about the life you left to become a Village artist."

"It was nothing exciting. I taught fourth grade in a small coal-mining village in western Maryland."

"Well, that explains everything." Jessie smiled. "Doesn't it, Rees?"

***

Maggie had enjoyed the teashop with Rees. He had a way of turning an ordinary afternoon into a pleasurable experience. Was it just his good looks, or something more? Maggie wasn't sure, but she knew she was already looking forward to seeing him again.

However, at the moment, she was looking forward to attending Mass and then having a chance to sketch again in the park.

St. Joseph's, a block west of Washington Square, was a building of simple design.

While many churches were composed of red brick, St. Joseph's was constructed of light gray, with two supporting white columns in front. A statue of St. Joseph was tucked in an alcove over the front entrance, and as with most Catholic churches, the roof held one single plain cross.

With reverence, Maggie entered the church and found a pew. Kneeling in prayer, she asked God to look kindly on her application to art school. She sat back and gazed at the altar with the Blessed Mother statue on the left and a companion statue of St. Joseph on the right.

Around the sides of the church were seven colorful stained-glass windows. The artist in Maggie marveled at the precise construction and placement of the windows allowing the sunlight to blaze through the glass and illuminate the small place of worship.

She vowed to come back on another day and pray the Stations of the Cross.

After having received the Eucharist and standing for the final blessing, Maggie genuflected and solemnly left the church. Outside the sun radiated out of a clear blue sky and she headed east to the park. A spring in her step accentuated her delight with the day.

She found her way to the same bench where she had sketched last week. Off to the side was the same woman feeding pigeons. Maggie took her art pad and graphite pencils and continued working on the rough drawing from last week.

An hour into her drawing, she looked up to find Officer Murphy smiling at her.

"I wondered if you would be back here again."

Maggie rested the pad on her lap. "Sundays are the only time I have to come here and sketch."

"What do you do for the rest of the week?"

"I work in my aunt's hat shop, Hats by Anne-Marie. Do you know it?"

"Can't say that I've been a customer, but I do know most of the buildings in the Sixth Precinct."

"I guess I don't have to ask you what you do the rest of the week," she smiled.

"Nope, I'm pretty transparent. Have you shown the drawing to Gladys?"

"Not yet. I'm waiting to get it just right."

"Well, don't wait too long." Then he nodded and strolled off on his rounds.

Later, when Maggie returned from her sketching time, Anne-Marie wore a wide grin.

"What are you so happy about?"

"Tomorrow starts July sales at Macy's. Make sure you're up early."

"How early?"

"Early enough that we'll be there when the doors open at 10:00 a.m."

***

The coffee was already brewing when Maggie awoke. Shopping had always been a pleasure in Riverton, and New York should have many more choices.

By 9:45 in the morning, Anne-Marie and Maggie stepped off the Sixth Ave El at West 33rd Street and walked down the stairs to street level. Macy's department store occupied the entire corner of West 34th Street. The name R. H. MACY & CO. hewn in stone sat over the ornate front façade.

Maggie looked up and counted eight stories. "Oh, my. I had no idea one store could be this big."

Precisely on the dot of 10:00, they entered through the double doors, and Anne-Marie pulled Maggie aside. "There will be huge crowds. Don't be shy. If you see an item you want, pick up the hanger. Otherwise, someone else will grab it."

Maggie stared wide-eyed in amazement at all the merchandise. And they were only on the first floor!

"Let's concentrate on getting you two lightweight summer outfits. And, a pair of lighter shoes. We can come here to shop each month if you like."

"I'd love to."

"Just remember, no hats! Macy's hats are strictly forbidden in my house. Although I do watch to see what styles they're carrying; then I design similar ones." She winked.

Lunchtime found Maggie carrying multiple shopping bags. She had found a lovely crisp white linen-cotton blend shirtwaist and had paired it with a dark-gray linen flared skirt. In a separate department, she snagged an orange linen dress with delicate piping on the sleeves and collar.

After dining on ham salad sandwiches that contained more diced celery and onion than ham, they finished their meal with a dessert of light sponge cake.

"Hats are so popular here."

"Because a hat gives a woman confidence. Even if she scrubs floors for a living, once she puts on a hat, it transforms her."

"I never thought about hats that way."

"Maggie, I don't sell hats, I sell dreams. The right bonnet helps you to be fashionable, to make a statement, and to lift yourself out of the ordinary."

"So, hats have power." Maggie chuckled.

"You're a quick learner."

"Where do you get the trimmings for your hats? The silk flowers and such."

"I buy them wholesale from Fleiss's Factory. That's where I met Mr. Steinberger, the manager there. Remember, we ran into him near the old Asch Building last month."

"I remember. Where is the factory?"

"Down in the East Village, on lower Broadway."

"You go there to make your selections?"

"I haven't been there in over a year. I usually put in my orders by telephone. Are you curious about the factory? Would you like to visit?"

"No, that's not necessary. But I am trying to understand the whole process. When did you get interested in hats?"

"I started dabbling in fashion during high school. A ribbon here, a belt there, but hats were always my specialty."

"You have a certain elegance about you. I hope I can learn to do the same."

"Just remember that fads come and go, but style lasts."

They left the tea room and ventured to the shoe floor, where Maggie discovered a pair of bone-colored Gibson's. The stylish cut-out design in the top leather, combined with a pointed toe and a two-inch French heel made Maggie feel instantly chic. They became the next purchase.

"Last stop is the fifth-floor bargain sales."

As soon as they emerged onto the fifth floor, Maggie spied Isabelle in the middle of the crowd of shoppers. She was haggling with a saleslady. Not sure if Anne-Marie would want contact with Isabelle outside of the store, Maggie didn't point out the girl's presence.

Instead, she waited until they were on the bus home when she had sagged into the seat with a mixture of exuberance and exhaustion.

"Aunt Anne-Marie. How did Isabelle come to work at the store?"

"I sat next to her at a Christmas Mass. Isabelle wore a fetching hat, and I complimented her on its design. She replied by telling me she had created it herself."

"But that doesn't explain how she came to work in the shop."

"I told her I owned a hat shop in the West Village, and if she ever needed a job, to come and find me. A month later, she did."

"Did she have references?"

"From a previous employer? No. She told me she had been given away in marriage at the age of fifteen to an older man her parents chose. She stayed a year, then ran away to New York City."

"She came to New York alone, not knowing anyone?"

"She lives with an aunt and uncle."

"That's all you know? Is she divorced? What's her last name?"

"You'll find people in the Village aren't interested in your previous life. Her last name is Levine."

"How did she support herself before she came to work for you?"

"You're nosy, aren't you? She was a chorus girl in a vaudeville show."

Maggie's eyebrows shot upward. "I can see her as a chorus girl." Then she hesitated. "Aunt Anne-Marie, I'm not sure you should trust her. There's something wrong about Isabelle. I can't figure her out, but my intuition says she could be trouble."

"If there's anything wrong with Isabelle, it's because she's had bad luck in choosing men."

"Is that why you handle all the money transactions at the shop?"

"Maggie, I wasn't born yesterday."

***

The summer air trickled to a non-existent breeze and business dragged with the oppressive heat. Maggie fanned herself.

"You'll see that business slows in July and August, especially on Wednesdays. Then begins to pick up again with the cooler temperatures in September."

"How do you compensate for the shortage of income?"

"I made good investments in the past, that help tide me over in the slow seasons. Why don't you finish up and go home? If your friend, Mr. Finch, shows up again, I'll tell him he just missed you."

Maggie blushed.

"Remember, Maggie, be careful. It's dangerous to fall for the first man you meet."

The blush deepened to a flame. "I haven't fallen for Rees."

Anne-Marie's arched eyebrow indicated otherwise.

"I'll stop at the deli and get dinner."

"That would be grand. Thank you."

After purchasing a quiche and fresh produce for a salad, Maggie entered the apartment building and went to the wall mailboxes. She scooped up their mail, tucked it under her arm, and pushed the elevator button.

After letting herself in the apartment, she plopped the mail on the kitchen counter and placed the food in the icebox. Then she poured a glass of cold tea and leafed through the papers when one envelope stopped her in her tracks. The return address was the Cooper Union.

Maggie tore open the envelope.

Dear Miss Canavan,

We have received your paperwork for the 1918 fall term in the School of Arts at the Cooper Union. Unfortunately, you did not adhere to the stated deadline. All applications were due in this office by the first of July.

We encourage you to re-apply for a future term.

Sincerely,
The Office of the Director of Admissions

Maggie stumbled into the living room. Didn't adhere to the deadline? Where was that written? Glancing up at the wall calendar, she realized she had picked up the application on July 1st. Why didn't the receptionist alert her? All she could remember was the woman had been talking on the phone and had waved Maggie away.

When the enormity of her mistake cascaded on her, Maggie burst into frustrated tears. She had to get into an art school to justify staying in New York.

With no appetite for fixing dinner, she went back to her bedroom and sat on her bed. Tears spilled down her angry face, and she wiped them away with a vengeance. Overcome with emotional exhaustion, she fell back against the pillow.

Anne-Marie returned within the hour. Since the mail lay on the dining room table, Maggie had already read it.

"Maggie, I'm home."

No answer.

"Maggie?" Anne-Marie approached the back bedroom and

knocked.

"Come in." An opened letter lay tossed on the bed. "I didn't get in."

"The Cooper Union? You heard already?"

"Oh, I heard all right. The board rejected my application because it arrived after the July 1st deadline."

"Deadline? Did you know that?"

"No. Oh, God, Aunt Anne-Marie. Now, what will I do?"

Anne-Marie crossed the small space to the bed. "I'm so sorry. Let me see the letter." She scanned the page. "I'm surprised they didn't advise you of the deadline." Her leveled stare bore through Maggie.

"Doesn't matter now. I'm off the list."

Anne-Marie softened her voice. "We'll put our heads together and formulate a new plan. I've grown fond of having you as a roommate." Then her tone shifted. "I did warn you that living in New York isn't always as glamorous as it sounds. The city often claims its tolls."

"I can't go back home, Aunt Anne-Marie. I have to be a success here."

EIGHT

Maggie found it hard to concentrate on the new shipment of trimmings. Around one o'clock she was surprised to see Rees standing in the shop's doorway. "Rees?"

"I've been standing here, wondering when you would notice me. It seems like your mind's elsewhere."

Maggie walked over to him. "My mind is occupied at the moment, but you're a welcomed diversion."

"Diversion, am I?" He chuckled. "I've been called worse. Now, what's happened to occupy your mind?"

"I didn't get into art school at Cooper Union."

He gave a low whistle. "They didn't like your art?"

"They never even saw my art. I filed my application after the July 1st deadline, by mistake. I didn't even realize there was a deadline." Her face reddened.

"Well, there's more than one way to skin a cat."

"How?"

"The Village is full of artists. Do you want to go and talk with Jessie? She might know someone who gives reasonable art lessons."

"Perhaps, but classes don't seem as professional as art school."

"You might have to start with classes first."

"I had such hopes. It would have been the perfect birthday present."

"Birthday? Don't tell me I've missed it."

"No, it's next week."

"And how old will you be?"

"A gentleman never asks a lady her age." She enjoyed bantering with him.

"Who said I was a gentleman?" He winked. "Let's see. You went to college, and you taught for a few years, so I'm betting you're turning…twenty-two. Am I right?"

Maggie laughed. "What you are is infuriatingly correct."

"Then we'll have to celebrate. First, let me take you out to a tea shop as soon as you close today so you can drown your sorrows about Cooper Union. Then, next Saturday we'll celebrate in style, and I'll take you to Webster Hall."

"Webster Hall?"

"A large ballroom. There's a hat party next Saturday, and several of my friends are going. It will be a lot of fun."

"All right. Sounds intriguing."

He hesitated. "Do you drink, Maggie?"

"I'm part French and part Irish. Does that answer your question?" She smirked.

"Good." He pulled out his pocket watch. "It's three now; I'll come back at five."

As he sauntered off down the street, Maggie's spirits lifted.

***

Two hours later Rees led her out the door. "I want to take you to the Mad Hatter."

"Like in *Alice in Wonderland*?"

"Oh, it's better than Wonderland. All sorts of interesting people will be there, and you'll forget about Cooper Union."

He steered her up Christopher Street to Sixth Avenue, then across to West 4th, where they headed toward the Park.

"Here we are. Duck your head; the tea room's in the basement."

"You're kidding!"

"No. It's true." He pointed to the inscription over the door.

Maggie peered at the letters, but they made no sense.

"I suppose you can read that." She pointed to the sign. ELOH TIBBAR EHT NWOD.

Rees laughed. "It says, 'Down the Rabbit Hole.' This is the Mad Hatter Tea Room, so you should expect the unusual."

Maggie let Rees lead the way, down the steps, and into the small tea room. Four tables with chairs sat near a few scattered wooden benches and two wall seats.

Rees kept walking into another room, and Maggie followed. Here, an impressive stone fireplace faced several opportunities for seating. There were no tables, but people lounged everywhere, eating and talking. Animated conversations filled the air.

Maggie was surprised to see that all the walls, plus the chimney, were covered with drawings of the characters from *Alice in Wonderland*.

"Rees, who did all these drawings?"

"Various people. I told you, the Village is teeming with artists. You've come to the right place to live. I'll get us refreshments. Coffee or tea?"

"Tea, please."

When Rees returned with the food, they found empty spots and sat down.

"What brought you to the Village, Rees? You never told me that on the train."

"I did tell you I wanted to become a newspaper photographer. The Village seemed to be the best place to start."

"Do you photograph all over the city?"

"Yes, but selling my pictures to the newspapers hasn't been easy. I often earn my living wages by taking photos of the military."

"The military?"

"I go out to the army camps and photograph the new groups of soldiers as they arrive on base."

"Not so glamorous, I guess."

"No, but it pays for my room at the boarding house."

Maggie mused over this information. He was always dressed so well that she had assumed he had money. Perhaps clothes were his one vice.

"Where do you live?"

"Not far from here. Sixty-one Washington Square South. I'm lucky that Mrs. Blanchard, the landlady, likes me. I rent the room that Willa Cather stayed in when she first came to the Village."

"Willa Cather, who wrote *My Antonia*?"

"The same. Our building got nicknamed the House of Genius because so many famous authors and artists have lived there."

"Like who?"

"In addition to Willa Cather, O. Henry lived there for a time as did Stephen Crane, and others."

"My, I had no idea you lived at such a famous address."

"I'll show it to you some time." He grinned. "Then it would be worth the $12.00 a month."

Maggie blushed.

The late afternoon digressed into early evening as they chatted with a man who regaled them with stories about the Czar trying to ruin Russia. His tales of the peasants revolting fascinated Maggie.

"I should be getting back, Rees. We told Aunt Anne-Marie we were only going for tea."

"All right, but when we go to Webster Hall, no early curfew. I'll walk you home now."

"That's not necessary. It's still light out, and I know how to get back to West 13th Street."

"What would your aunt think of me if I let you go home alone?"

"All right, we can go to the El together, and wait till I get on board."

They left the restaurant and Rees guided Maggie around the block to the elevated train platform on Sixth Avenue.

"I'll come for you next Saturday at eight. But you'll need to tell me your address."

Would Aunt Anne-Marie object to Rees knowing where they lived? "Come to the shop next Thursday, and I'll give you my address."

"Till then, Maggie, dear." He leaned over and gave her a lingering kiss on the cheek. "Keep your wits about you. The El is a favorite hangout for pick-pockets."

She smiled as she climbed up the steps to the train platform, her bag tucked tightly under one arm and the other fingers resting on the spot that still held the warmth from his kiss.

**

The week of Maggie's birthday started with Maggie and Anne-Marie having brunch at the Brevoort Hotel on Fifth Avenue to celebrate Bastille Day.

The hotel reminded Maggie of the hotel in Washington D.C. where she spent the night with her parents. Just like that hotel, the Brevoort's lobby contained ornate chairs and lounges. Guests were busy reading and talking.

Life here is so different from Porters Glen. I bet none of the girls from my school have ever been to a swanky hotel like this. Still, I have to remember to be cautious and save the money I make helping Aunt Anne-Marie.

Anne-Marie led Maggie to the hotel restaurant and smiled as a waiter led them to their table.

"Did you celebrate Bastille Day when you and my mother were growing up?"

"*Certainment,* as Grand-papa would say. You know how proud he is of his French heritage."

"What did you do?"

"He would remind us of how the peasants stormed the Bastille Prison, and then he would treat us to strawberry crêpes for breakfast."

"Hasn't it been hard, never going back home? Never seeing Grand-papa?"

Anne-Marie stared down to her lap. "Of course, it has. But I made my decision to move to New York. I never intended to go back to Porters Glen."

"Why didn't you ever come home to visit?"

"I've led a busy life here with my shop. How is my father doing?"

"Good, except for his arthritis. But he still comes to the bakery on most days."

"Maggie, you do know that our family store isn't a true French bakery."

"What do you mean?"

"An authentic French bakery sells bread and rolls. If you want sweets, like pastries and tarts, you go to a *patisserie*."

"Why would Grand-papa call it a bakery then?"

"Because he's smart. When he arrived in Porters Glen, there was Drum's Store and Mackenzie's Grocery. He needed a special edge to compete with them, so he called his store Charbonneau's Bakery."

"And the villagers didn't know the difference."

"He offered what the other stores could not; French bread and rolls, special cookies, cakes, and tarts."

"He does have a loyal following."

Anne-Marie smiled, then looked off over her shoulder. "Does he ever talk about me?"

"Of course, he does! When I said I wanted to go to art school in New York, he reminded me how brave you were to leave home."

"Yes, I was, wasn't I." But her voice sounded flat.

"Aunt Anne-Marie, Rees is taking me to Webster Hall on Saturday to celebrate my birthday. Is it all right that I give him our address?"

"I certainly don't want you sneaking out to meet him. A young man always picks you up at your residence. When he stops in at the store this week, give him the address."

"Thank you."

"One more thing about Webster Hall. Everyone will be drinking. Remember to pace yourself."

"All right."

"Now, let's think about your birthday. I've thought of two choices of how we can celebrate. A fancy dinner or even a show? The

Ziegfield Follies just opened at the New Amsterdam Theater. Everyone is talking about it."

"I'd love to go to the theater!"

"Wonderful! I've read that the costumes are magnificent." Then Anne-Marie playfully leaned forward. "So, tell me. Are these crêpes as good as Grand-papa's?"

Maggie laughed. "Nothing is as good as Grand-papa's."

***

Summer seemed to move faster in New York than it did in Porters Glen. Two days before Maggie's birthday, the newsboys on Sixth Avenue harked the headlines that the Russian Czar and his entire family had been executed. Maggie thought back to the man at the Mad Hatter and his hatred for the Czar. Had it been necessary to kill the whole family as well?

On July 18th Maggie turned twenty-two. Her parents called from the bakery to wish her a happy birthday.

"Hello? Maggie? It's Papa and me. We wanted to wish you a happy birthday!"

"Thank you. Aunt Anne-Marie and I are going to the Ziegfield Follies tonight!"

"The Follies, oh, how special. Wait, here's Grand-papa."

"*Bon Anniversaire*, Maggie!"

"Oh, Grand-papa I'm having the best birthday ever. We're going to the Ziegfield Follies."

Then her father got on the phone. "Happy birthday, Maggie. We all miss you."

She cringed, glad they could not see her reaction. "I miss you, too, but I'm getting to sketch each week in Washington Square, and I love working in the shop with Aunt Anne-Marie."

"Remember, school starts on the first of September."

"I haven't forgotten."

After Maggie replaced the phone receiver in its cradle, she

turned to Anne-Marie. "I'm deceitful. They have no idea that I don't want to return home."

"Don't be so hard on yourself, Maggie. You still have a month before deciding. Just enjoy the Follies tonight."

"I also didn't mention that you've had your cast taken off."

"That shouldn't have any bearing on you staying here. Our agreement was for the entire summer."

Maggie selected the new orange dress that she had purchased at Macy's. Anne-Marie had counseled her not to wear a large hat to the theater. She would be asked to remove it for the performance. So, Maggie selected one of the smart new Milan styles with a decent crown and modest brim.

They took a hansom cab. When Maggie stepped out of the hack, she felt like Cinderella. Although it was summer and the sun would set later, all the theaters on 42nd Street had their lights turned on, and the resulting sparkle lit up the street with a dazzle.

Maggie and Anne-Marie ventured into the lobby of the theater with its Art Nouveau décor, and Maggie spied a theater poster announcing that Lillian Lorraine would be performing. Maggie moved all around the vestibule, looking at everything. Then they found their seats and read through the program. The Follies would be staged in two halves with a break for intermission.

The lights flickered, and the theater dimmed.

All at once a crescendo of music resounded off the walls, and the luxurious silk stage curtain rose into the air.

Maggie let out a light gasp. The stage rotated under shimmering lights as rows of showgirls dressed in lavish white feathered costumes climbed onto a moving spiral staircase. Amidst this splendor, the lead actress, Lillian Lorraine stepped out to sing.

Everything about the performance was stunning. The stark white plumage covered the girls' torsos, then spun up to magnificent headdresses of peacock-like white feathers that dipped and twirled as the girls moved. From the waist down, the girls were dressed in white sequined tights and sparkling white tap shoes, and the effect took

Maggie's breath away.

Each act was more evocative than the last, and each new set showcased the chorus girls in opulent new outfits.

The first half of the show concluded, and the theater lights illuminated the audience once again. Maggie sat back in her seat, drained by the extravaganza.

"Aunt Anne-Marie, I have never seen such magnificent feathers in all my life. Were they real?"

"I think so. I read that it takes 250 seamstresses to sew the costumes and 1,000 workers to put on one of these shows. The feathers were ostrich plumes, but with the new Migratory Bird Act, it's now illegal to kill birds for plumage."

"Where did you hear that?"

"I ran into another milliner at the hospital when I went for the removal of my cast. She gave me the news. I know the treaty will protect millions of birds, but we'll have to see how it will affect business."

"If it's now illegal to use plumage, the suffragists will be happy."

"But I'm not sure how the general public will react. No plumage will mean a bigger demand for silk flowers."

On the ride back, Maggie asked, "You said that Isabelle worked as a chorus girl. Was she a Ziegfield girl?"

"Oh, I doubt it. More likely, a chorus girl in vaudeville. Probably over on Second Avenue."

Maggie mused. *So, that was where Isabelle had probably learned to flirt.*

NINE

Saturday dawned with a tarnished silver sky, and New Yorkers awoke to the smell of impending rain.

But nothing could dampen Maggie's preparations for the evening. From the rental section in the store, she found a man's top hat and decorated it to fit the character of the Mad Hatter from *Alice in Wonderland*. She wanted Rees to get the connection from their time in the tea room.

Rees came to the apartment and played the part of a true gentleman, coming inside to talk with Anne-Marie and promising to have Maggie home at a reasonable hour. Back outside, he slid his arm around Maggie's waist as they walked up to 14th Street to hail a cab.

Goodness, I hope he can't hear my heart leaping. I've danced with boys before, but have never had a young man be so bold during daylight. I like it.

The cab pulled up to Webster Hall, and Maggie could almost believe they were back in western Maryland. The front facade reminded her of large saloons in Riverton.

Once they stepped inside, Maggie stopped in her tracks. The large open ballroom contained a stage with upper-level balconies.

"Enormous, isn't it? And it's safe here; you don't have to worry. It's not like a black and tan."

"What's a black and tan?"

"Where both blacks and whites gather to drink beer and dance.

Those places attract a rough crowd, down around Minetta Place, south of the Park."

"Have you been to one?"

"I go where I can get good photographs, remember?"

Rees maneuvered Maggie through the crowd. Everyone was wearing eccentric hats. There were Rembrandts and pirates, Napoleons and cowboys. Rees wore a British tweed cap, which he insisted had belonged to Sherlock Holmes' assistant.

Glad I took the time assembling my hat; I fit right in with the crowd.

Her dress of orange silk rustled as she followed Rees through the crowd and to their table.

"Hello, boys. May I introduce my date, Miss Maggie Canavan of Maryland."

"Welcome, Maggie," two men stood up in unison. Next, they introduced their dates, a girl named Nancy and one named Sally. Maggie noticed right off that the two girls were dressed in outfits that showed off their ankles.

Maggie had no sooner sat down at the table when the band struck up the melody of "Over There," the wildly popular song written by George Cohan. Everyone in the ballroom stood up and placed their right hand over their hearts and sang along to the patriotic tribute.

Maggie flushed with excitement.

"I'll get us something from the bar," Rees announced as soon as the song ended.

Maggie started to tell him what she wanted, but he left.

"So, Maggie. Tell us about yourself."

Maggie looked at the two couples. "Not much to tell. I'm from a small town in western Maryland, and I came to New York to study art."

"How did you meet Rees?"

"On the train."

Did those two girls exchange a knowing glance? God, I hope neither of them used to date Rees.

"Here you go, gin and tonic. Maybe we could get more

adventurous and order a sidecar as the night goes on." He grinned.

Maggie had no idea of what was in a sidecar.

"Thanks, I'll stay with gin."

She'd never had a gin and tonic before either, but if that was the preferred New York drink, she told herself to get on board.

The band switched to a softer tune of "Till We Meet Again."

"Take off your hat, Maggie, so we can slow dance."

Out on the dance floor, Maggie stepped into Rees's arms. They fit as if their two bodies were meant to be together. He guided her around the floor with finesse. The next dance was the new popular foxtrot. Maggie silently thanked her mother for teaching her the steps before she came to the city.

The night progressed. Maggie sipped at her drinks, while the rest of the table outdrank her. When the band took a break, Maggie excused herself and went to the Ladies Room. After using the facilities, Maggie stood in front of the mirror to reapply her lipstick when Isabelle walked in and wobbled over, reeking of cheap perfume.

Isabelle slurred, "Well, if it isn't Maggie Canavan, out for an evening with her beau."

"I didn't expect to see you here, Isabelle."

"You're in my territory now."

Maggie ignored the comment.

"You may be a year older than me, but I've already had a man." She jabbed a finger in Maggie's face. "And you'd better hold onto your precious Mr. Finch. Any real woman could steal him away."

Isabelle stumbled over to a toilet stall.

Maggie's ears reddened. Whether from the alcohol or Isabelle's words, she couldn't tell, but she wanted to distance herself. Maggie left the Ladies Room a bit shaky. Not wanting to be a bumbling fool like Isabelle, Maggie forced herself into complete composure.

She is not going to ruin my evening.

As the band continued to play, Maggie pretended to sip at her drink.

The announcement came for the last dance of the evening, and Rees led Maggie onto the dance floor. With the lights low, the music soft, and plenty of alcohol-fueled desire, he slid his hand partway inside the back of her dress. Startled, but also pleased with the sensation of having his hand on her bare skin, Maggie floated around the dance floor in his arms.

Outside the club, Rees hailed a cab. When they arrived at West 13th Street, Rees told the cabbie to wait. Maggie opened the main door to the building, and Rees followed.

"I'll return you to your apartment, just like I picked you up." He smiled, but in a silly way. Inside the elevator, he took Maggie into his arms and kissed her with a crushing passion that riveted her entire body. He continued kissing her, barely stopping when the elevator reached her floor.

In the hallway, he moved her up against the wall and kissed her again. As he pressed up against her body, she could feel the hardness of his cock. Feelings of apprehension melted as a sexual urge shot through her body, surprising her with the intensity.

Dear God!

"Maggie." He groaned. "Please go inside, or I might ravish you here in the hallway."

She walked to her door as calmly as possible, turned, and gave him a coquettish smile.

Entering the apartment, she leaned against the wall, savoring the rush she had experienced. She wanted to learn to become the type of woman who could hold him.

***

A few days later Rees popped into the shop, loaded with camera equipment.

"Maggie, I had a great time with you at Webster Hall. I'd like to take you with me on an assignment this coming Saturday. Would that be all right with your aunt?"

"I'll have to ask her. Where would we be going?"

"I'm taking a series of photographs to showcase innocence of childhood in the city. I'm hoping to sell the photographic essay to the *New York Daily News.*"

"And how would I help?"

"You'd be my assistant."

Anne-Marie had been lingering nearby. "Where exactly and when, Mr. Finch?"

"We'll be walking around the West Village, and it would be late Saturday afternoon, so it shouldn't impact your business." Her gave Anne-Marie a well-practiced smile.

"All right. Come to the shop at three. One of these days, I want to see your photos."

"Yes, ma'am." He tipped his hat.

***

Precisely at three on Saturday, Rees strolled with Maggie down Christopher Street until they came to Sheridan Square, then Rees turned east on 4th and Maggie followed.

"You still haven't said where we're going."

"You'll see."

A few minutes later, Maggie recognized the area. "I know where we are. St. Joseph's is over there." She pointed.

"Do you go to church there?"

"Most Sundays, yes."

After one block, they made a quick right and stopped in front of 27 Barrow Street.

"What is this, Rees?"

"It's a settlement house, set up to help immigrant families get accustomed to life in New York City. I want to photograph the children here. You can help or watch if you prefer."

Rees went into action as he cajoled the woman who answered the front door to allow him access to the back yard to photograph the children playing. Maggie listened to his claim that he was on assignment for the New York Daily News.

"Yes, Ma'am, I'm shooting a photographic essay documenting the help that settlement houses provide to the newly arrived immigrants."

Maggie saw him flash a brilliant smile at the woman. Moments later, he winked at Maggie and ventured off toward the back.

"Are you his assistant, like he claims?" the receptionist asked Maggie.

Swallowing the lie, Maggie responded, "Yes, but I need to use the lavatory first."

"You'll have to go up to the second floor." She pointed to an iron staircase off to the left.

Maggie climbed the stairs and used the toilet. When she walked out, she found herself on the floor with a variety of rooms. Rees was nowhere in sight. Neither was the reception woman, so Maggie strolled down the corridor to explore a bit.

She peeked her head inside one of the rooms. It contained two bookcases, a large rug, and two tables with child-sized chairs. Intrigued, she stepped inside.

Looks like a small library, or maybe even a classroom?

Maggie was ready to leave when a little girl with a full head of jet-black curls came tearing into the room. Without hesitation, the child went to the bookcase and pulled a book off the shelf and then skipped over to Maggie and held the book out to her.

"Oh, thank you. Is this for me?"

The little girl nodded and plopped herself down in front of Maggie.

"Do you want me to show you the book?"

The child nodded again.

Maggie looked around, but they were alone. Well, showing a book wouldn't be breaking the law.

"All right. Let's see. The title is *Mr. Prickly Porky*. That's funny, isn't it?"

The child giggled and put her hands over her mouth.

With no adult chair in the room, Maggie sat on the floor. The little girl climbed into Maggie's lap.

"All right. Let me begin."

Maggie had no sooner finished reading the book when the little girl squealed in delight, "Again!"

At that moment, a professionally dressed woman entered the room.

"Gabriella, is this where you ran?" Her smile thinned when she turned to Maggie. "And who are you? I know you're not part of Gabriella's family, and we do not let anyone come into the facility without registering."

"Oh no, Ma'am. I'm here to help Mr. Finch take pictures for a newspaper essay. I needed to use the lavatory, and when I came out, I poked my head in one of the classrooms. I used to teach back home."

"What did you teach?"

"Fourth grade."

"And do you always go 'poking' into rooms when you are an uninvited guest in a building?"

Maggie reddened. "No, of course not. I'm sorry that I trespassed."

"How did you get Gabriella to come in here?"

"She walked in and pointed to a book. I guess my teacher instinct took over. I do apologize for any intrusion. I'll go back downstairs and find Mr. Finch."

"I would like to know your name."

Maggie's heartbeat quickened. "Why? I haven't done anything wrong."

"No, you haven't. But we could use a person with teaching experience. I am trying to start a nursery program here."

"I came to New York to take art classes, not teach."

"And I'm not offering you a job. What I need is a volunteer. Someone who has experience with young children to come on Sunday afternoons for one hour. You would read a story to the children and then help them with an art project."

Maggie didn't respond, and the woman went on, ignoring the silence.

"Can you do art activities with children?"

"Yes."

"We service the newly arrived immigrant families with free classes in English, cooking, and homemaking. And we serve afternoon snacks to the children. Would you be comfortable with children of immigrants?"

Maggie stood up taller. "Of course. My mother started a night school for immigrant women back home."

"Then you understand that mothers are the guardians of the home. If we can help them acclimate to living in America, the entire family benefits."

"Where are the families from?"

"Mostly Italy and now living in the tenements of the South Village. A large percentage of the women work in the needle trade, assembling silk flowers for hats. Sunday afternoons are the only semi-free time they get during the week. Plus, we offer a simple hot meal at half-past five for anyone on the property."

"Does the volunteer bring the art supplies?"

"Heavens, no. We have a wealthy sponsor from the Upper East Side. At a nickel a box, we could never afford to replenish the crayons on our own. Well, are you interested? You seemed to be a natural with Gabriella."

Gabriella pulled on Maggie's hand. The cherubic smile on Gabriella's face tugged at Maggie's heartstrings.

"Yes, I think I'm interested."

"You still need to tell me your name."

"Maggie Canavan."

"Well, then, Maggie Canavan. Please arrive by one o'clock tomorrow, and I can take you on a tour of our building. If you agree, you can start your first volunteer hour at two. My name is Mrs. Simons, and I'm the head of Greenwich House."

***

"Tell me again why you've agreed to volunteer at Greenwich House?"

"I told you. Rees took me there yesterday on one of his photo shoots. He was taking pictures of the children for his upcoming project called *Faces of Innocence.*"

"I'm not sure that Rees should be taking you to Greenwich House."

"Oh, for goodness sake. We've gone to lots of places in the West Village. The Greenwich House isn't in a bad area."

"And how would you know?"

"Rees drew me a map of the safe sections of the Village."

"He drew you a map?"

"Yes, showing the important spots of the Village, and the areas to avoid. Greenwich House is a couple of blocks from the hat shop."

"There might be a few…down-on-their-luck men who frequent Greenwich House."

"I only saw children."

"And the Italians of the South Village are known for their high rate of tuberculosis."

"Mrs. Simons, the woman who runs the place, said they need a volunteer for one hour on Sunday afternoons to read to the children. One hour can't put me in any danger."

"And you want to do this?"

"Yes, I think so."

Later that night, Maggie found herself unable to fall asleep. She climbed out of bed and opened her art satchel, locating her pencils and sketch pad. Back on the bed with her knees drawn up, she balanced the pad and begun to draw some quick lines.

Without hesitating, she began a rough sketch of the little girl she met at the settlement house.

The next day Maggie slipped out of the apartment house after lunch and headed south down Sixth Avenue. This route had become Maggie's main street, and she knew all the storefronts by heart. She turned the corner on Barrow, and her breath quickened with anticipation.

Perhaps she would get the opportunity to sketch a few of the immigrant mothers.

I shouldn't be nervous. I taught a whole class of fourth graders for two years. One hour of reading to younger children should be easy.

She opened the door and walked in, noticing right off the cleaning smell of lemon and vinegar water.

Maggie fanned herself. Lord, the heat was oppressive, but she knew it had to be worse in the tenements.

I'm glad I used the new smoother Anne-Marie gave me, and the stick of Odo-ro-no.

She smiled wondering if little Gabriella would return to Greenwich House today.

"I'm glad to see you back, Maggie." Mrs. Simons had silently glided into the room.

"Thank you. I'm looking forward to helping you. I like to sketch on Sundays, but I can always do that after I read to the children."

"So, you're already an artist? I thought you came here to become an artist."

"I'm hoping to become a better artist while living in the Village."

"All right. Let's start with a tour of the house."

They climbed the stairs as Mrs. Simons recounted the history of Greenwich House. Maggie surmised that Mary Simons was a woman of action and not content to sit back and wait for life to unfold.

They started the tour on the top floor of the six-storied building.

"You have a gymnasium!"

"We believe everyone benefits from exercise." Mrs. Simons stated.

As they worked their way down each level, they passed rooms devoted to sewing, bookkeeping, and language classes. The fourth floor contained the kitchen, dining room, and cooking classrooms.

When Maggie asked about the kitchen, Mrs. Simons told her they grew their vegetables on the rooftop garden to provide a hot, nutritious meal each day. Other items like pasta, milk, and cheese, they had to purchase.

"I'm impressed. I didn't know that settlement houses even existed."

Mrs. Simons nodded, but Maggie detected the hint of a smile

skimming across the older woman's face.

At a quarter to two, Maggie entered the reading room and began organizing the materials.

Thank goodness I came early. Whoever used the books last, tossed them into the bookcase.

As Maggie rearranged the books, the middle shelf suddenly gave way and books tumbled to the floor with a crash.

Oh, dear God.

Before the entire bookcase might collapse, she reached out to the other shelves.

"Whoa, what happened?"

Maggie turned. A young man rushed into the room and went to the bookcase.

"I don't think it will collapse. Wait a minute, and I'll get my tools to reinforce the shelf."

He left the room, and Maggie silently thanked God that help had appeared in the nick of time.

A moment later, he was back, replacing the shelf, and hammering wooden supports on either side to hold everything in place.

"Thank you."

"Not at all." He studied her. "Wait. Aren't you the girl who sketches Gladys in the park?"

"Excuse me?"

"Gladys, the pigeon woman."

"Yes." Maggie studied his face. "You're the policeman from the park."

"Guilty as charged. But I also volunteer here as a handyman. I'm Sean Murphy, by the way."

"Well, Mr. Murphy, I'm indebted to you for saving the bookcase. I didn't recognize you without your uniform."

Just then, Gabriella ran into the room and straight to Sean.

"Up?" the little girl questioned.

"Of course." He held open his arms and scooped Gabriella up

into the air, as the child squealed with delight.

Back on the ground, Gabriella walked to Maggie and pointed to the book from yesterday.

"All right, Gabriella, but we need to wait a few minutes for the other children to arrive." Maggie turned back to Sean. "Thank you again, Mr. Murphy, for rescuing the bookshelf."

"If you need anything, I'm down the hall."

Then a dozen young children tumbled into the room, all giggles and shy smiles.

"Come sit here, children. My name is Miss Maggie, and I'm going to read you a wonderful story called *Mr. Prickly Porky.*"

As Maggie sat down with the children at her feet, she caught a glimpse of Sean Murphy smiling as he left the room.

TEN

When Maggie commented to her aunt that she hoped she'd see Rees again, soon, Anne-Marie stopped fussing with a hat and turned to face Maggie.

"Maggie, you might think I don't know what I'm talking about when it comes to young men, but I do."

Oh lord, she sounds like Mama.

"I know you are infatuated with Rees, and he may be a perfectly wonderful gentleman, but men, all men, are more intrigued when the woman isn't easily captured."

"What do you mean?"

"Develop your interests here in the city. It's dangerous to allow the man to become the center of your world, because if he leaves, then your world would crumble."

Finished with her comment, Anne-Marie returned to the hats, while Maggie remained unusually quiet.

***

Mid-week, Rees appeared unexpectedly at the shop.

"Hello, Mr. Finch."

"Hello, Miss Charbonneau. Is Maggie available for a moment?"

"Just a moment?" Anne-Marie's left eyebrow arched.

"Perhaps a few moments?" He grinned.

"Rees! I thought I heard your voice; I was in back, organizing the new trimmings."

"Sounds exciting." He winked and waited for Anne-Marie to leave them in privacy, although Isabelle hovered nearby. "I know this is short notice, but I have another 'assignment' you can help me on. Next Saturday, about three again?"

Maggie hesitated. She wanted to go but didn't want him to think she was always available.

"I think I can persuade my aunt, but I can't take off every Saturday afternoon."

"All right, we can switch to Sundays, then." He grinned.

"I accepted a volunteer position at the Greenwich Settlement House. I started last Sunday."

"Did I miss something while I was photographing the children there?"

"Mrs. Simons, who runs Greenwich House, asked me if I might help out and read to the younger children on Sunday afternoons."

"Why didn't you tell me this before?"

"I hadn't decided, and didn't think you'd be interested."

"All right, how about we plan to see each other on Sunday mornings? I can pick you up early and take you over to Bleeker Street, which has the best bakeries in the Village."

"I usually go to Mass on Sunday mornings."

"What is this, Maggie? Are you playing hard to get?"

"No, but we have to be flexible with our schedules. We could always go to Bleeker Street on a Monday."

Rees's face had the beginning of a scowl. "All right. Can I at least count on you to come with me this Saturday? We'll be visiting a garment factory. Safe, I assure you."

As soon as he said "garment factory," Maggie knew she had to go. "We'll need to leave by noon."

"I'll be ready."

Rees left rather abruptly. Maggie turned and saw Isabelle.

"I'd be careful if I were you. Cancel your volunteering and be available."

"But you're not me." Maggie looked her square in the eye.

Isabelle sashayed to the back of the store, humming a tune from Webster Hall.

∗∗∗

At noon on Saturday, Rees arrived at the shop and took a look at Maggie's outfit.

"Take off your necklace and choose a plain hat."

Maggie cocked her head; she didn't care for his authoritative tone.

"You don't want to stand out, where we're going."

Anne-Marie walked over, and Rees's face brightened.

"Can you tell me where you'll be taking my niece?"

"I want it to be a surprise, but I'll take good care of her; thank you for letting her go with me today." Then he flashed his most charming smile. "We'll be gone all afternoon."

"That doesn't answer my question."

"I plan to photograph children down on lower Broadway."

Doffing his hat, he guided Maggie out of the shop and steered her to the El station. "Hurry; we need to catch the next train."

No sooner had they climbed the platform, then the roaring rumble of a train made it impossible to talk. The train screeched to a stop. Rees paid for them both and sat down next to Maggie. "We'll take this to Bleecker Street. After that, we walk."

The August heat had Maggie's clothes already clinging.

"All right. I agreed to this adventure." She attempted to smooth out her skirt. "But now I insist you tell me which factory are we visiting."

"One that still hires underage children."

Maggie's breath quickened. "We're going there so you can photograph children working illegally?"

Rees nodded. "Lewis Hines has been doing it for years. I know the laws have changed. Children under the age of fourteen are not supposed to work in factories, but many owners turn a blind eye to the regulations."

Maggie remained silent a moment. "And what will I be doing?"

"You'll be distracting the factory manager, pretending to apply for a job. While he's occupied with you, I'll slip up to the next floor and photograph the children."

"How do you know which floor they're on?"

"I've been there before."

"What?"

"Don't ask more questions; just help me out in this."

"Where is the factory?"

"Lower Broadway."

The El rumbled to its stop, and Rees and Maggie departed the train.

"How many blocks is it?"

"Four short blocks and one long one."

As they walked along Broadway, Maggie noticed fewer eating establishments and more signs indicating the needle trade.

"There, on the corner." Rees pointed. "Let's cross. Act the part of a young woman looking for work. Remember, you're single."

"Of course, I'm single."

"In this neighborhood, no married women work in factories; they work out of their homes."

He's referring to the homeworkers.

They entered the lobby and went to the elevator, but not before Maggie saw the sign for which tenants were on which floor. Her face turned pale.

"Rees. You didn't tell me it was the Fleiss Factory! That's where my aunt gets her trimmings."

"So?"

"My God, Rees. It's a sweatshop. The women up there sew artificial flowers!"

"You mean women and children. I'm taking pictures so I can expose the atrocities still going on in the garment industry."

She did not respond.

"Use a false name. No one up there will know who you are. And think about how you are helping the plight of the disadvantaged."

The elevator doors opened and clenching her fists; Maggie stepped in with Rees. The elevator climbed each floor level, and sweat stains formed under her armpits.

All she could think of was, 'What would my mother do?'

The answer came quickly: she'd dig in her heels and help expose the atrocities.

They reached the fifth floor, and the elevator door opened. Across from the elevator, a sign proclaimed, *Fleiss Factory, Millinery Supplies.*

Maggie cleared her throat.

"Come on, think how you're helping the children of this city. All you have to do is go in and inquire about a job. I'll climb the stairs to the next floor and quickly snap a few pictures."

Rees turned toward the stairway door.

She took a deep breath, turned the handle, and walked inside. A man immediately walked over to her.

To her horror, it was Mr. Steinberger, the manager who knew Anne-Marie. All at once, Maggie remembered why she knew his name. He'd been the factory manager at the Triangle Factory the year of the fire.

Now she knew it was no coincidence that she had come here.

"Yes, can I help you?"

"I came…to apply for a job."

He scrutinized her face, almost as if they had met before. "How old are you?"

"Twenty-two."

Then he thrust his chest out with a gleam in his eye. "You married?"

"No."

He smirked. "Don't see why not. You're pretty enough. Do you have good eyesight?"

"Yes."

"Come over here then, and I'll show you where you'll make

violet bunches."

Maggie followed him further into the factory where dust and fabric litter rested in puffballs all across the floor. They turned a corner where two long tables crammed with young women sat side by side fashioning silk violets. Wire strings of inverted finished flower bundles hung above tables jammed with wire stems, petals, leaves, jars of paste, and scissors.

God, this is just like the Triangle!

By a quick count, she estimated that at least forty girls worked in this small room. Maggie's eyes instinctively darted, searching for windows and exit doors.

Steinberger interrupted her thoughts. "You'll arrive at eight in the morning, get a one-hour break for your noon meal, and closing time is half-past five. Starting pay is $4.00 per week. At six months you go up to $4.50 a week. After year two, if you're still here, you can work up to a $5.80 weekly salary."

Good God, how insulting! "Can you tell me what I would do?" She knew she needed to keep the conversation going.

"You'd make flower bunches. What did you think?" He pointed to the tables of the working girls.

"Course, if you are one of my best workers, we can always find a way for you to advance." He winked.

Maggie kept her composure. *I want to vomit on your shoes and tell you that you deserve to be in prison.*

"So, can you start tomorrow?"

"Tomorrow? I didn't realize you'd have an opening so soon. I'll be going out of town for a week or so. Can I come back then and start work?"

Steinberger glared. "Hey, what is this? Why are you here?" He stared hard at her face. "Are you a reporter?" His jaw tightened. "Get out. And I'll remember you, girlie. Don't ever come back."

Maggie did not wait for him to say anything else. As she marched to the exit, she glanced at the rows of young working girls. One of them looked up at Maggie for a moment. Their eyes met, then the young girl busied herself in her work.

Maggie hurried out into the hallway. The stairwell door opened and Rees joined her. "Let's get out of here. We'll take the stairs."

Holding hands, they dashed down the steps.

Once they reached the street, Maggie let out a rush of breath. "I hope you got your photographs, Rees. Because I can never go back there; he knows my face."

"Wasn't it great to have pulled this off?" Rees grinned with the flush of success. "Maggie, a few of those girls I saw can't be older than ten. They were a bit shy, and I had to hurry before anyone came in, but I got the shots I needed. I couldn't have done it without you."

His contagious spirit made her relax, then grin.

"It does feel good to be proactive. The factory was horrible. The young women work crammed at tables like fish in a barrel. Dust piles litter the floor, and the only real light comes from the front windows. It was suffocating."

"What about the manager?"

"His name is Steinberger. Did you know he was once the manager of the Triangle Factory?"

Rees let out a low whistle. "No, I didn't."

"Thank goodness he didn't realize I was related to my aunt. He was nasty, hinting I could advance more quickly if I became one of his 'best workers.' I should report him."

"He's been reported before. That's how I knew about this factory."

"Rees, what will you do with the photos of the children?"

"Hopefully make a name like Lewis Hines is doing. No twenty-three cent dinners of Spanish rice with buttered bread forever. I plan to make real money."

Maggie smiled and let him have his moment of triumph.

"Come on; I'll take you to the studio space I share with Jessie."

When they reached the intersection of Bleecker and Carmine, Rees stopped. "That's where the studio is." He pointed to the large red brick building hugging the corner. "We're up on the fifth floor. Hope you don't mind climbing the stairs. It's a walk up."

By the time they reached the fifth floor, Maggie felt a bit winded and had a new-found admiration for Rees's physical prowess. She only had to carry her purse, while he lugged the camera equipment up each flight of stairs.

Once he opened the door, Maggie stared at the amount of sunlight that flooded the large studio, especially in contrast to the poor lighting at the Fleiss Factory.

"This is where we work to compose photos with models. The back room is where we develop our film."

"Just you and Jessie?"

"No, there's five of us who share the rent on this space."

"What happens if two of you need the studio at the same time?"

"We have a sign-up system. I already signed up for this afternoon. Go ahead and poke around. I'm going to unload the equipment in the back room."

"Are you going to develop your pictures today?"

"Later, after I take you home. I need to be alone to concentrate on the chemicals."

As Rees retreated into the back room, Maggie moved around the studio. All the furniture sat on one side of the room. The arrangement, she supposed, was to take advantage of the light and allow the photographer to shoot from the best angle.

On the couch were several ladies' hats, a long-feathered boa, and a variety of silk scarves.

"There, done. I wish I could offer you a bite to eat, but we don't keep food here. There are so many eating places nearby."

"Are you hungry?"

"I am, but I'm not thinking of food. Maggie, we have the rest of the afternoon to ourselves." He walked over and pulled her into his arms, still full of excitement from the success in the factory. His kiss went deep.

Maggie's body responded in kind. Then he led her to the sofa, and they both sat down. The kissing became more passionate. Maggie could not stop her body from reacting to his, nor did she want to; but she also knew where this would lead. The next few minutes would determine the course of their relationship.

"Rees…" She pulled back.

He looked at her with a silent question on his lips.

"I'm still …"

"A virgin? I suspected as such. Then let me be your first. You have to know I've been crazy for you ever since we met."

"I feel the same way about you. But I don't know if I'm ready for this."

"Ready for me, or ready to take the next step?"

"The next step. Back home, girls didn't …"

"Didn't sleep with their beau outside of marriage? Oh, but Maggie, I can assure you that did happen at times."

Maggie remained silent, not sure of herself.

"I'll be tender, I promise. Your first time should be with someone you trust."

Part of Maggie wanted to proceed, but she chickened out. "I can't. Not yet, anyway."

"I won't force you, Maggie. But I would be honored to be the man who taught you what love in the afternoon means."

"Please, Rees."

"This is the Village, Maggie. No one stays a virgin forever."

"I don't intend to stay a virgin forever, but I want it to feel right, and this feels too rushed. Don't push me. I'll know when I'm ready."

He let out a sigh, then smiled. "All right, not yet." Rees got up and offered a hand to Maggie. "Then let me show you my collection of photos. You'll be able to see that I do want to report on the lives of city children."

He led her to the back room, and there, clipped to wires strung across the walls were the black and white photos he had taken, capturing city children in alleys, on the streets, and in the parks.

Maggie recognized his talent right away and smiled at the photos of the children in the backyard of Greenwich House Settlement.

ELEVEN

The next day was the first Sunday in August. Maggie planned the story and art project she would do with the children. She selected *The Tale of Peter Rabbit*. While the children might not know about gardens, they would have a favorite food they could draw.

She arrived at Greenwich House with plenty of time to arrange the chairs and put out pieces of drawing paper and crayons so the children could share the colors.

Ten minutes before her reading time was to start, Sean popped into the room.

"Checking that the bookcase is still intact." He smiled.

"Yes, thank you."

"What story are you going to read?"

"The Tale of Peter Rabbit, do you know it?"

"I do. My Mam used to read it to me when I was little. I think she used it as a cautionary tale about minding your parents." He laughed.

"I'm going to use it to coax the children to draw pictures of their favorite food."

"Well, I doubt any of them will draw carrots," he laughed.

Just then, the children arrived with their mothers. Each woman nodded a silent greeting to Sean, but the children all squealed a hello or waved as they toppled into the room.

Once the mothers left to attend their classes, Maggie settled the children. She taught them that when she sat, so should they. It was also the signal for everyone to become quiet so that Miss Maggie could read.

When the hour finished and each child had proudly shared their pictures, Maggie was surprised that every one of them had drawn macaroni as their favorite food.

The mothers came to collect their children, and Gabriella held onto Maggie's hand. Then an older girl with matching black curls walked into the room.

"Hello, I'm Maggie Canavan, the teacher."

"Hello, I'm Tessa, Gabriella's older sister."

Maggie wasn't sure, but she thought she recognized Tessa from the Fleiss Factory. Not wanting to pry, she decided not to ask. "Gabriella certainly loves to listen to stories. I'm glad she's a part of the group."

"Thank you. Come, Gabi, it's time to go home."

The young child got up and followed her sister. But as she walked out the door, she turned and flashed a huge smile at Maggie.

Maggie waved back.

***

The following Sunday, Maggie finished her volunteer time, and on her way out, she saw Mrs. Simons in conversation with another woman.

"Ah, Maggie, I'm glad you're still here. I'd like you to meet a friend."

Maggie smoothed her skirt.

This is Crystal Eastlake, who often drops by. She and her brother publish a magazine here in the Village."

"How do you do…" Maggie stuttered, not knowing the proper protocol.

Crystal extended her hand. "Please, call me Crystal. Mrs. Simons tells me you have a gift with children. Now, are you a Miss or a Missus?" Crystal Eastlake let a grin slowly spread across her face.

"A Miss. My name is Maggie Canavan."

"What do you do when you're not volunteering?"

"I work at my aunt's hat shop. Hats by Anne-Marie."

Crystal Eastlake looked at Mrs. Simons. "That little millinery store on Christopher Street?" Facing Maggie, she offered a genuine smile. "Yes, I know the shop, and I've met your aunt. Have you come to New York to become a milliner?"

"No, I came to New York hoping to attend art school, but I missed the deadline at the Cooper Union."

"Deadline?" Crystal Eastlake turned to Mrs. Simons. "Do you think there was a quota?"

The director shrugged her shoulders.

Maggie furrowed her brow. "What do you mean?"

"Meaning that the Cooper Union had already admitted their chosen number of women for the year."

"Oh, I don't think so. My rejection letter said I missed the date for admission."

"What the letter stated versus the true reality might never come to light."

"That wouldn't seem fair."

"A lot of things aren't fair for women. But, perhaps there's a way around Cooper Union. You could still study art with a good teacher."

Maggie nodded politely.

"Many artists here offer classes. What type of art interests you?"

"I wanted to be a sketch artist and draw fashions for working girls."

"Please assure me you will not succumb to painting the Gibson girl image. Real women are nothing like that. Fashion magazines portray us as silly little tootsey-wootseys. I would hope you would use your talent for a more noble pursuit."

Maggie reddened.

"We should recruit you for the cause."

"What cause?"

"Women's rights."

"You mean the suffragists' cause?"

"What do you know about the suffragists?"

"I sold hats to two ladies who marched in the Fourth of July Parade. They carried a banner that said VOTES FOR WOMEN."

"Other than those two women, have you met other suffragists?"

"I don't think so."

Crystal Eastlake smiled at Mrs. Simons. "Well, Maggie. You have. Both Mrs. Simons and I are suffragists. We're also feminists."

"Isn't that the same thing?"

"Suffragists campaign for a woman's right to vote. Feminists want women to have that right, but also legal control over their bodies, and the right to pursue meaningful careers."

Maggie digested the information.

"Do you think those ideas are radical?"

"Not really."

"Classes here at the settlement house empower immigrant women to help themselves."

"My mother teaches English classes to immigrant wives of coal miners."

Crystal Eastlake smiled. "Seems like you have an inherited trait of compassion, then."

Maggie blushed again. It was the first time anyone had ever compared her to her mother.

"Who is giving lessons, now? Edward Hopper?" Mrs. Simons asked Crystal Eastlake.

"No, I don't think he's teaching, just painting. Maggie, let me investigate for you. Your desire to be an artist should not be wasted."

"Thank you, but I don't have money for art lessons right now. I expected the Cooper Union to be free."

"Leave that to us. And if you'd like to learn more about women's rights, why don't you join us this Saturday at our next Heterodoxy Club lunch? You'll be my guest. We meet at Polly's."

"I've not heard of that club."

"We're a group of outspoken females who believe women

deserve to have the same rights as men. Our luncheons are quite spirited, and we often have an outside speaker like Margaret Sanger."

"Oh, I heard her speak at the Cooper Union back in July. She gave an illuminating talk on women's rights to birth control."

"And did you agree with her statements?"

Maggie thought about the correct answer. "I did learn a lot."

"Meet us at Polly's, then, this coming Saturday at noon."

"I would need Polly's address. I've not met her."

"You are a newcomer, aren't you? Polly is Polly's Restaurant. She used to have one on MacDougal, but she relocated to 5 Sheridan Square."

"Oh, I do know Sheridan Square. It's near Jessie's art gallery."

"You know Jessie?"

"We've eaten shortcake together."

"Well then, you're not as green as I thought."

Maggie's smile changed into a grin.

TWELVE

"Aunt Anne-Marie, I would like to attend their lunch meeting."

"Maggie, you just met Crystal Eastlake, and you know little about her."

"I know she's a suffragist and a feminist."

"Yes, and a radical one, to boot. All the women there will be older than you and have arduous notions about women's rights."

"I'd still like to go."

"It means Isabelle will have to carry your load on top of her own."

"It's only for a few hours. I don't think Isabelle will have that much extra work, and I'll be back as soon as the lunch is over."

Anne-Marie scrutinized Maggie. "What did they tell you about the club?"

"Not much, except that the members support women's rights and they have outside speakers like Margaret Sanger."

"How did Crystal Eastlake meet you?"

"Mrs. Simons introduced us. I thought you would be supportive of me going. You believe in women's rights, don't you?"

"Of course, I do. However, I don't believe you have to be radical about it. Battles can also be fought and won by feminine wiles."

"But are those the important battles?"

Anne-Marie narrowed her eyes. "If you're so intent in learning about the club, go ahead and attend the lunch. I seem to recall that they meet at Polly's Restaurant."

"Yes, at 5 Sheridan Square."

"Crystal Eastlake is a powerful connection here in the Village. Don't get swept up with any extremist ideas. And don't come back here assuming you can convert me into a feminist."

Maggie let out a sigh. *Lord, I don't want to alienate Aunt Anne-Marie, but I had no idea how independent-minded she would be.*

***

Rees left Maggie a note at the shop that he was going out of town to photograph soldiers on a New Jersey army base. He asked her to save next Monday morning for him because he wanted to take her to Bleeker Street for the best pastries in the Village. He'd come by the apartment at eight.

Maggie smiled at his thoughtfulness. But this was Saturday, and all her thoughts were zeroed in on the luncheon.

She found Polly's without any trouble.

"Maggie! I'm delighted you're here."

"Thank you, Miss Eastlake."

"I told you to call me Crystal. Now, come sit next to me; our speaker today is one of us."

Maggie glanced around the table. Anne-Marie had been correct; the ten women were older than Maggie. Each woman's outfit showcased quality fabric, but none of them wore elaborate hats.

"Let me introduce you. Ladies, this is Maggie Canavan who volunteers for Mary at Greenwich House."

The women smiled, and one by one gave their names: Ida, Henrietta, Susan, Neith, Frances, Edna, Alice, and Margaret. Maggie already knew Mary Simons.

Everyone sat down. No one offered a grace, so Maggie dipped her spoon into the bowl set in front of her. The meal was a vegetarian goulash, even though meat rationing no longer existed.

As the group enjoyed their dessert of simple pound cake and coffee, a no-nonsense woman named Frances stood up and addressed them.

"I want to talk today about our sisters who have been working in the factories, stepping into the shoes of the brave American men who went off to war.

"My question is, what will happen when the men come home? Should the women be coerced into giving up employment, or should the companies find them similar jobs? The women are not being paid anywhere near what the men earned for those same positions, and the women have not been given any health benefits.

"I say that if a woman has done a man's job, then she is entitled to the same pay and benefits as the man.

"The only way we can right these wrongs is by ensuring that women get elected into office. Then, unfair laws can be changed. We cannot sit back, proud that New York women can vote, when our less fortunate sisters, like the women of Maryland, have been consistently denied that right. We will not rest until all twenty million women in America have won the right to vote, guaranteed by the United States Constitution."

The women burst into applause.

"I urge each woman here to consider giving a speech, or design a billboard poster or visit a politician in his office, stipulating our concerns that women's equality has to be addressed. I hope I can count on every one of you."

Applause followed once more and then quick, spirited conversations broke out around the table about the possibilities brought forth.

Maggie was both astonished and energized.

She didn't even know that New York women already had the vote. It wasn't fair that your address determined such an important right. Maryland women deserved the right to vote as much as anyone else.

By the time the luncheon was over, Maggie had found herself intoxicated with the ideas of the women around the table. She might not be able to give a speech or visit a politician, but she could design a billboard poster.

"Thank you so much, Crystal, for inviting me. I found the discussion to be thought-provoking and I would like to draw a few posters. I could show working women voting at the polls."

"Good. Here, I found an Edith Young Lecture for you to attend."

Maggie opened the envelope to find an admission ticket to a YWCA lecture on "An Introduction to Fashion Drawing."

"Oh, my. Thank you."

"She is one of the premier art instructors in the fashion world and runs a school in Newark, New Jersey. She occasionally comes to New York and gives lectures. I think you'll find a wealth of information from listening to her."

"This is very generous of you."

"You can pay us back by creating posters for the equality cause."

Maggie could hardly wait and share her news with Anne-Marie.

***

"Slow down, Maggie. I'm trying to listen, but you are going too fast. So, there were ten women plus you at the luncheon. Were any of them wearing one of our hats?"

"Not that I could tell. The hats were simple in style but well-made. What I want to tell you is about the speaker and a lecture on fashion drawing that I can attend."

"Who was the speaker?"

"Frances something. I didn't catch her last name, but she talked about the women who have taken over the factory jobs once held by men. What will happen to those women when the men return from war? Have you ever thought of that?"

"No, because it doesn't affect me."

"But you should be concerned."

"And why is that?"

"Because we need to support other women and help all of us gain the equality we deserve."

"It sounds to me like you're parroting what you heard at the luncheon."

Maggie reared back. "Aunt Anne-Marie, are you saying you're against women's rights?"

"What I am, is a proponent for my rights, the right to own my business and the right to express my views without any other woman thinking less of me."

"But you are such an accomplished woman, owning your shop."

"Yes, and the feminists didn't help me get there. You need to be careful about those women, Maggie. If you don't watch out, they'll expect you to help them."

"But I want to help them. Poster artists are needed."

"And how are you going to do that?"

"Crystal Eastlake has given me a ticket to an Edith Young Lecture on fashion drawing. After that, I intend to use the knowledge I'll learn to design a poster showing a woman in attractive work clothes casting a vote."

Anne-Marie arched her left eyebrow. "You do realize that once you make a poster for them, you will be beholden to their cause."

"Is that such a terrible thing?"

"Well, I don't want to see you marching in any of their parades."

"Honestly, Aunt Anne-Marie, I can think for myself."

"At least put one of our hats on the woman in the poster, and sign your name only as MC."

"Why?"

"In case you regret in later years having your artwork associated with the Women's Rights Movement."

"I doubt that will happen."

Anne-Marie threw up her hands and left the room.

**

Bright and early on Monday morning, the apartment buzzer rang. Minutes later, Rees knocked at the apartment door.

"I have a surprise for you, in addition to the best pastry in New York."

"What is it?"

"If I told you, it wouldn't be a surprise, so you'll have to wait. Good-bye Miss Charbonneau. I'll take good care of her."

In the elevator, Rees leaned over and kissed her.

"My, Mr. Finch, this is a pleasant way to start the day."

"Good. I'm glad you feel that way."

Outside, Maggie waited to see which way they would head, although she knew Bleeker Street was south of the park. Maggie loved Rees's sense of adventure; it added to his intrigue.

"Maggie, today you'll ride in style to Bleeker Street. We're taking the subway!"

"The train that goes underground?"

"Yes. Have you ridden it yet?"

"No. We stick to the Sixth Avenue El."

"Come on."

Maggie closed her eyes and said a quick Hail Mary when Rees helped her navigate down the steep steps leading to the hidden station. She shivered with the memory of miner' stories about rats as big as squirrels that lived in underground tunnels.

The temperature dropped, but the odors did not. The smells were worse than on the streets above.

Reese purchased their nickel tokens and guided Maggie to the train platform. A distant rumble increased into a screeching vibration of metal scraping metal before Maggie could figure out what was happening. Then a subway train ground to a halt alongside her.

"Quick, Maggie, you don't want to get left behind."

Swallowing any fear, Maggie surged into the car which looked like an enclosed omnibus. In an instant, the doors slammed shut, and the train sped off.

Maggie tried to look out the window, but she only saw total blackness. The train screeched along the tracks, swerving left and right. Then the train slowed and pulled into a lit station stop.

"We get off here at Christopher Street."

Maggie held onto Rees's arm as they stepped out of the train.

"Wasn't that fun!" Rees's eyes were shining with delight. "See the wall tiles that spell out Christopher Street? All the subway stops have tiles to alert you to your location."

Maggie was relieved they were going up to the real world again.

They ascended the steps into the bright morning light, and Maggie spied Sheridan Square. "Rees, Jessie's tearoom is down this street."

"Very good. I didn't realize you had developed such a good sense of direction." He teased.

"Yes, thanks to street signs. Now, where is Bleeker Street?"

"Due south on Seventh."

The foot journey took less than ten minutes. On Bleeker Street, every other building was a food establishment. There were meat shops, pastry shops, cheese shops, Italian groceries, and cafes.

Maggie thought how Bleeker Street resembled the main street of Porters Glen, where the butcher sat across from Grand-papa's store, and McKenzie's Grocery nearby. However, when they arrived at Roma's, the sign read Pasticceria Roma, which meant it was a pastry shop, not a bakery.

Do I enlighten Rees on the matter? Probably not.

Inside the shop, Maggie was smacked by a bolt of homesickness, not for Porters Glen, but, for Grand-papa. The air inside Roma's dripped with the smells of warm pastries fresh from the oven. She imagined her grandfather dressed in his baker's apron sampling the goods.

Rees nudged her over to the tall glass displays of pastries, cookies, and small cakes.

"What would you like?"

"I'm not sure. What do you usually get?"

"I like everything here, but I often choose a cornetto." He pointed to one.

"They look like a treat my grandfather makes called a croissant.

I'll try a cornetto with you."

They sat at a table covered in red and white oilcloth and Rees ordered two cups of cappuccinos. When their order arrived, Maggie waited to see what Rees would do with his coffee.

"Have you ever had a cappuccino, Maggie?"

"No. At home, we drink café-au-lait. Coffee laced with steamed milk."

"Not that much different then. Except this coffee is espresso, so it will be stronger than what you might be used to."

Maggie took a small sip. The coffee was strong and hot, but she enjoyed it. Then she bit into the cornetto. The soft dough tickled her lips. It was sweeter than a croissant, and Maggie swore she tasted sugar and vanilla. Whatever the ingredients, the pastry was delicious.

Rees broke into a smile, but not at Maggie.

"Why, Mr. Finch, I didn't know you frequented Roma's. You must know all the best spots of the Village."

Maggie choked. She recognized the voice. Isabelle's! Turning slowly around in her seat, Maggie mustered a weak smile. "Well, hello, Isabelle. I'm surprised to find you in this neighborhood. Aren't there any good pastry shops on the Lower East Side?"

Isabelle ignored Maggie. "I see you ordered a cornetto, Mr. Finch. So much better than those puny French pastries, don't you think?"

"Let me get you one."

Before Maggie knew what was happening, Isabelle sat in Rees's seat while he ordered at the counter.

"Isabelle, what are you doing?"

"As I said, I came for a pastry." Isabelle looked at the counter and saw that Rees was still waiting to order. "Look, Maggie, there's something I need to say. I feel that we got off on the wrong foot when you came to work at the shop. I'd like for us to be friends."

Maggie tried not to choke. "Isabelle, we don't have anything in common."

Isabelle blanched. "Why? Because I don't come from a family of schoolteachers? You have no idea, Maggie, of how lucky you are to have a family supporting you."

"You know nothing about me."

"That's where you're wrong. You might need my help one day."

"I doubt that very much."

A fleeting look of hurt crossed Isabelle's face.

But Maggie did not trust the girl, especially around Rees.

"Here we go. One cornetto."

"Thank you, Mr. Finch." Isabelle lowered her eyelashes. "I'll eat it as I walk. Good-bye, Maggie."

Maggie returned to her pastry, but the taste had lost its appeal.

"What's a matter, Maggie? You don't like the cornetto?"

"What I don't like is Isabelle."

"She's a harmless flirt."

"Honestly, Rees. When women are working so hard to get the right to vote, among other things, girls like Isabelle are the very opposite of the image we hope to project."

He raised his eyebrows.

"Maybe not all women are meant to vote."

"That's easy for you to say, you're a man. You've had the privilege since birth."

"Maggie, this was supposed to be a quiet morning sharing delicious pastry—not an opportunity for getting into an argument."

"Until men understand that women deserve the right to vote, there will always be an argument."

Rees sat back from the table. "Wow, Maggie. I didn't expect this from you."

"I'm sorry. I didn't mean to spoil our morning."

"At least now, I know you're an advocate for women's rights."

"I can't change what I believe to be right."

"No one is asking you that. Come on, let's get you back to the hat shop. I have work to do."

The remnants of the pastry lie untouched in the now subdued atmosphere.

THIRTEEN

Tuesday was the date Maggie had been dreading. She had waited until the last possible day to call home and let her parents know she intended to stay in New York.

"I hate making this phone call, Aunt Anne-Marie. I know Mama is going to be upset, and then Papa will be angry with me because I'm going back on my word."

"Would you rather go home and resume your life there?"

"No."

"Then be honest with them. Explain what you want to do with your art and how much you love the city."

"Mama's biggest fear is that I won't ever come home."

"Of course, you'll go home. You just don't know when."

"But you didn't. You stayed in New York and made your life here."

"My life story will not be the same as yours. Answer me this: If Rees Finch were not here, would you still want to stay in New York?"

Maggie didn't hesitate. "Yes, I'd still want to stay."

"Then give yourself a year. If things don't work out, you can make other changes. But please, don't go back to Porters Glen just for your parents. You deserve your own life."

"All right. Thank goodness the bakery isn't on a party line."

Maggie picked up the receiver and asked the operator to place a long-distance call to Charbonneau's Bakery in Porters Glen, Maryland.

Anne-Marie stood up to leave the room, but Maggie beckoned

her to stay.

"Mama? Hello, it's me."

Anne-Marie beamed a smile of encouragement.

"Yes, I've been well. Yes, I've gone to church regularly. What date am I coming home? That's why I'm calling. I want to extend my time and stay on for a bit longer." Pause. "Hello? Are you still there?"

Maggie looked up in fright at Anne-Marie.

"Yes, I know I promised to return before fall. But I've found a job here reading to young children at a settlement house. They're immigrant children. I'm following in your footsteps. And I have an opportunity to attend art lectures, which I could never do back home."

Anne-Marie reached for the phone. "Annie? This is Marie. Maggie hasn't come to this decision lightly, and I did not suggest she stay. She's made friends here in the city and has become quite involved with the Settlement House. She wants an extension, not forever."

She gave the phone back to Maggie.

"Mama? Please call back after you've had the chance to talk this over with Papa. I've already written my note to the Allegany School Board, asking for a one-year leave of absence. Yes, I do understand. All right. Good-bye. I love you both."

As soon as she put the phone back in its cradle, Maggie began to cry.

"I knew she'd be upset. I hated telling her I wanted to stay here instead of going back home."

"Maggie, after a full year in the city, you'll know if you're meant to stay."

"God, I hope so."

***

Two days later the phone rang in the hat shop. Not expecting her parents, Maggie cheerfully answered with, "This is Hats by Marie, how can we help you?"

"Oh, Papa, it's you." She listened patiently as he gently chided her for going back on her word, but that he and her mother had talked over the situation and wanted Maggie to be happy.

Maggie began to cry. "I didn't want to disappoint you, and I know we depended on my paycheck last year. But right now, more than anything else, I want to stay. At least for the school year."

Her father carried on the conversation, telling Maggie that they would expect her to write letters regularly and call home each week. She was not to worry about family finances; her father had already planned on teaching a full load again at the college.

Maggie breathed a sigh of relief. "Thank you, Papa."

Now that the decision had been made, Maggie felt lighter. She would get ten whole months to live in The Village, take art classes, and date again. Her world was suddenly filled with delightful possibilities.

Her relationship with Rees, however, warranted extra thoughts. Her perception of sex had shifted. She knew she wasn't quite ready, but when the time did arrive, she would carry douche tablets as a precaution. As Rees had said, this was the Village, and no one stayed a virgin forever.

***

On Sunday, Maggie was lost in thought and didn't see Sean enter the Reading Room.

"Maggie?"

"Oh, hello. Sorry, I didn't hear you come in."

"I wanted to ask you to consider staying for the evening meal. It's going to be a real treat, spaghetti."

"I don't even know what that is."

"Well, it's new. Think of macaroni, but with long slender pieces. It is all the rage right now, and Mrs. Simons thought it would be fun to prepare it for dinner."

"Thanks, but my aunt will be expecting me for dinner."

"Can't you call her and tell her about this special meal? Afterward, we're all going to the Garrett for ice cream."

"Ice cream? That would be hard to pass up."

"They'll only have vanilla, but it will be good."

What would Rees think about this? Then she shrugged. He

didn't always share his schedule with her, so she wasn't obligated to tell him everything she did.

"Maggie, it's summer! It's the season to do unexpected things."

"All right. Let me call my aunt and let her know. It's three o'clock. I can go home and come back."

Sean thought for a moment. "We could visit the park instead, and I could introduce you to Gladys. I assume you're still sketching her?"

"The park? Yes, I'd like to meet Gladys."

As they walked from Greenwich House to Washington Square, Sean recounted stories to Maggie about the park.

"Did you know the park was once a potter's field? When the city decided to build the park in the 1800s, they knew that approximately 20,000 unnamed graves rested in the ground."

"Where did they move the bodies?"

"They didn't. Each time I walk through the park, I think of all those souls resting below."

Maggie shuddered. "I'd rather sketch people who are on top of the ground."

As they approached the park, Sean stopped. "See that gigantic elm?"

Maggie nodded.

"It's a witness tree."

"A witness tree?"

"The oldest living resident in the Village. It's also called the Hangman's Tree because it was used as the gallows a hundred years ago. Think of the stories it could tell."

Maggie looked up at the strong linear branches and decided maybe not all the stories warranted telling.

They walked through the arch and looked for Gladys. As soon as they saw a flock of pigeons swooping down to land, they headed for that section.

Gladys sat on a bench holding a paper bag. She pulled out pieces of bread, tore them into smaller pieces, and tossed them into the air.

"Hello, Gladys. How are you today?"

"Good as long as I have my feathered friends come to visit. Why aren't you in uniform?"

"It's one of my Sundays off. I didn't realize you'd miss me."

"I know all the good-looking men in the park." She cackled. "And her," she stared at Maggie. "She's an artist. I've seen her sketching me."

Maggie smiled. "I didn't mean to be secretive. I wanted to respect your privacy."

"Privacy? Hah! That's a laugh. There's no privacy in the Village. Everyone knows what everyone else is doing. And that includes you."

She pointed a boney finger at Maggie, and Maggie swallowed a nervous laugh.

"Maggie and I are out for a stroll. We'll leave you to the birds while we go watch a chess game."

Sean led Maggie over to the east side of the park where several men were engrossed in playing chess.

"Sean, I know nothing about the game."

"All right, we can sit and talk, then."

"About what?"

"Tell me what you did this week."

Maggie smiled. "Well, I went to a fascinating luncheon."

Maggie found herself telling Sean all about the Heterodoxy Club. He was a good listener, and his eyes never left her face.

When she finally stopped to catch a breath, he laughed. "Whoa! Can I ask a question? Are you thinking about becoming a suffragist or a feminist?"

"I think women should have the vote, and I also think women should be paid the same salary as men if they are performing the same job."

She waited to see his reaction.

"My Da is probably rolling over in his grave, but I agree. There's no reason why a woman shouldn't be able to vote. As for the salary issue, I don't know many instances where women perform the same job as a man."

"Women should get equal pay. Period."

"Life's more complicated than decreeing that everyone deserves equal pay."

"Well, what if women made a higher salary than men? What

would you think then?"

"I think we should head back to Greenwich House, before tackling any more of the nation's issues." He grinned.

The spaghetti dinner turned out to be one of the most enjoyable meals Maggie could remember, and she loved the novelty of the thin pasta strands covered in thick, tangy tomato sauce. About twenty people stayed to dine, and they pushed the tables together like at a party.

Most of the group went for ice cream after the meal, including Maggie and Sean. As they ventured out, Mrs. Simons walked over to Maggie and informed her that next Sunday would be the annual end of summer celebration. They would all be going out to Coney Island for the day. She hoped Maggie would attend.

Coney Island? I wouldn't miss it!

When she climbed on the El to return home the long summer day had trickled to an end, sending the sun off in a blaze of purples and blues. Maggie smiled. Deciding to stay in New York was one of the best decisions she had made.

***

Maggie wasn't sure when she'd see Rees again. It irritated her that his schedule was so inconsistent, but there was little she could do other than make her own plans.

When Rees finally appeared at the shop, he explained that he had been out of town on a variety of assignments and now had the opportunity to take photos for a classy inn in the Catskill Mountains.

Maggie had never heard of the Catskills.

"That's all right, Rees. Greenwich House is having an outing to Coney Island on Sunday, so I'll be busy on the weekend anyway. Come into the shop when you get back."

He looked around and seeing no customers, leaned over and kissed her on the lips with a kiss that lingered. "So, you won't forget me while I'm gone."

"Then, don't forget me either." Her left eyebrow arched.

FOURTEEN

Maggie woke with a smile. Today she would see the ocean!

Although she had picnicked on the shores of the Casselman River with her parents, Maggie had never been any place where one could swim in deep water.

In celebration of the outing, she had gone to Bonwit Teller's and purchased a real bathing suit. The saleslady called it a Jantzen and said it functioned as two pieces with a belted tunic made out of navy-blue light-weight wool. The top came down to Maggie's knees and covered the short trousers underneath. She was a bit surprised that the short cap sleeves did not reach her elbows and the plunging neckline revealed never-before-seen skin. But this was New York where fashions differed drastically from back home.

The saleslady further explained that Maggie would also need a pair of light-weight woolen stockings and buttoned-up canvas shoes for walking in the sand. If she thought she might go into the water, then she needed a rubber swim cap as well. By the time the lady rang up Maggie's purchase, the sum had exceeded more than Maggie had wanted to spend. She rationalized the purchase by telling herself that any modern New York woman would have made the same purchase.

The aroma of fresh coffee drew Maggie to the kitchen.

"Aunt Anne-Marie! You made café au lait."

"I did. It's a special day. I also took the liberty of getting you a travel bag for your bathing suit and a soft-brimmed hat for walking around the town."

"There's a town? Isn't Coney Island a beach?"

"It's a large area. Now, tell me how many children are going."

"Mrs. Simons said eighteen, and I won't be the sole chaperone. Mrs. Simons will be there, of course, and five more adults. I'm hoping to have four children in my group."

Maggie wanted to savor the café au lait, but her excitement about the day got the better of her. She gulped down the coffee and polished off a piece of buttered toast and a poached egg.

Knowing that the steamboat left Pier One in lower Manhattan precisely at nine forty-five, Maggie took no chances in being late. She finished dressing in a light-weight cream-colored linen shirt-waist, and her navy gored skirt. To tie her ensemble together, she switched the white ribbons on her hat to navy ties matching her outfit.

A quick kiss to Anne-Marie and Maggie sprinted out the door.

She walked up to 14th Street and waited for the El. The ride was quick, only one stop and she waited patiently for a young mother and her three rambunctious children to exit in front of her.

By the time Maggie reached Greenwich House, Mrs. Simons had everyone standing in line, listening to instructions.

"Dear children, I know how excited you are, but there are rules to be followed. I will put you in groups of four, with an adult. You will at no time, ever, leave on your own. If you must use the toilet, tell us and one of us will take you there. Is that clear?"

All the children nodded, but Maggie heard them giggle to one another. Energy flooded the atmosphere like high tide.

"Mrs. Simons, please indicate who my four charges will be."

Mrs. Simons handed her a list. Scanning the names, Maggie saw that she had six children, including Gabi and Tessa.

"All right, everyone. We must leave to catch the next El to South Ferry, where we'll board the boat. Adults, please round up your group. Children, please hold hands with one another as we walk to the 8th Street station."

Everyone went into action. Maggie retrieved Gabi and Tessa,

and the four other children on her list. Amid the commotion, Maggie felt a tap on her shoulder.

There stood Sean.

"I thought perhaps you could use an extra pair of hands with the children. I know you have the largest group, and I already cleared it with Mrs. Simons." His smile, warm and genuine, diffused the chaos.

"I'm delighted you'll be with us."

By the time the group arrived at the South Ferry Terminal, the excitement among the children had crackled like electricity in the air. Seagulls screeched overhead, and the pervasive smell of salt and fish saturated the air.

A warm feeling of happiness spread over Maggie. Few of these children had ever left their section of Greenwich Village, much less board a boat to Coney Island.

Mrs. Simons handed the tickets to the station agent and proceeded to shepherd all the children on board. "Remember, stay with your teacher!"

"Come with me, Maggie, I know the best viewing place."

Maggie followed Sean, with her six charges. "I had no idea I would be this drained already!"

The paddleboat steamer took them down the lower part of the East River and out into Upper Bay. The excursion would take an hour before they docked at Coney Island. Mrs. Simons walked the deck, checking in with each group. When she came to Maggie and Sean, she sat down.

"It seems as if everything is in order."

"Mrs. Simons, how are the children paying for their tickets?"

"They're not. Remember the patron who supplies us with crayons?" Maggie nodded. "She also makes this outing possible."

"How expensive is it?"

"It costs 35 cents per child to ride the ferry and gain admission to all 25 attractions in Steeplechase Park. Add in another 5 cents for a Nathan's red hot for lunch. None of our families would ever be able to spend that much on one child. Not when you consider that the sum of

40 cents is almost equal to a day's rent."

"The children each brought a paper bag. Is that for their bathing suits?"

"No, they'll swim in their one-piece union suits." Maggie shook her head, and Mrs. Simons clarified, "Their underwear."

Maggie blushed, while Sean grinned. "Then what's in their bag?" Maggie asked.

"Lunch. Each mother was asked to pack a sandwich for their child, although I imagine most of the sandwiches are mainly pieces of bread spread with olive oil. That's why we make sure each child gets a red hot."

"A red hot?"

"A frankfurter. Goodness, Maggie, didn't they have frankfurters in your home town?"

"I'm not sure. My family is French, and we never ate one."

"Then, Sean, please make sure Maggie gets to eat a red hot today." She smiled and got up and continued on her walk around the boat.

The salt air and steamboat plodding through the bay made Maggie giddy. She might not have known what a red hot was, but she could tell this was going to be an adventure.

While the children laughed and pointed to seagulls, Maggie and Sean sat back and enjoyed the breeze.

Maggie stole a glance at Sean. He was every bit as good-looking as Rees, but not out to impress. His dark brown eyes crinkled when he laughed, and his policeman trained physique was honed. She smiled and turned to look out over the bay.

They chatted easily about her love of painting, and he admitted to her that he played an Irish tin whistle sometimes in bars. This intrigued her, and she made him promise to share a tune with her sometime.

When forty-five minutes had passed, the boat turned east. Sean pointed out Coney Island ahead on the left, then told Maggie to look right. There lay the Atlantic Ocean.

The enormity of the Atlantic on the horizon held Maggie spellbound as sunlight seemed to dance upon its surface.

If only I could capture colors the way the sky and the sea present themselves, I'd be a real artist.

When the steamboat pulled up to Steeplechase Pier, the passengers moved down to the departure deck. Tessa grabbed Gabi's hand, and then Gabi grabbed the hand of the boy next to her in line. Sean held hands with two of the children, leaving Maggie to negotiate with the last child.

As they disembarked, Sean stayed close, like a mother goose herding goslings.

Once out on the pier, Maggie let out an audible gasp.

Their tickets were for Steeplechase Park, but off to the right were signs for Luna Park and further east a sign for Dreamland Park. Who knew that Coney Island had three amusement parks!

She peered at the view of Steeplechase Park. A tall steel tower stood out on the landscape with a huge Ferris wheel and large buildings proclaiming to be Fun Houses. From far away, she could hear the excited screams of visitors already on the rides.

If I am this thrilled, I can imagine how the children are reacting. She looked over at Tessa and Gabi. Both girls' stares fixated on the magical landscape.

Mrs. Simons appeared and reminded everyone that they couldn't stop to lollygag; they needed to walk the entire length of the pier to get to the entrance of Steeplechase Park.

Even the seagulls were celebrating the day as they swooped down out of a sky hoping to snag morsels of food bobbing in the water.

Maggie tied the ribbons of her hat and then glided along the pier, trying to act mature, but feeling like an exuberant child.

***

After their group had walked around Steeplechase Park and looked at all the rides, the children announced they were hungry. Sean led the group to Nathan's Red Hots while the sun beat down on the walkway, making Maggie perspire.

Sean demonstrated how to spoon mustard over the frank and then pick up the roll and take a bite. Maggie followed his directions, but when she bit into the concoction, mustard squirted out and landed on her plate. The children burst into simultaneous laughter.

"Well, Maggie, now you've had a red hot!"

She grinned and made a second attempt. This time her mouth managed to capture the entire bite. The meat tasted a bit spicy and deliciously juicy. It reminded her a bit of her grandfather's smoked pork shoulder, but the red hots were a lot more fun to eat.

Licking her lips as she finished the last bite, Sean politely handed her his handkerchief.

Once the children had finished their red hots, the group walked around looking at the attractions along Surf Avenue, before going back inside Steeplechase Park to cool off in the Pavilion of Fun.

Inside the Pavilion, the children squealed with delight as they climbed on the carousel with its variety of barnyard animals and three separate platforms revolving at different speeds.

"How about it, Maggie? Ever been on a carousel?"

"No, we don't have those back home." A sly smile spread across her face as she dashed to the ride, gave the operator a nickel, and climbed onto the biggest horse she could find. The carousel started up, calliope music filled the air, and the sea breeze blew through her hair.

As her mechanical horse moved up and down, Maggie laughed. The children watched from their animals, amazed at seeing a grown-up indulging in pleasure like a child. When the ride ended, Maggie disembarked, her cheeks flushed and her eyes sparkling. She thanked the ride operator, who gave her a smile showing crooked, tobacco-stained teeth. Even that sight could not dispel her happiness.

Next, the children begged to ride the Ferris Wheel. Each enclosed car could hold all eight of them. Maggie asked Sean if he thought it would be safe.

"I think so."

They herded the children with them into a car, then waited breathlessly as the compartments slowly rose into the sky with a clinking of the machinery below.

"Look, Maggie. There's the Atlantic Ocean. We could almost swim to Ireland!"

Their car rose to the top of the arc, and Maggie looked out through the glass to a stunning vista of horizon and sea. By the look on Sean's face, he was enjoying every minute of the ride as well.

When their car came back down, the children pleaded to go again, but Sean suggested they get changed and go to the beach.

"Maggie, rent two towels in the bathhouse. One for you and the other for the girls. You'll need them for the showers. Then meet me outside, and we can go to the beach together."

Maggie wasn't sure about changing in front of the girls, so she asked Tessa to supervise while Maggie went to use the toilet. She slipped into her bathing suit. Tessa smiled when Maggie emerged in the costume.

"You look pretty, Miss Maggie."

"Thank you, Tessa. You're not changing?"

Tessa shook her head. "I'll dip my toes into the water and watch over Gabi."

The girls moved outside where the boys were already waiting. Maggie tried not to stare at Sean's trim figure in his one-piece woolen bathing costume.

"I'll bet the girls back home don't have an outfit like that." He pointed to her Jantzen.

"I'll have you know the saleslady at Bonwit Teller told me this was the newest swim fashion and soon to be all the rage."

He smiled. "Did you show it to your aunt?"

"Absolutely not. I don't think she'd approve of bare arms!"

They took the children down to the edge of the water and told them to splash all they wanted, but no further than up to their knees.

"You can take your hat off, Maggie."

Maggie slowly untied the ribbons. The salt breeze caressed her face, and a new sense of freedom emerged. Its warmth brought a glow to her skin.

The children splashed each other with squeals of laughter. Sean turned to Maggie.

"Are you going swimming?"

"I don't know how."

"Then don't go further than the children do. Waves can come fast and knock you down."

"You sound like you've been here before."

"I have. My Mam and Da would bring me each year on my birthday." A melancholy smile tugged at his lips.

"Sounds like you miss them."

"I do. No fun being an orphan, even as a grown-up."

"I'm sorry. I don't realize how lucky I am to have both my parents and Grand-papa still alive. So, you have a summer birthday?"

"Late August. Just last week."

"Then we should have a toast for your birthday."

"I'll let you do that later with a birch beer."

"I don't usually drink beer, but I could make an exception."

Sean broke out in laughter. "A birch beer isn't real beer. It's like a root beer."

"Oh."

"But I might hold you to your promise."

She grinned.

All of a sudden, Tessa came running. "Miss Maggie, where is Gabi?"

"Isn't she with you and the other children?"

"I told her to stay here while I went to use the toilet. Now I can't find her!" Tessa's eyes widened.

"Don't worry; I'll go find her. Maggie, you stay here with the other children." Sean ran up the beach.

A sinking feeling of disaster washed over Maggie. Dear God, she was the one responsible for her group. What would she say, that she had been chatting with the good-looking policeman while one of her charges wandered off?

Instantly, she said a prayer to St. Jude.

Sean doubled back; a worrisome expression plastered across his face. "I didn't see her on the east side. I'll go check the west."

Maggie did not want to alarm the other children, but Tessa had dissolved in tears.

"Whatever is the matter?" Mrs. Simons had arrived on the scene.

"One of the children, Gabi Brunelli, has wandered off, and Sean is searching for her."

"However did that happen?!"

"I honestly don't know. Gabi was playing with the other children, splashing in the water, then when I looked up, she wasn't there."

"Good God. We have to find her."

Mrs. Simons took off, running along the shoreline, calling out Gabi's name.

Maggie tried to keep her feelings of panic in check.

Sean returned empty-handed. "I didn't see her in the water or along the beach. She must have gone off to a building. Perhaps she needed to use the toilet? Maggie, check the bathhouse and I'll stay here with the children. Don't worry; I promise we won't give up until we find her."

How long had it been since Gabi wandered off? Maggie was furious with herself that she had not been more diligent with her responsibilities.

"Tessa, you stay here in case she comes back."

Frantic, Maggie ran into the bathhouse calling out Gabi's name. When there was no response, she stopped and listened. Was that soft crying? She called out again. No answer. Then Maggie walked by the toilets until she came to one particular stall.

"Gabi? It's me, Miss Maggie. Nothing's wrong sweetheart, and no one is mad at you. Can you talk to me, Gabi?"

A tiny voice replied, "I need help."

Maggie knocked on the wooden stall door. "Gabi, open the door so that I can help you."

A moment later the door opened to reveal Gabi standing in front of the toilet with her union suit around her ankles, soiled with feces.

"Oh Gabi, I'm so glad you're safe. What happened?"

"I had to go to the toilet, but Tessa wasn't there to help, so I walked to it myself. I had to go really bad, and I couldn't get my union suit undone in time. I dirtied myself." The crying resumed.

"Gabi, listen to me. I can fix this. Step out of your union suit and let me have it."

"But it's smelly."

"That's all right; I'll take it anyway."

Maggie retrieved the one-piece underwear and left the stall. She turned on one of the shower spigots and held the soiled fabric under the stream of water, forcing herself not to gag. Little by little, the feces rinsed away.

The problem now was what to do with Gabi. Her union suit dripped and still smelled. Maggie thought of turning the mini-disaster into a game.

"Gabi, do you want to play a game with me?"

Gabi's curly head peeked out from the toilet stall.

"I'll help you rinse off in the shower. Then you can put on your wet clothes again. They're all rinsed out and don't smell too bad. We can race down to the beach and jump in the water and sit down in the sea. How does that sound?"

Gabi came out of the stall and walked over to the showers. After rinsing off, she climbed back into the soggy union suit and holding Maggie's hand, followed her outside.

"Ready, set, go!"

Maggie dashed down the beach path and smiled as Gabi streaked across the sand and jumped into the water.

"Gabi!" Tessa ran over to her sister. But before she could yell at her younger sister, Maggie was at Tessa's side.

"She had a bathroom accident. Let her sit in the sea water and splash around. She's safe."

"But she should never have left the group!"

"No, but she had to go to the toilet. I'm sure she thought it was all right."

Tessa dropped in the sand, her shoulders convulsing. "If anything had happened to her, my mama would kill me."

Maggie knelt. "You are a wonderful sister, Tessa, but now we're all wiser from this."

At that moment, Mrs. Simons returned and saw Gabi playing in the water. "Where did you find her? Oh, thank God she's safe. Lord, please no more commotion with any of the children today."

"Amen," Sean whispered, his face flushed with relief.

***

Late in the afternoon, the summer sky shifted from cornflower blue to softer tones of muted violet. With the oncoming dusk, the Greenwich House party boarded the steamer for the return passage to Manhattan.

The children promptly fell asleep on the ship's benches.

Maggie stared out at the water. This day had been the most delightful part of summer, and Sean had played a major part in it.

As the boat cleared Upper Bay, Maggie rested against her bench and fell asleep. Lulled by the full day of activity, the hot afternoon sun, and the episode with Gabi, her body finally relaxed.

***

Sean shifted slightly on the bench being careful not to disturb Maggie, her head now lying against his shoulder.

A tender smile graced his lips.

GREENWICH VILLAGE, NEW YORK CITY

FALL 1918

The week after Coney Island, plodded along. Maggie may have thought about Rees, but it didn't stop her from looking forward to the Edith Young lecture.

After a quick Saturday lunch, she maneuvered to the subway, switching lines till she exited at Lexington Ave and E 53rd Street. Gazing up at the impressive ten-story brownstone building, she hurried inside and made her way to the lecture hall.

She found a seat, and turned around, fully expecting to see an audience full of women. However, several men attended. Maggie took out her notebook, gave a contented sigh, and reminded herself to enjoy this experience. Edith Young's talk would be Maggie's first introduction to fashion design, and she wanted to saturate herself with new techniques.

Once Edith Young took the stage, a hush fell over the crowd. She advised the audience that they were free to take notes, but serious attendees were invited to apply to the Albert Studio of Fashion Drawing in Newark, New Jersey, where she presided as director.

Then she launched into her presentation.

Maggie took pages of helpful notes, from the advice of having multiple pencils starting with the HB medium hardness to carrying an emery board in her purse so she could always be able to sharpen the pencils on the go.

She copied down the name of the best pens for inked drawings,

Gillott, even though she didn't intend to sketch in ink, and the name of the best ink, Higgins. She made a note in the margins that the best ink brushes came from camel hair.

As the lecture continued, Maggie became overwhelmed at all the items that were deemed necessary for fashion artists. When Edith Young spoke about watercolors, Maggie tried to picture how her pencil sketches would look if she switched to that medium.

She dutifully noted that the best watercolor brushes were sable hair #2 and #6. Then the paint color names of yellow ochre, madder brown, crimson, vermilion, burnt sienna, umber, and cobalt blue stirred her imagination of Gladys in full regalia. Perhaps her colored pencils were not professional enough for fashion drawing. She made a resolve to set aside money for watercolor paints and brushes.

The lecture progressed, more and more technical, and Maggie began to suspect that she was a real novice and needed to enroll in the Albert Studio in New Jersey. It had all seemed so simple back in Porters Glen. She would need to find out how to commute to Newark and pay attention to any deadlines for applying.

The other obstacle was that Edith Young never mentioned the cost of attending the classes. Maggie hoped that information would be on the application.

By the time the lecture hour ended, Maggie had tried to ignore the little voice in her head telling her she might not be accepted because her art was only mediocre.

That thought lingered.

***

"So, tell me, how was the lecture?"

"It was both fascinating and intimidating."

"Intimidating?"

"Just because you own a successful millinery business doesn't mean that I possess the same level of confidence."

"Oh, Maggie. I learned to have confidence. It didn't happen

overnight. Now, tell me the details."

"Edith Young gave explicit information about the correct supplies for fashion designers and a lot of technical data on how to execute a proper drawing."

"How did that intimidate you?"

"It made me realize I have a lot to learn. I'll send away for the application to her school. Hopefully, they'll provide directions for commuters."

"Where is it located?"

"Newark, New Jersey."

"New Jersey? You can't commute there."

"Why not?"

"It's too far, and too dangerous for a young woman to be going on her own."

"Let me worry about that."

"Let you worry? I'm the one who's responsible for you. New Jersey is out of the question; don't waste your time with the application."

Maggie stalked off to her bedroom and slammed the door.

Furious, she grabbed her sketch pad and drew bold strokes of a dark river with land on one side she labeled New Jersey; then slashed through the drawing. Once her anger had defused, she tried to see the situation from Aunt Anne-Marie's point of view. Maybe New Jersey was unrealistic. She flopped back on the bed, drained.

After sleeping, Maggie heard Anne-Marie calling her for dinner.

Then the bedroom door opened, and her aunt stood there with a gentle smile.

"I know you're hungry. Let's eat and then we can talk about art options."

"But where will I be able to take classes?"

"I'm not sure, but you'll have to find a location here in the Village, or at least nearby."

"Aunt Anne-Marie, I'm sorry I acted like a child. It's just that I was so sure the New Jersey classes could be real. I'm disappointed that the school is so far away."

"I know you are, sweetie."

∗∗∗

To smooth over their disagreement, Anne-Marie bought a package on her lunch hour the next day and placed it on Maggie's bed.

It was a new set of colored pencils with a note that read, "To help you further your dream."

∗∗∗

Rees showed up the following Thursday at the shop, as the noon hour started. Maggie tried to act nonchalant, but her heart beat double time at the grin on his face.

"Maggie, did you miss me?"

"I've been so busy; I hardly missed you at all." Her smile said otherwise.

"I know this is your lunch break, so let's walk over to the Waldorf Cafeteria and share a meal. I want to tell you all about the Catskill Mountain Inn and the people I photographed."

As they walked to the restaurant, Rees dominated the conversation with the descriptions of the inn, the well-to-do patrons he photographed, and the newspaper family from Chicago he met.

They sat down to eat. "Maggie, what are you hungry for?"

"To tell you about my week."

"I'm sorry. I took over the conversation, didn't I? Go ahead. How was your week?"

Maggie wanted Rees to be impressed with how she took care of the children on Coney Island. But instead, she chatted about how much she enjoyed the beach. Then she added in a bit about the Edith Young Lecture.

"Good. I'm glad you're enjoying yourself. Are you thinking of enrolling in Edith Young's school? I think it's in Jersey."

"Yes, and that makes it too far to commute."

"Speaking of commuting, do you think your aunt would let you spend all day Saturday with me? I'm going to be shooting pictures on the Lower East Side for the shopping frenzy of pushcart vendors."

"I'll have to ask her."

"We can have lunch together afterward and go back to the studio." He grinned.

Maggie blushed.

Once they returned from lunch, Maggie asked Anne-Marie in front of Rees if it would be all right for her to accompany him on Saturday for a photo shoot.

"Where?"

"We'll be on the Lower East Side photographing the pushcart peddlers, but I assure you that Maggie will always be in my sight and never in harm's way."

Anne-Marie demurred.

"After the photo shoot is over, I'll take her out for a nice meal and a stroll in Washington Square."

Anne-Marie stared at Maggie's hopeful face.

"All right, but have her back by late afternoon."

"Yes, ma'am." He tipped his hat.

"Wear a simple outfit, Maggie, and no large hat. You don't want to stand out."

***

Early Saturday morning, Maggie met Rees in the lobby of the apartment building.

Checking that no one was looking, he gave her a long kiss. Then, grabbing her hand, he led her out of the building.

"I'm surprised your aunt did not put up a protest."

"What do you mean?"

"My taking you to the Lower East Side."

"I think she trusts you, Rees, as long as we won't be there come nightfall."

"I'd like to take you there at night, to the Jewish theaters on Second Avenue. They have wonderful shows."

"I think it'll be a while before she would agree to that."

Rees steered them north to 14th Street where they caught the Sixth Ave El.

"How far is it?"

"We'll get off on Grand. Then it's four blocks to Orchard. So, tell me, the most memorable part of your day at Coney Island."

Maggie's heart soared with delight that he remembered. Now, how to best answer him. "I guess I could narrow it down to three things: the Ferris Wheel, the ocean, and eating my first red hot."

Rees laughed. "Maggie, you are so easy to impress."

"That doesn't sound like a compliment."

"It means you're delighted by life. I like that about you."

Within twenty minutes the El had reached the Lower East Side, and they disembarked. Walking the blocks toward Orchard, Maggie marveled at how different the storefronts and buildings appeared from the West Village.

She heard Orchard Street before they arrived. A cacophony of pushcart voices competed to attract customers, women screamed at children, and animals squawked at the top of their lungs. Added to that was the constant movement of the people that never seemed to stop. The combined noise was deafening.

Turning the corner, Maggie stood transfixed. The scene of dense humanity packed shoulder to shoulder lining both sides of the street overwhelmed her. Each vendor had a pushcart that allowed him or her to display wares and haggle with the customers for an exact price.

It was hard to tell which was more crowded, the sidewalks or the street. The pushcarts lined the road, and shoppers stood four and five deep, scrutinizing the merchandise. Maggie watched as two women tried to purchase the same scarf and got into a shouting match, while a ragged young boy stole an apple off the adjacent pushcart and then disappeared into the crowd.

Maggie had thought that Union Street in Mount Pleasant on Christmas Eve was a happy madhouse of activity when all the holiday merchandise became reduced. But here, it appeared that everyone in New York was out hunting for a bargain.

She did notice that the men grouped, and the women stayed separately. Was this a tradition from their old country? Or was she being overly sensitive to the issue of Women's Rights?

Before she had further time to think about that, the odors hit. A combination of manure, spoiled food, urine, garbage, and humans in need of a bath saturated the air. Thank God they were here early; the stench would worsen as the day wore on in the September heat.

Rees nudged her elbow and helped her into the street. Now she knew why he had suggested she dressed plain. The women she spied all wore full-length black dresses with dark scarves over their heads.

They passed by fruit vendors and men selling undershirts, pushcarts full of tools and women selling pickles from barrels.

"Rees, what type of pickles do they sell?"

"Kosher I think, but if you get a pickle, make sure there are no teeth marks in it."

"You mean someone would have been eating on it?"

"No, rats. The barrels are left unattended at night."

Maggie's stomach heaved, any vestige of appetite disappearing. "Where do they keep their pushcarts at night?"

"They rent them daily. The pickle barrels go back to their tenement rooms. I'm going to start taking photos. Stay close by me."

Maggie wanted to see everything, but she trailed behind Rees. The memory of how quickly Gabi got lost at Coney Island still preyed on her mind. As Rees composed his shots, Maggie listened to all the voices, most of them in a foreign language she didn't understand.

After a while, she became acclimated to the sights, sounds, and odors. Although when they passed a dead cat in the gutter Maggie's stomach lurched once again.

When Rees was satisfied with his shots, he suggested they get an egg cream as a treat.

"An egg cream? What is that?"

"It's a drink, a Jewish treat if you will."

"What do you mean, a Jewish treat?"

"Most of the Lower East Side is Jewish; you didn't know that?"

Maggie shook her head.

"You'll love the egg cream. We have to catch the bus on Second Avenue and take it to 7th Street."

By the time they reached Auscher's Restaurant, Maggie's clothes clung to her, and her throat was parched. Rees however, managed to appear fresh. His eyes danced with energy, spurred on by the crowd.

They walked in, and Maggie was surprised to see a large room with what looked like a soda fountain off to one side. Rees steered her in that direction. He ordered two egg creams, and they went to sit at a table with three chairs, two for them and one for the camera equipment.

Maggie sipped her egg cream through a straw. "Rees, this is delicious. I had no idea. How do they make it?"

"Each store has its own fiercely guarded recipe, but the drink is a combination of milk, seltzer water, and dark chocolate syrup. I like Auscher's. They serve their egg creams in fancy glasses, not paper like the cheaper establishments."

"So, there is neither an egg nor cream in it?"

"All part of the marketing, I guess." He grinned. "We'll need to grab a more substantial meal. Are you willing to try a Jewish delicatessen?"

"Of course."

They walked a bit further on Second Avenue and found a deli that served corned beef sandwiches. Rees ordered for them and brought the sandwiches and two drinks to the table.

"Smells delicious. What type of drink did you get?"

"Birch beer. Ever had one?"

Maggie thought of Sean, and that Rees knew nothing about him.

"No, but I understand it's a bit like root beer."

"Nothing gets past you, Maggie." He grinned.

After lunch they made their way back to the Village, arriving at the studio at Carmine and Bleeker.

"Let's go upstairs so I can put the equipment away."

Maggie caught her breath. I hope he doesn't pressure me.

They trudged up the five flights, and when Rees opened the studio door, the sunlight streamed in, dancing off the walls.

Maggie turned toward the windows and studied them as Rees put the equipment in the back room.

"What's so interesting about our windows?"

"You have the perfect exposure of northern light."

"Of course, we do. This room is an art studio, after all. How did you learn about the northern light?"

"Edith Young mentioned it in her lecture."

"I bet she didn't mention this…" Rees put his arms around Maggie. As their kissing progressed, her pulse raced. Then she pulled back.

"Don't tell me; you're still not ready?"

She slowly shook her head. An awkward silence hung in the room, and her eyes searched his face for a reaction.

"Okay, Maggie, but I don't understand. I can tell your body is responding to mine."

She leaned herself up against his chest. "I need to ask you a question."

"All right."

"Are you seeing anyone else except me?"

He pulled back and stared at her. "Is that what you think? No, there's no one else. I've been with other girls in the past, but right now there's only you."

Maggie supposed she should feel relief, but his words did not reassure her about giving up her virginity, not yet.

***

After Rees walked Maggie home, he wondered why she was holding back. Perhaps she had had her heart broken before and was now distrustful of men. He could tell she was genuine with him, so he needed to be careful with her heart. Lord knew he wanted her, but he also did not have any desire to strap himself in marriage.

SIXTEEN

The next afternoon, Maggie resolved to engage Tessa in a conversation so she could learn more about the family. Her goal was to sketch the mother and daughters who came to Greenwich House, and she had hoped to start with the Brunelli family.

Tessa arrived a few minutes before two o'clock.

"Hello, Tessa. Gabi always seems so happy to come here; I wondered which of the classes you're taking."

Tessa peered up from under her long black eyelashes. "I'm taking bookkeeping so I can get a job as a bookkeeper."

"What do you do now?"

"I sew silk flowers for ladies' hats."

"Do you work at the Fleiss Factory?"

Tessa nodded. "I saw you there a few weeks ago."

"Yes, well, I won't be going back."

Tessa nodded again as if she understood why.

"Are you the only two in your family who come to Greenwich House?"

"My mother comes to the cooking classes now and then, but my father only likes Italian food." She smiled a sheepish grin. "I'll come back for Gabi after my class."

"Of course. It was nice chatting with you."

Maggie threw herself into the lesson and took delight when the children squealed with laughter when the pig in the story fell into a mud puddle.

Afterward, Maggie straightened up the room. She was hoping to talk with Tessa again when Sean stuck his head in the doorway.

"How did it go today?"

"Good, thanks. Little Gabriella has stolen my heart."

"Children have a way of doing that, don't they? You must enjoy teaching. Your whole face lights up when you are reading to them."

"It does?"

"Yes. The afternoon is still early. Would you like to go for a cup of coffee or tea?"

Was there going to be a special meal later he wanted to invite her to join?

"Or we could go up to the fourth floor and indulge in tea and a snack up there. I like it when most of the people leave, and Greenwich House settles itself."

"All right."

Upstairs, Maggie sat at one of the tables, and Sean brought over a plate of cookies. "There isn't any coffee. I hope the tea is okay."

"Tea is great, thanks."

"So, Maggie, how did you discover Greenwich House?"

"I bumped into it. Then Mrs. Simons asked if I would volunteer."

"How did you come to volunteer here?" she asked.

"The church bulletin at Our Lady of Pompeii stated Greenwich House needed part-time help. It's a nice change from the precinct."

"Do you enjoy your job as a policeman?"

"Most weeks. But there are always difficult times. Just this week, we learned that a rash of deaths occurred down in the South Village."

"What from?"

"No one is sure. But within days many people sickened and died. Those tenements are so crowded and unsanitary; I guess diseases easily jump from building to building."

Maggie wondered where Tessa's family lived.

"How are your sketches of Gladys coming along?"

"I need to keep working on them, but I do enjoy sketching her."

Sean drained the last of his tea. "You make Sundays more pleasant, Maggie. I'm glad you stayed for tea."

She blushed at the compliment.

***

The following week Rees came to the shop on Friday and asked Anne-Marie if Maggie could accompany him once more on a Saturday photo shoot. This time he would be shooting pictures of an Italian Street Festival next weekend on Mulberry Street.

"You'll be there in the daylight, correct?"

"Yes, Miss Charbonneau, I'll have Maggie back during the afternoon. I'll need to develop the pictures as quickly as possible. I hope to sell them to the *Sun*."

"You know that area was once near the worst slums of New York."

"I do. Five Points, right?"

"Just because they tore down the tenements and built a park, doesn't mean the area is completely safe."

"Not meaning to argue, Miss Charbonneau, but there's probably no place in any city completely safe."

"I'll bring my sketchbook, Aunt Anne-Marie. Hopefully, I might find interesting people to draw."

***

The following Saturday, Maggie dressed in a light-weight camel skirt and paired it with a cream-colored blouse. Knowing they would be walking for a couple of hours, she wore her sturdy oxfords. Even if they weren't her most fashionable shoes, they would keep her feet comfortable. To complete the outfit, she donned a straw hat with a caramel colored hat band.

They set off on the Sixth Avenue El and disembarked once again on Grand Street. Maggie's enthusiasm for the outing matched Rees's spontaneity.

A block away from their destination, came the noises of Mulberry Street. Sounds of musical instruments mixed with humanity combined to make a melody of celebration. Unlike the smells of the Orchard Street push carts, Maggie detected the more mouthwatering aroma of onions and peppers frying.

They turned the corner on Mulberry, and the throngs of people in the street were not just Italian immigrants, but other nationalities as well. The food plus the music and festive atmosphere drew everyone together.

Like the Lower East Side, vendors crowded the streets, canopies shaded the merchandise, and children dashed among the stands. Rees and Maggie stepped into the crowd, amidst the tantalizing smells of hot sausage and onions on rolls. Maggie looked around for an idea to sketch. Men in straw hats stood together devouring street food while women shopped among the stalls.

This time, Maggie didn't need to hover near Rees. "Let's split up. You go get your pictures, and I'll sketch."

"All right, we'll meet at half-past one, in front of the Catholic church. It's north on Mulberry. You'll be able to find it."

As Rees left, Maggie stepped out on her own with a sense of independence. She was by herself at an Italian street festival in New York, ready to practice her art.

She wandered among the crowd. A vendor might make an interesting subject. She had to find one who struck her fancy.

Two blocks up the street sat a flower lady. The woman appeared to be around Anne-Marie's age, but with a foreign flair of beauty. Maggie stared at her. This was how Tessa might look like as an adult. The woman wore her ebony black hair tied back with a scarlet ribbon and stood under a green and white striped umbrella. Maggie glanced at the woman's hands. Chipped fingernails showed she worked with flowers.

"Can I interest you in my flowers, pretty girl? You can take them home and make your table more beautiful for the evening meal."

Maggie leaned forward. "I stopped because I would like to sketch you."

"Me?"

"Yes."

The flower woman hesitated. "Will you give me the sketch when you are finished?"

"I'm afraid not. I'll want to add it to my portfolio."

The flower lady assessed Maggie up and down. "I'll agree to let you sketch me if you buy a bouquet of my flowers."

"All right, I agree."

Maggie needed to sit down to sketch. She looked around, hoping to discover a chair behind the flower display.

"What do you need?"

"A chair."

"I have crates but no chairs. Can you sit on a crate?"

"Yes."

The woman dragged forth a sizable wooden crate that held traces of floral scents.

Maggie positioned the wooden crate off to the side, out of the way of the foot traffic. She started with an outline of the woman's face; the way Edith Young had suggested. Then she drew lines for the woman's body, the dress she wore, the way she tied her hair back, and a few of the flower containers.

Time flew, as it always did when Maggie sketched. After she had finished the rough composition, she took out her new colored pencils and went back to color in the drawing.

The umbrella with its bright green with white stripes provided a contrast against the woman's dress of pearl gray. Flowers in the containers showcased blues, yellows, whites, and mauves.

Maggie sat back, pleased with the picture. "Do you know the time?"

The flower lady looked up at the sky. "Past the noon hour; that's all I can tell."

"Well, thank you for letting me sketch you. Would you like to see it?"

Maggie turned the sketchbook.

"You made me look pretty."

"You are pretty."

"*Grazie.* Now, which flowers will you buy?"

"How much is that bunch there?"

"For you…eight cents."

Maggie dug into her purse and pulled out a dime. "Here, please take this. I can't carry flowers. They would wilt before I get home. But the picture will help me remember you. My turn to say, *Grazie.*"

The flower vendor smiled, and Maggie gave her back the crate.

Minutes later, Maggie became swallowed up by the crowd as she searched for the Catholic church.

She wasn't sure when or where they would eat, but her stomach growled. It had been hours since breakfast. Stopping at one of the food vendors, she bought a thick roll split down the middle, piled with a mixture of sausages, peppers, onions, and tomatoes.

Looking around, she saw no tables or chairs, so she stepped out of the crowd and ate standing up with her art satchel resting against her leg.

Oh, my, this is delicious.

She devoured the delicacy. Then she picked up her satchel and continued walking north.

When she found the Precious Blood of Jesus church, Rees was nowhere in sight. She went inside to say a few prayers.

As always, the hushed sanctuary of a Catholic church soothed her. She knelt to pray, thanking God for this time in Greenwich Village and the people she had met. She thanked him for Rees. Then she surprised herself by adding an extra prayer for Sean.

Emerging into the sunlight, she spied Rees leaning against the church fence.

"There you are. I didn't expect you'd be inside."

"I knew it would be cool, and I wanted to say a few prayers."

"Did you get a chance to eat?"

"I did. I ate an incredible sandwich roll with onions, peppers, sausage, and tomatoes. And I was able to sketch a wonderful flower vendor."

"Good, then we don't have to stop to eat. I want to get back to the studio right away so I can start developing the pictures. I hope you don't mind that I need to work."

"Of course not." She linked her arm through his, and together they walked back to the El.

Once they were on the platform, Rees asked to see her sketch. "My goodness, Maggie, I didn't realize how good you are at drawing."

She beamed. "Thank you, Mr. Photographer. But I still need to paint the catchlights in the eyes."

"So, you did pay attention to me when we were on the train to New York!" He laughed.

Maggie let a sly grin spread across her face.

SEVENTEEN

Reading the newspaper during the last week in September, Maggie discovered an ad for Van Groot's Costume Agency.

"Aunt Anne-Marie, do you know of Van Groot's Costume Agency?"

"Yes, they're quite well known. They make theater costumes."

"Do they have an art department?"

"I'm sure they do. Why?"

"Now that I know I'm staying in New York, and both Edith Young and the Cooper Union didn't work out, I'm thinking of maybe getting commercial art training. Perhaps I should go to Van Groot's next week and apply for a job in their art department. Sound like a good idea?"

Anne-Marie smiled. "Isabelle won't be thrilled, but yes, go ahead and apply. You'd be learning art on the job, and getting paid. Once the holiday season approaches, I would still need you on Saturdays."

The phone rang in the apartment that afternoon.

"Charbonneau residence."

"Maggie, oh thank goodness I got you right away."

"Mama, what's wrong? You're upset."

"I need to know what you and Marie are doing to protect yourself from influenza. It's spreading through Mt. Pleasant like wildfire."

"Influenza?"

"Yes, even the college has suspended classes."

"Is Papa, all right? And Grand-papa?"

"Yes, they're both fine, but Mt. Pleasant has been hit hard. The Miners Hospital can't keep up with all the new cases."

Maggie thought about Sean's comment on disease wracking the South Village. "It doesn't seem to have hit our part of Greenwich Village. At least not yet."

"You remember the Shea family?"

"Of course."

"Their oldest son, Frank, came down with the flu last week and died within four days. My God, Maggie. He was only a few years older than you. God help his young wife with a newborn baby."

"I promise we'll be careful."

"I think you should skip Mass for the next several weeks."

Skip church? Maggie felt a prick of alarm.

"And what about that settlement house where you volunteer? God knows what kinds of germs the people bring in there."

Maggie's back stiffened. "Not any more than your coal miners' wives would bring to the night classes."

"I've suspended the night classes until the sickness stops."

"We haven't been told to stop volunteering."

"Let me talk to Marie."

"She went for a walk."

"Maggie, please be sensible and stop volunteering. And ask Marie to call me back."

"Of course, I'll tell her. Good-bye, Mama, I love you."

Maggie returned the receiver to its hook. She had read the headlines warning people to avoid crowded places. Lower Manhattan had the most cases reported, but Maggie hadn't realized the severity of the situation.

She had been with the immigrant children on Sundays and eating in the dining room with their mothers, all of them straight out of the tenements. Had she already been exposed?

Maggie made the sign of the cross.

She was due at Greenwich House within an hour. Once there, she would ask Mrs. Simons' opinion about the likelihood of catching the flu from the children.

When she reached the settlement house, Maggie was surprised to see a notice tacked to the front door proclaiming that all classes and non-essential activities were suspended due to the flu. She turned to leave when the front door opened and Mrs. Simons stepped out.

"You've read the sign?"

"Is it that bad?"

"The Board thought it more prudent to close. We're still offering one soup meal at five o'clock each day. Don't worry, Maggie, you'll be able to restart your reading sessions once the flu is over."

"But this is all so sudden."

"I know. However, we cannot take any chances."

Maggie nodded and said good-bye. On the walk home, she found herself disappointed on two accounts. She had grown fond of reading to the children, especially little Gabriella, and she would miss seeing Sean Murphy. For a reason she couldn't quite explain, she enjoyed his company more and more each time they were together.

***

Then, everything changed within one week. Deaths from the flu soared into the thousands in New York City. The pharmacies in the Village poured the red liquid into their front window globes, alerting everyone that the flu had reached an epidemic situation.

October descended on the Village with the pall of death. Newspapers reported a daily toll of the number of victims. Houses at first hung a black curtain in a front window to announce the passing of a family member. However, entire families were now succumbing, and no one paid attention to the black cloth – every family had lost at least one person, usually more.

Priests driving make-shift coffin wagons stopped daily at houses and waited for the family to bring out bodies of the dead. With so many dying, funeral masses were held hourly.

Foot traffic and shopping slowed all over the city. Days without any customers were now quite usual at the hat shop. Anne-Marie graciously offered to pay Isabelle a half month's wages and told her to stay home for the remainder of the month. As altruistic as the offer appeared, both Anne-Marie and Maggie knew that the Lower East Side had the most flu cases. No need for Isabelle to bring those germs to the shop.

The doctors still did not know what caused the flu or how to stop it, but they knew it was highly contagious. Cases were reported where the victim had been healthy the previous day, became ill during the night, and expired within twenty-four hours. The most pitiful cases were the young mothers desperately trying to save their babies, only to die from it themselves and leave motherless children behind.

Anne-Marie established new rules. No going to church, no going to mid-town to shop, and no going out with Rees Finch. Maggie had protested, but Anne-Marie explained that Rees went all over the city for his photography, and he would most likely have been exposed, possibly on multiple occasions.

Anne-Marie and Maggie would still shop at the greengrocer and the deli, but meals out in restaurants or even tea shops had to be suspended. Even Maggie's plans to apply for a job at Van Groot's was placed on hold.

To make matters more depressing, Maggie's mother called each week to check on their health, and then report the weekly casualties of Porters Glen. The majority of the victims were in the prime of their life, and previously healthy. Anne-Marie commented that she had expected the flu to take the very old and the very young, not strike down an entire generation of healthy young adults.

Eventually, 33,000 deaths would be confirmed in New York City.

With the Great War raging in Europe, American soldiers who had been infected at home carried the flu virus with them to the battlefields of France. Within months, the flu ravaged multiple continents and became a pandemic, pushing the numbers of deaths into the millions worldwide.

Rees stayed in touch with Maggie by phone. Anne-Marie would ask to talk with him, then grill him about where he had been. She explained once more why he could not visit Maggie. The two women kept the shop open, but no one appeared. Maggie and Anne-Marie spent their days watching the street sweepers, the mailman, and the traffic policeman all wearing gauze masks as they performed their jobs.

At the end of October, Anne-Marie asked Maggie to man the shop while she slipped out to the deli and brought them back lunch.

A few minutes later, the shop bell tinkled, and Maggie looked up, hoping for someone other than the mailman.

"Sean! You're a sight for sore eyes! I am so glad to see you."

"I'm on the beat, but I wanted to come and see if you were all right."

"Yes, we're fine. My aunt has stepped out to get lunch. Shouldn't you be wearing a mask?"

He took one out of his pocket. "I usually keep it on everywhere I go. I miss seeing you at Greenwich House."

"I miss being there, too. This flu has been horrible. Have any of the patrolmen gotten sick?"

Sean nodded. "The disease doesn't discriminate. Maggie, do you have the number to the precinct house?"

"No."

"Here, I'll write it down. Call me if you need anything. God willing this will all be over soon."

"Not soon enough." Then she smiled at him. "Thank you for coming here. You are always so thoughtful."

"You're not on my beat, but I made an exception. Stay healthy, Maggie."

"You, too, Sean."

When Anne-Marie returned with lunch, Maggie was smiling.

"Did we have a customer?"

"No, just Sean Murphy, the policeman from over at Greenwich

House."

"What did he want?"

"Checking on us to see if we were all right."

Anne-Marie looked at Maggie. "Anything else you want to add?"

"No, he didn't stay."

Anne-Marie shrugged, then unpacked their lunch.

After the meal, Maggie took out her sketchbook and started sketching Anne-Marie and the hats.

Even the Heterodoxy Club had temporarily suspended their luncheons.

Life was at a standstill, waiting for the disease to wear itself out.

***

As October ended and November began, the number of flu deaths plummeted, and everyone hoped that the epidemic had ended. Doctors, however, cautioned that the flu could resurrect itself with another wave. Wearing gauze masks in public was still recommended.

Maggie celebrated the new freedom by going to the park to sketch.

She quickly found Gladys and decided to sketch her in a different pose. Drawing hands was always a challenge, and Maggie struggled with it again today.

An hour or so later, she had erased Gladys' hands for the umpteenth time.

"Why don't you draw her with one hand in the paper bag and the other hand beneath the bag?"

Maggie looked up to find a man peering at her sketch.

"That is a good suggestion; thank you."

He nodded but did not leave.

"Do you draw?"

"Actually, yes, and I know how hard hands are. You might also want to blend a few of your colors to create more nuances."

Maggie stared at him.

"But you've captured her likeness in a good way. I'm impressed."

"Thank you, Mr.....?"

"Vincent Fox. Here is my card, so you can see that I am a legitimate artist. I take on private students, too. If you are ever interested."

Maggie reached for his card and tucked it in her art satchel. "Do you sketch here often?"

"Yes, but mostly on the other side of the park. Have a nice day." The man veered off, down the path.

Maggie returned to her sketch, drawing Gladys's hands the way Mr. Fox had suggested.

**

The next week Maggie announced she would apply to Van Groot's as soon as the pharmacy globes held yellow liquid. Anne-Marie had suggested perhaps waiting for the green would be safer. Maggie, yearning for freedom after one month of flu-imposed imprisonment, couldn't wait.

By mid-week, she arrived at Van Groot's armed with her satchel and a selection of her best artwork. She took the elevator up to the third floor and held her head high. Pushing open the door, she faced a sour looking woman who acted like a front office sentinel. Perhaps she was.

"Good morning. I have come to apply for a job."

The woman turned and eyed the clock. The hands indicated 10:01. "We opened an hour ago. You'll need to fill out the application, then take a typing test."

"I'm applying for a job with the art department."

"Did you receive a letter from the company informing you of a vacancy?"

"Well, no. I assumed there would be vacancies from time to time."

The woman turned back to the clock once more. "And now it

is 10:06." She handed Maggie the application papers. "You did bring a pen; I hope."

"Of course." Maggie found herself mumbling. She placed her art satchel to one side.

The application papers were straightforward, asking if the applicant had graduated high school, any previous jobs held, unique talents, and current typing speed.

Maggie filled everything out, adding that she had taught school, worked in her grandfather's bakery, and was currently employed at a hat shop in the Village.

She handed the papers back to the woman, who read them over.

"You did not include your typing speed."

"I don't know it."

"Then follow me." The woman opened a door and led Maggie into a hallway and then into another room. At least thirty women sat in this room, all of them typing. "Sit there."

Maggie sat down. Now, what was she supposed to do?

"Well, put your paper into the typewriter!"

A pounding headache started.

"Ethel will time you. The piece you are to copy is next to your machine."

Then the woman left.

Thank God she's gone.

Ethel approached her. "Go ahead and get comfortable. Once you're ready, open to page one and copy the letter while I time you."

She should tell this Ethel that she was a hunt and peck typist, at best. But this might be the only way to get her foot in the door.

Maggie opened the book, said a quick prayer, and started typing. She knew she was making mistakes, but couldn't stop to fix them. She finished the task, took the paper out of the typewriter, and handed it to Ethel.

Without saying a word, Ethel walked off with the paper, into the hallway.

They'll see I'm not a typist, and realize I have other talents.

After several minutes, the door opened, and Ethel walked back in with a man. Instantly all the women in the room focused on their typing.

"Are you, Miss…Canavan?"

"Yes."

"And this is your application and typing score?"

"Yes."

"Please follow me."

Maggie had an insane hope that he would take her directly up to the art department. Instead, they walked into another room. By the arrangement of the furniture, Maggie could see it was an office.

"Is this a joke?"

"Excuse me?" Her body stiffened.

"This is the most miserable typing score I have ever seen. I'm Mr. Reggio, and I have been screening Van Groot girls for years."

"I'm not a real typist. I came here to interview for a position in the art department, drawing fashion sketches."

"Oh, you did, did you?"

"Once you see my sketches, I think you'll agree that my art is better than my typing."

"All of Van Groot's girls start in the secretarial pool."

Maggie let out her breath. "If I agreed to take a secretarial position, how long would I have to work before I could move up to the art department?"

He narrowed his eyes and chewed on an unlit, foul-smelling cigar. "Why don't you tell me about your so-called artistic talents."

Maggie's nose wrinkled, whether from the smell of his tobacco or his after-shave, she couldn't tell. "I have been drawing since I was a young girl and have always been fascinated with fashions. I came to New York to study art and learn from a reputable institution like Van Groot's."

He scoffed. "You don't understand that girls like you are a dime a dozen. You come to the big city expecting to land the job of your dreams, without realizing what the city demands in return. Everyone, including you, has to pay their dues to get ahead."

Maggie held her tongue. *What a pompous ass.*

"Now, if you would be willing to start paying your dues today, then Van Groot's might be able to find a position for you."

"I'm not sure I understand."

"Go over to that window."

A strange request in an interview, but she complied.

"Bend down and pick up the pen."

Maggie's antennae went on full alert. However, she wanted the job, so she bent down as delicately as possible and retrieved the pen.

"Now, bring it to me."

"I don't understand how this is part of an interview."

As she handed him the pen, his hand shot out like an arrow and his fingers flicked across her chest, skating across the path of her nipples.

Maggie's face turned beet red with anger. "Mr. Reggio!"

"As I said, you have no idea of what the city demands. Are you willing to work for me?"

"Certainly not! And I intend to report you!"

"To who, dearie? And it would be my word against yours. Don't let the door hit your fanny as you leave."

Mortified and irate, Maggie stormed out of his office. She reached the front room and glared at the woman who had to know about Mr. Reggio, or perhaps she had already paid her dues to stay with the company.

Rather than wait for the elevator, Maggie took the stairs down to the street level as fast as she could, feeling dirty, even though none of it had been her fault.

***

Maggie told Anne-Marie all about the job interview but didn't want anyone else to know what had happened. Anne-Marie hugged Maggie, assuring her she had done the right thing by leaving right away.

"I shouldn't have been so naïve."

"So now you are wiser."

"First the Cooper Union, then Edith Young, and now Van Groot's. Am I ever going to find a way to study art?"

"Have faith, Maggie."

Maggie walked into her bedroom and looked at her windows with their northern light.

She could hear her grandfather's voice about God helps those who help themselves.

I know what I'll do. I'll make this room into a small art studio and practice daily.

She sat on the bed and made a list. First, I'll need a tabletop easel I can put on Aunt Anne-Marie's card table. Then, if I want to experiment with watercolors, I'll need paints and brushes, illustration board and pieces of special art paper. Maybe I need to visit Jessie and ask her advice on what other materials to buy.

Feeling satisfied that she was taking action, she pulled out her last sketch of Gladys and propped it up on her dresser.

Out loud, she declared, "Gladys, you will be my inspiration. And, as of today, I've paid my dues."

EIGHTEEN

"Good morning, Mr. Marositz."

"Morning, Maggie," his voice was muffled by the gauze flu mask he wore.

"Reading about the war?"

He looked up from the pages in his hand. "No. I'm reading about that crazy lady down in Washington, D.C."

"What crazy lady?"

"Her name's Alice Paul. It seems she's in trouble again for picketing at the White House. She and her group are angry over that suffrage amendment not passing."

"Here's my nickel." Maggie took a copy of the morning paper off the stack. Walking to work, she scanned the article on Alice Paul.

On August 28, 1917, Alice Paul and nine other suffragettes were arrested for picketing the White House. They were threatened with imprisonment at the infamous Occoquan Workhouse if they dared to picket the White House again.

This week Alice was arrested for unauthorized picketing of the U.S. Capitol Building. She and the other members of the National Women's Party are still demanding the right to vote. As of this date, the amendment is still two votes shy of gaining the required two-thirds votes by the individual states.

Two votes! I need to make another poster and deliver it to Crystal Eastlake. It's the least I can do to help get the word out.

***

On November 11, Americans heard the joyous ringing of church bells throughout the land. The Great War in Europe had ended.

In New York City, people danced in the streets. Office workers and shoppers spilled out of buildings. Thousands made their way to Fifth Avenue and began an impromptu celebration. After four years and a hundred thousand American soldiers killed on foreign battlefields, the war was finally over.

For the time being, people forgot about the flu.

Anne-Marie and Maggie locked the hat shop and made their way to Washington Square where hundreds of Villagers were celebrating. A man raced through the crowd and passed out small hand-held American flags. Caught up in the fervor, Anne-Marie and Maggie waved their flags, then danced with each other in front of the Washington Arch.

"Maggie, I have to get back to the shop and open it. Women will want victory hats, and I have to make some quick."

"How will you do that?"

"With red, white, and blue ribbons. I left the jobber's new phone number at home. Without much business lately, I hadn't planned on contacting him for a ribbon order. Thank goodness that's all changed. His phone number is in a small book on the secretary desk."

"All right. I'll go get it and meet you at the shop."

The two parted, and Maggie hurried home to the apartment.

She rummaged through the top drawer of the desk and found a copy of the Bible, which she laid aside. Then she picked it up again.

Perhaps I should say a prayer of thanks that the war has ended.

She opened the Bible, looking for the Book of Psalms. Paging through the book, she discovered an embroidered bookmark.

It appeared to be about five inches in length and approximately three inches wide. Beautifully sewn with a red heart near the center, it included a border of bluebells embroidered down each side. But the most intriguing aspect was the name Ed stitched diagonally near the bottom. There, the bookmark had been cut on the bias.

Was this a gift from a beau of Aunt Anne-Marie's? But if so, why cut it in such an unusual manner?

She placed the bookmark back in its place, found a familiar Psalm, and read it.

Then she closed the Bible and placed it back in the drawer. Underneath a small stack of papers, she found the phone book. Once she had that, she walked out of the apartment and back to the shop.

"Did you find the phone number?"

"Yes. Here."

"Good. I know we'll need more ribbon. See these hats I've finished."

Maggie couldn't help but smile at Anne-Marie's creativity. Her aunt had quickly repurposed a few summer hats into victory hats.

"Aunt Anne-Marie, I also found the most curious item in your Bible."

Anne-Marie froze, but Maggie didn't notice.

"What were you doing with my Bible?"

"I was rummaging in the secretary and decided to read a Psalm as a thank-you prayer for the war ending. I thumbed through the Bible and stumbled across the most unusual bookmark. Well, more like a decorated ribbon with the name Ed embroidered at the bottom. But the ribbon had been cut off, almost like it was unfinished."

Anne-Marie sank into a chair. "I don't want to discuss this, and I don't want you looking through my Bible again."

"I'm sorry. I didn't realize the Bible was personal."

"Well, it is." Anne-Marie brought her hand to her forehead. "I have a terrible headache starting. I need to go home. You'll have to deal with any customers and then close the shop."

Maggie stared. "By myself?"

"Yes, you'll have to handle it. Most of the customers will appear tomorrow."

After Anne-Marie left, Maggie sat down. *How could I have*

known the Bible was off limits?

***

Later, after Maggie returned home, the evening became a subdued affair with neither of them talking. The specter of the Bible hung between them like an unwanted talisman. Maggie couldn't think of what to say or do.

After dinner, which Anne-Marie only picked at, Maggie retreated to the living room and read for a while. Anne-Marie announced she was going to bed. Maggie stayed up for another hour and then went to bed as well.

Dear God, this day has been a disaster, and I don't know how to fix it.

Several hours later, Maggie woke, hearing sobs emanating from Anne-Marie's bedroom. Maggie lay still. As the sobbing continued, Maggie got up and walked through the living room and out into the hall. She knocked quietly on her aunt's door. Anne-Marie did not answer.

Maggie gently opened the door and saw Anne-Marie curled in the fetal position, rocking back and forth and crying so hard, it hurt Maggie's heart. Maggie tiptoed over to the bed and sat down next to her aunt and stroked Anne-Marie's back. After what seemed like an eternity, the sobbing ebbed.

Maggie switched to stroking Anne-Marie's hair and gently shushing her. "Aunt Anne-Marie, the Bible shouldn't be upsetting you this much."

Anne-Marie looked up. Her tear-streaked face resembled that of a child. In a quiet voice, she whispered, "It isn't the Bible; it's what you found in the Bible."

"You mean the bookmark?"

In the same waifish tone, Anne-Marie replied, "It isn't a bookmark. It's a birth ribbon."

Maggie sat up. "A birth ribbon? Whose birth ribbon?"

"My baby's. My tiny Edward, it's his birth ribbon."

Maggie sat, stunned.

Anne-Marie let out a soul-wrenching sigh. "I've kept my secret for two decades…" She did not finish the sentence. Then she reached for Maggie's hand. "You must swear, you'll never tell anyone."

"Of course. I promise."

Anne-Marie remained quiet and then began. "A few months after I arrived in New York I met a man and fell in love.

Maggie studied her aunt's face.

"I lived with Aunt Hulda's cousin at the time. She warned me about the men of New York, how young women could be deceived. But Martin swept me off my feet, and I thought Freda was a sour old spinster lady.

Now Anne-Marie studied Maggie's face.

"However, Martin was already married. After being with him for six months, he promised he would divorce his wife and marry me. By fall, I discovered I was pregnant. I lied to Freda and told her I planned to move in with a friend from work. Martin moved me to a boarding house here in the Village. I assumed we would get married, but we fought about the pregnancy.

I finally had to quit work at the hat shop in Chelsea; my pregnancy became too obvious. Miss Genevieve, the owner, agreed that I could design hats at home and send them to her.

I gave birth to a fine baby boy at St. Vincent's. Martin never even held him. The next day, Martin told me he could go through with the divorce if I gave the baby to the nuns—just for a week until he could settle things with his wife."

Fresh tears streamed down Anne-Marie's cheeks. Maggie held her aunt's shaking hands.

"I was so trusting, Maggie. I named my baby Edward and left him with the nun in charge. I explained to her that I would return for him in one week. I'd made an identification ribbon for him with a blue-flowered border. In the hospital, I embroidered his name diagonally and stitched a red heart to show my love for him.

The nun cut the ribbon in half and gave the top half back to me. The bottom half she pinned to his nightshirt, telling me I could claim him with the top half of the ribbon."

A cold apprehension crept into Maggie's heart.

"But when I went back a week later, I learned he had been sent to the Foundling Hospital the day after I left St Vincent's. According to the nun, babies sent to the Foundling Hospital were always put up for adoption. I cried and screamed and threatened to call the police, but the nun told me a man had come in a few hours after I left Edward and given his permission for my baby to go to the Foundling Hospital. That man was Martin."

"My God, Aunt Anne-Marie, that's illegal!"

"Martin was wealthy and well connected in the city. I tried to get legal recourse, but I was never successful."

"And you told no one? Not even Mama?"

"Your mother had given birth, and all the attention was on her baby—you. I was so ashamed of what had happened that I never told the family."

"What about Martin?"

"I finally located him. He told me his wife had refused a divorce and threatened to ruin his name if he didn't get rid of the baby and me. So, you see, Freda knew what she was talking about."

"Didn't you try to find Edward?"

"Of course, I did. I went to the Foundling Hospital every week and pleaded with the nuns. They told me Edward had been adopted, and this was God's punishment for my sin.

"Then, the adoption record went missing. I even hired a detective, but Martin had covered his tracks."

Maggie's stomach twisted with the unfairness of it all.

"A day doesn't go by that I don't think about my baby."

"Aunt Anne-Marie, it was two decades ago, Edward would be grown by now. Maybe I can help you locate him."

"No, Maggie. I don't want you involved. You must keep your promise. I resigned myself years ago to my tragedy. Perhaps it was a penalty for loving a married man."

The two women held onto each other. Then Maggie slid down and lay next to Anne-Marie, tenderly stroking her shoulder. "There has to be a way, Aunt Anne-Marie. God wouldn't want a mother torn from her baby."

The two women lay spooned next to each other and fell back into a deep sleep. Morning found them in the same position.

***

Maggie sat down to her now-usual breakfast of a bagel, poached egg, piece of fruit, and cup of coffee.

"Thank you for coming into my room last night. I feel like a huge weight has been lifted off me. In telling you about Edward, it brought him back to me."

"But, Aunt Anne-Marie, it wasn't fair, and I still think you have recourse to find out about your son."

"It's a little more complicated."

"How?"

Anne-Marie took a deep breath. "I blackmailed Martin."

"You did what?"

"When I found Martin, I told him I would go to the police, the newspapers, and his wife unless he agreed to set me up in business with my own hat shop and pay twenty years' rent."

"My God, Aunt Anne-Marie, blackmail is a criminal act!"

"I had to survive, and I truly believed I would eventually find Edward and then have the last laugh on Martin."

"I'm speechless."

"Twenty years ends on June 1, 1919."

"That's only six months from now. What will you do after that?"

"Instead of spending money on rent for the shop, I invested the savings. As long as the Stock Market stays strong, I shouldn't have a problem."

"I don't know if I could have done that."

"You don't know what you would do until you're faced with surviving." She paused. "I hope you understand now why I've been so adamant about Rees. I don't want you making the same mistake I did."

"But Aunt Anne-Marie, Rees isn't married."

"Are you sure? "

"I would know."

"Would you, Maggie? Promise me you'll be careful and for god's sake, take precautions—don't get pregnant out of wedlock. You can see the repercussions of my error."

Maggie nodded but did not answer. "Is Martin still alive? Have you ever seen him again?"

"I think he's still alive, but after I set up the blackmail, I never wanted to see him again. He ruined my life, Maggie."

Maggie sat back, the remains of the poached egg no longer appealing.

All the more reason I need to get some douche tablets.

NINETEEN

The phone rang at the shop the next day. Annie wanted to share the joy that the war had ended and wanted to know how Maggie and Anne-Marie had celebrated.

Anne-Marie put her finger up to her closed lips.

"We went to Washington Square Park to celebrate with all our neighbors, and then we went back to the hat shop and began making victory hats to sell."

"Marie has always been clever with hats. Put her on the phone."

Maggie held the receiver out to her aunt.

"Annie? It's so good to hear your voice."

"Marie, I think it is ingenious of you to be creating victory hats. Bravo."

"Thank you. You've always been my best supporter."

"Please put Maggie back on. I'll wait."

Anne-Marie handed the phone back to Maggie.

"Maggie, are you and Marie still taking precautions about the flu?"

"Yes, Mama. The crowd in Washington Square Park yesterday was the first crowd we've been in since early October. We're careful."

***

The following day the phone rang again, this time it was Crystal Eastlake.

"Maggie? The club is getting back together to celebrate the end of the war. Can you join us on Saturday? We're all wondering how you enjoyed the Edith Young lecture."

"It was very informative, and I thoroughly enjoyed it."

"You can thank me at the luncheon. We'll expect you at Polly's. Same time, the same place."

"All right. Thank you again."

"Who was that?"

"Miss Eastlake is asking me to join her club for lunch on Saturday. I need to go. She's the one who paid for the Edith Young ticket."

"Of course, you should go. But just because a person gives you a gift, doesn't mean you're beholden to reciprocate."

Maggie had no sooner digested this piece of advice when the phone rang again.

"Maggie?"

"Rees! Are you all right?"

"Yes. I've been following the papers, and it seems the flu cases are finally subsiding. I'd like to see you. Can we get together on Saturday?"

Oh, God. I haven't seen him in seven weeks, and now I've promised Saturday to Ms. Eastlake.

"Rees, I can't on Saturday. I'll be at the Heterodoxy luncheon. Can we choose a different day?"

"I didn't realize you had become so popular. Is next Saturday spoken for, too?"

"No."

"Good, then I claim it. I'll come to the shop around lunchtime. Till then, Maggie."

"Yes, till then."

***

Maggie was ready to leave for the Saturday luncheon when she turned back and packed up her drawing of the Italian flower vendor.

The speaker this month was Helen Keller. Maggie listened in rapt attention as the blind and deaf Miss Keller expounded on the subject of a woman's right to marry whomever she chooses.

After the luncheon, when the ladies stood up, Maggie cleared her throat.

"Before we adjourn, I want to take this opportunity to thank Miss Eastlake for having me as a guest and for sending me to the Edith Young lecture. I wanted to share with all of you my latest endeavor."

Maggie pulled the drawing out of her bag. Murmurs flew around the table.

"My, my. Maggie, is it for sale?"

"What? Oh, no, not yet. But thank you for the compliment."

"Nonsense. I was sincere. I wish to purchase it."

"Thank you, Miss Widener. I'll remember that." Maggie stifled a nervous giggle.

The group lingered as always with the ladies talking among themselves.

When Maggie arrived back at the hat shop, she couldn't wait to tell Anne-Marie that a member of the club had offered to buy the drawing of the flower lady.

"Who was it?"

"Miss Widener. She's a poet."

"Don't sell yourself short, Maggie. I bet she has a keen eye for good art and is probably speculating that you'll be famous one day and then she can brag that she bought your first piece."

"Oh, Aunt Anne-Marie. I doubt that very much."

Anne-Marie's left eyebrow arched. Then she softened. "I trust you did not mention the birth ribbon to anyone?"

"Of course not."

"Tell me about the luncheon. Who was the speaker?"

"Miss Helen Keller. Do you know who she is?"

"Yes, she's a blind and deaf woman who is an inspiring orator."

"She spoke to us about women's rights; specifically, the right to marry whomever we want. Her parents tried to force her into an arranged marriage, but she was in love with another man."

"A difficult situation. I can see why she's an advocate."

"But I noticed something at this luncheon that I hadn't before."

"What?"

"Two of the women."

Anne-Marie kept silent.

"One of them kept draping her arm over the other woman's shoulder. They seemed to be quite affectionate with each other."

"It's possible they have a Boston marriage."

"What's that?"

"When two independent women decide to live with each other, instead of with a man."

"Like us?"

"No, a Boston marriage is different. The women have committed themselves to each other, like in a marriage. Have you ever heard the term, lesbian?"

Maggie shook her head, no.

"A woman may have many friends in her lifetime, but some women fall in love with another woman, rather than a man. Legally they cannot marry, so they enter into a Boston marriage."

"I don't know any women like that."

"The Village attracts a liberal lifestyle. Boston marriages are accepted here."

Maggie remained pensive.

"Does that bother you?"

"I guess not."

"Try not to judge other people, Maggie. The world isn't always fair. Did you know it is illegal for whites and Negros to marry in many parts of America?"

Maggie shook her head.

"Some social clubs won't admit Jews. Even the Catholic church won't permit you to marry an outsider unless the children are raised Catholic."

"I didn't know that either."

"The real problem, Maggie, is that people are often afraid of others whose lives do not match theirs."

"I did feel a little awkward."

"Now that you know, it shouldn't bother you. If you stay in New York, you'll meet a lot of different people. It's part of what makes the city so exciting."

"What about the other women in the club? Are all of them in Boston marriages?"

"I doubt that."

"I do think several of the women are feminists."

"That doesn't make them lesbians."

"Are you wary of feminists?"

"I'm wary of anyone who tries to push their ideas onto others."

"Even if their ideas would make the world a better place?"

"A better place for who? I doubt the men of America think the world would be better if the feminists were in charge."

Maggie grinned.

"Formulate your own ideas, Maggie. Don't allow yourself to be swept up in the tide of emotions that other people are espousing."

Maggie thought back to the lively discussions at the Heterodoxy Club today. The ideals of feminism were tugging harder.

***

On the following Saturday Rees arrived at the hat shop beaming a wide grin. "Maggie, I have the most wonderful surprise for you."

"And what would that be?"

He withdrew a slim envelope from his breast pocket. "I have two tickets to a new play tonight at the Provincetown Playhouse."

"My, Mr. Finch, you seem to know all the right places." Anne-Marie smiled at him.

"Well, a client of mine bought them and can't use them."

"That's wonderful, Rees. What kind of show?"

"It's by a fairly new playwright, Eugene O'Neill. The show starts at eight o'clock. I'll swing by your apartment at seven. The theater is on MacDougal Street, and we can go for drinks afterward."

As Anne-Marie turned and walked to the back, Rees leaned in and gave Maggie a quick kiss. Isabelle, standing off to the side, didn't miss his gesture.

After Rees left and Maggie turned around to get back to work, Isabelle smirked and whispered, "Sleeping with him, yet?"

Maggie instantly flushed and stalked past her.

***

The night at the theater provided pure enchantment. Even though the Provincetown Playhouse only sat eighty-eight patrons, the entire audience buzzed with glowing remarks after the play.

"How about we visit a new place called the Russian Room? It's a short walk over to West 4th Street."

They entered the restaurant, and Maggie was struck by the numbers of people dining at this late hour. Tables filled with patrons drinking and talking sat side by side with other tables occupied by the actors they had seen—also drinking and talking.

"Gin and Tonic, right?"

Maggie nodded with a smile, pleased that he remembered.

For the remainder of the evening, they discussed the play and talked about life in the Village.

"How about visiting the studio for a drink?"

"I'm afraid the late hour would make my aunt suspicious."

"Maybe we should switch to afternoons again?"

Maggie smiled. "Yes." *I guess now is the time for me to get protection.*

***

On Sunday morning, Mrs. Simons called to tell Maggie that

Greenwich House had re-opened and would Maggie be resuming her volunteer schedule? She also asked Maggie to come for a celebratory spaghetti dinner.

Maggie couldn't wait to see the children again, and Sean, too.

She arrived early and went about choosing a book and an art activity for the children. As she put out the paper and crayons, she heard a noise at the door.

"Sean! How good it is to be back here."

"I'm glad you're here, too, Maggie. Are you staying for the spaghetti dinner?"

"I am. I plan to stay for Sunday dinner each time I volunteer. That way, I can get to know more of the women who take classes."

The children arrived, tumbling into the classroom and running up to Maggie and hugging her. Little Tony Costa, one of the regulars, was missing. "Is Tony here? " she asked, and then saw Sean shake his head.

"Go ahead and sit down on the carpet, children, and I'll get our book."

As the children sat down giggling, Maggie walked back to Sean.

"He didn't make it through the flu," Sean whispered.

Maggie paled, then caught herself and forced a smile as she walked back to the front, sat down and began the story.

When the volunteer time concluded, Sean appeared at the door. "Want to take a stroll through the park? We have about three hours until dinner. We could check on Gladys."

"Let me straighten up and then yes, it would be nice to go for a walk."

Without being asked, Sean walked over and helped her clean up the room. They soon fell into easy conversation about the upcoming Thanksgiving holiday.

"Are you going back home to see your family?"

"No, my aunt and I have been invited to a friend's for dinner. It's a long trip back to western Maryland, and once there, my parents would try to convince me to stay. How about you?"

"I usually volunteer to work on Thanksgiving so one of the married guys can be home with his wife and kids."

"That's nice of you."

Sean shrugged. "I would hope that one of the guys would do the same for me."

They entered the park, relieved to see Gladys on her usual bench.

"Hi Gladys, glad to see you made it through the flu."

"Can't kill an old buzzard like me." She winked. "What would the pigeons do if I upped and died?"

They stayed a while chatting with her.

"Maggie, how about getting a cup of tea? We could venture south of the park."

Maggie knew that Rees's boarding house was south of the park.

"Let's stick closer to Greenwich House, so the time doesn't get away from us."

They settled on the Crumperie on West 4th Street, and Maggie hoped that Rees would not be at Jessie's gallery, right nearby. Of course, she wasn't doing anything wrong, having tea with a friend. Was she?

"So, tell me about your art. I'm guessing you did a lot of drawing during the last few weeks, quarantined by flu."

"I did. I took the time to sketch my aunt and the hats in the shop. We had so few customers."

"The hats? Good practice for a fashion artist."

"I'm touched that you remembered that."

"You're hard to forget, Maggie."

She blushed. "What did you do during the last weeks?"

"Police precincts don't shut down, and we still had our fair share of customers."

Together they laughed and chatted until it was time to return to Greenwich House for dinner.

LINDA HARRIS SITTIG

GREENWICH VILLAGE, NEW YORK CITY

WINTER 1918

TWENTY

December brought northeast winter weather to New York. Maggie knew cold, but she wasn't prepared for the blast of cold air that incessantly raced across town from the Hudson to the East River.

She knew Rees had spent Thanksgiving with his aunt and uncle, and presumably was now off on a photo shoot at an army base.

Maggie glanced at the calendar. There were three and a half weeks until Christmas.

She wanted to give Anne-Marie the gift of finding out about Edward. Even though she had promised not to pursue anything, Maggie was sure she could find pertinent information.

On Sunday, she announced, "I'm going to the New York Library after Mass to do some art research for my Women's Rights poster."

"All right. You'll be home in time for dinner, though?"

"Yes."

She dressed in her dark gray flared skirt and a new matching jacket. The colors matched both her mood and the weather. She kissed Anne-Marie good-bye, reminding herself that she didn't lie, she would visit the library, after St. Vincent's Hospital. Mass would have to wait.

Walking west on 13th Street, she turned south on Seventh Avenue until the hospital loomed in front of her with its dusty brick walls. Taking a deep breath, she opened the door and walked inside. A nun sat behind a large reception desk.

"Can I help you?"

"Yes. Where do I go to find out about hospital records—birth records to be exact?"

"Are you the mother?"

"No, my aunt is."

"Then she would need to come in person to make the inquiry."

"Well, that's not possible. My aunt is… no longer mobile. And the birth happened over twenty years ago."

"As I said, the mother of the infant needs to request birth records."

Maggie swallowed. "I understand there are rules, but my request is for an unusual, but important reason."

"And what might that be?"

"After my aunt gave birth, her baby was taken from her without her consent."

"Did this baby go to the Foundling Hospital?"

"I believe so, but he, the infant, wasn't a foundling. The father of the baby signed the paperwork without telling my aunt."

"The hospital does not interfere in matters between a husband and wife."

"But they weren't married."

The nun looked at Maggie with complete understanding. "In that case, the baby would be considered a foundling. I'm sorry. The birth records would be at the Foundling Hospital. I can give you their address: 175 East 68th Street."

"Thank you."

"I wouldn't get my hopes up. Many of the children who went to the Foundling Hospital were sent west on orphan trains."

Maggie's face blanched. "But he wasn't an orphan!"

"In the eyes of the law, he was an abandoned infant. Same thing."

Shaken, Maggie walked out of the hospital. My God, did Aunt Anne-Marie know of that possibility? If Edward had been sent west, then the hopes of finding him were even slimmer. With a determined stride, she set out for the subway station.

Once inside, she consulted the map. It showed that she could transfer at Grand Central Station and take the new Lexington Line, which stopped at E 68th Street.

Thank you, Rees, for showing me how to maneuver through the system.

When she finally disembarked at East 68th Street, she said a prayer about the orphan trains, hoping that Edward had not been placed on one.

The Foundling Hospital appeared as a forlorn six-storied building with a front door similar to St. Vincent's. Once again, Maggie took a deep breath.

And once again, she was greeted by a nun.

"Can I help you?"

"I hope so. I've come from St. Vincent's Hospital. The nun I spoke to, advised me to come here in my quest."

"And what is that?"

"I'm looking for any information on the birth or adoption of my cousin."

"I see, so you are not the mother?"

"No. My aunt gave birth to a baby boy twenty years ago. He was taken from St. Vincent's without her consent and sent here."

"Somebody had to sign for him to be released."

"The father did."

"We do not interfere in family decisions."

"But my aunt was never told her baby had been sent here."

"Her husband didn't tell her?"

"They weren't married."

"Oh, I see."

Do I imagine this, or did this nun's composure change?

"But the man was the boy's father?"

"Yes."

"Then he had every right to relinquish his child."

"But he lied to my aunt! He led her to believe he was going to marry her."

"My dear, that story is as old as time. Your aunt should have been more careful."

"But he had no right to sign the papers without telling her."

"I am afraid he had every right. And, anyway, adoption papers are sealed by the court. There is nothing I can do to help."

"What if he went on an orphan train?"

"Then it would be almost impossible to track him. I'm sorry."

"There has to be a way my aunt can bring closure to her heartache."

Compassion filtered the nun's gaze. "There's nothing I can do."

Maggie nodded. With leaden feet, she exited the building.

Why does life have to be this unfair? I thought for sure I could find information. Maybe City Hall has copies of the birth records. I'll go there tomorrow.

Maggie reversed her subway trip and disembarked at Grand Central so she could visit the New York City Library.

Standing in front of the massive library with the huge stone lions flanking its entrance, Maggie told herself to venture inside and take a quick look around, in case Aunt Anne-Marie might have questions about the visit.

***

The next day Maggie headed out to City Hall, preparing herself for the expected questions.

The lady at the information desk was polite, asking Maggie what she needed.

"I need to obtain either birth or an adoption record for my cousin."

"Adoption records are sealed."

"Yes, but the birth occurred over twenty years ago."

"The date doesn't matter; the records are still sealed."

"How would I find out if my cousin had been put on an orphan train?"

"The Foundling Hospital handled the orphan train children."

"I've already been there."

"Do you have the child's full name?"

"Yes. It would be Edward Charbonneau."

"And the year?"

"1896."

The woman shook her head. "Unfortunately, a lot of the records from that year were destroyed by mistake. I don't think I can help you."

"What else can I do?"

"Talk to your aunt and uncle. They must have copies of the birth certificate."

Maggie trudged back outside. No wonder Aunt Anne-Marie gave up. What a mess. If women had the vote, these unjust laws could get changed.

***

Maggie had yearned to tell Anne-Marie about her inquiries, but she knew that without any answers, Maggie's attempts would only bring additional heartache. She wasn't sure if there was anything else she could do.

After a quick Sunday lunch, Maggie headed off to Greenwich House with an idea for a holiday activity for the children. Since most of her charges were Italian, it might be fun to listen to a Christmas story about La Bafana and have the children draw their favorite holiday treat. She hoped their pictures would show more than macaroni.

Sean was in the reading room when she arrived.

"Hello, Sean. Did your neighbors save you any turkey from Thanksgiving?"

"They did. Well, Mrs. O'Connor did. She always looks out for me. How about you, Maggie. What have you been up to?"

"I've been busy with my sketching. I'm coloring in my drawings, but I want to experiment next with watercolors. Did you know it takes different brushes for each type of art?"

"No, I didn't. Maybe you should be a food artist?" He grinned.

"But you would have to show restraint and not nibble on the subject."

"Actually, my next project is going to be a poster for the Women's Movement."

"I think food would be an easier subject." He laughed.

"There's nothing humorous about women's rights, Sean."

He held up his hands in mock surrender. "All right, a truce then. Let's join the others. I hear tonight is Romy Marie's famous goulash."

***

When Rees walked into the shop a few days later, Maggie's heart skipped a beat. She had not seen him in two and a half weeks.

"Hello, Maggie."

"Hello. Are you back in town for a while?"

"The rest of the month. And you've not experienced Christmas in New York, so we should spend a day walking along Fifth Avenue in midtown, exploring all the Christmas decorations."

"Sounds lovely."

"How about Saturday, then? We can make a day of it, visiting the window displays, eating out, and having time together."

"Let's meet in a location other than the shop. I don't want to run into Isabelle on a day I'm taking off."

"I guess coming to the apartment at ten in the morning is out of the question?"

Maggie nodded.

"Then I'll meet you outside your apartment at ten o'clock sharp. We'll take the midtown bus up to Herald Square and start there."

***

She only had two days to prepare.

On Friday, Maggie announced she would be shopping on her lunch hour. What she didn't say was where she would be going.

She left Christopher Street and crossed Sixth Avenue to

Bigelow's. Hoping she would not see Mr. Otis, she scanned the sales floor for help. Near the back of the pharmacy, Maggie spied a saleslady and asked to speak about a personal matter.

"Of course. We have a small room for private consultations. Follow me."

Maggie slid the dime store ring she'd bought yesterday onto her left hand, while the saleslady closed the door. "Now, how can we help you."

Maggie took a deep breath. "I need to purchase an item that would prevent pregnancy."

"I assume you mean a pessary? Do you know which kind?"

A mild panic rose in Maggie's throat. "I didn't realize there were different choices."

The older woman nodded. "Why don't I bring in the most popular brand? Then you can examine it privately."

"Thank you."

The woman left for a few minutes and then returned with a small, unobtrusive cardboard box. She sat down and opened it, pulling out an object that looked similar to a tiny rubber hat.

"It's called a Dutch Cap. We had to order these from France in the past, but now they are available in America, too."

For the next ten minutes, the lady explained how Maggie would need to insert the 'cap' into her body, pushing it in far enough to accommodate sexual relations. Then, afterward, she would remove the cap. It would still be advisable to douche. That way, the birth canal would be cleansed from any errant male semen or stray germs.

"Do you need douche equipment as well?"

Maggie's face blanched. "Yes, please." By now, Maggie's armpits were sweating in spite of the winter temperatures.

The saleslady left the room and returned with a different small box. She opened it and pulled out a rubber bulb the size of a small onion. A thin hose lay next to it.

"This is called an Omega Spray. You mix a douche powder packet with the specified amount of water and pour the mixture into the bulb. Then reattach the slender hose and gently shake the bulb. You insert the other end of the hose into your private area and squeeze the rubber bulb firmly, so the mixture goes into the hose then is released inside you. Wait a few moments before urinating." The saleslady smiled. "It isn't as difficult as it sounds."

Maggie prayed she would never see this woman again.

"You can come outside and pay for your purchases. I'll put everything into a plain paper bag."

Maggie exited the room and promptly bumped into Isabelle. The horrified expression on Maggie's face caused Isabelle to smirk.

"Been to the consultation room? I can only guess why."

"Mind your own business, Isabelle." Maggie retorted with a false sense of bravado. Then she forced herself to saunter up to the pharmacy counter and pay for her package. It took all her courage not to glance back to see if Isabelle headed to the consultation room, as well.

TWENTY-ONE

Saturday dawned with a blast of chilly air, but not cold enough to prevent Christmas window shopping. Maggie chose her black woolen coat to keep her warm, glad that her mother had thoughtfully sent it with Maggie's winter clothes.

Rees showed up right on time.

They walked arm in arm over to Sixth Avenue and caught the bus heading uptown.

Departing at 34th Street and walking to the corner, they saw the area already busy with people. Rees maneuvered Maggie to the front of the crowd.

"Oh, Rees! I had no idea!"

In Macy's front windows where merchandise was usually staged, Maggie set her sights on a magical winter wonderland of whimsy. Colorful sleighs pulled by mechanical swans, moved across the display while toy circus horses and toy reindeer pulled other vehicles. Miniature knights in shining armor guarded toys scattered in the foreground. Tiny white electric lights illuminated each scene in a fairyland spectacle.

Maggie stood rooted to the ground, enjoying it like a child.

"Maggie, let's go inside."

"I've shopped here before."

"Not at Christmas time, you haven't."

They politely pushed their way through the crowds and entered the store. Once again, Maggie registered surprise. Everywhere she looked, the shelves, the counters, the walls, and even the salespeople wore vestiges of the holiday season.

The pungent aroma of balsam and cedar brought back the poignant memory of attending Christmas Eve Mass at St. Bridget's. This Christmas would be her first one away from home, and all she had known as a child.

"Rees. I want to buy my parents their Christmas gifts here today. Will you help me?"

They walked over to ladies' accessories, where Maggie selected a warm pair of gloves made from luxurious merino wool. "This will keep my mother's hands warm. Now, I need to go to the men's department and select a warm scarf for my father and a hat for my grandfather."

Once the purchases were made, and Maggie carried a Macy's white shopping bag with the iconic red star blazoned on the front, Rees stopped.

"Maggie, what would you like for Christmas? I'm not a good shopper when it comes to women."

"Women? You mean you buy gifts for other girls, too?" Her voice held a teasing edge.

"That's not what I meant, and you know it."

Maggie thought of the watercolor paints she wanted but decided those should come from Anne-Marie. "How about perfume? I've never used anything other than lavender water."

"Then, I shall surprise you for Christmas."

They left Herald Square and walked over to Fifth Avenue where they continued window gazing, but none of the displays were as enchanting as Macy's.

By lunchtime, they changed course and walked down Fifth Avenue until they ventured into the Chelsea district. Here, they found a small restaurant catering to the weekday lunch crowd. Maggie was fully prepared to stand behind the customers at the lunch counter, but Rees procured a small table for them in the back.

"Rees, this day has been so much fun."

"Let's cap it off with a visit to the studio. It's been weeks since I held you in my arms."

"Shh. Someone will hear."

"No one here knows us, and besides anyone with half a brain could see that we want each other."

They left the restaurant and went directly to the studio. Maggie was lugging a larger than usual purse, but Rees never commented on its size.

Inside the studio, he took her in his arms. Their kissing became more and more urgent.

"Rees, I went to Bigelow's. I should go prepare myself."

"Maggie, that'll take time. I'll use a condom, so you don't have to worry."

"Will it be enough?"

He nodded and then began to kiss the back of her neck, and then her throat.

Then, before she could talk herself out of it, she unbuttoned her shirtwaist.

"Let me help."

Rees removed her clothes, one piece at a time until all she wore was her princess slip and undergarments. Then he untied the satin ribbon and the slip fell to the floor.

Maggie shivered, not from being cold but from every nerve fiber standing on edge.

"Go ahead and unhook your brassiere."

Maggie did and then pulled down her silk bloomers, standing now in complete nakedness.

He led her to the coach and gently lowered her down. Then he undressed. Maggie had never seen any man or boy naked, and at first, she was alarmed at the size of his swollen penis encased in a condom.

Before she could register any fear, he climbed on the sofa and leaned next to her. Soon, his fingers were tracing an imaginary line down each of her arms, then back to her throat, then her chest. He cupped each breast and leaned over and suckled on her nipples, which by now were achingly firm. Lastly, his fingers caressed her inner thighs.

In a quick but subtle movement, he climbed on top of her and guided himself inside. At first, she experienced a sharp pain, but then their two bodies became like one as they moved together in a rhythm as old as time.

When their lovemaking finished, they lay wrapped in each other's arms.

"I hope I didn't hurt you."

"Not terribly much."

"Was it what you expected?"

"I didn't expect it to be so intense."

Rees stroked her arm. "I hope you liked it."

Maggie smiled. "I did."

The pessary lay untouched in her purse.

***

Life had changed, and Maggie knew it was more than just giving up her virginity. She was now making her own decisions as a woman.

What she had failed to anticipate, was how she would feel around Sean.

Sean did not know about Rees, and for some unexplained reason, Maggie didn't want him to know.

This Sunday would be the last date that Greenwich House would be open in December. Then it would close for three weeks for the holidays and thorough cleaning.

Everyone had been asked to bring a dish for a holiday potluck supper. Maggie made Grand-papa's onion tart.

The dinner had been loud with everyone talking, laughing, and telling stories. Sean sat next to Maggie.

Later, when the dishes had been cleared, washed, dried, and stacked, everyone put on their coats, picked up a candle, and ventured out into the neighborhood. When they came to the first apartment building, the group lighted their candles and sang Christmas carols. Then they repeated the procedure as they walked down Barrow Street until they had serenaded the entire loop.

Maggie stood next to Sean, caught up in the joyful atmosphere, and glad to be participating in the night's events. When they found their way back to Greenwich House, everyone yelled *Merry Christmas!* And *See You in the New Year!* Maggie breathed a sigh of contentment.

My life is filled with good people.

Sean nudged her. "Maggie, don't leave yet." He took a small rectangular box out of his coat pocket. "Merry Christmas." Then he leaned over and kissed her on the cheek.

Momentarily stunned, Maggie stammered. "Sean, I didn't realize people would be exchanging gifts. I didn't bring anything."

"That doesn't matter. I wanted you to have a gift from me under your tree."

Maggie leaned up and kissed him on the cheek. "You are such a special friend, Sean Murphy. I hope you know that."

He blushed and turned his head aside. "Good night, Maggie, and Merry Christmas."

"Merry Christmas, Sean."

As she walked back to the El, Maggie cradled the small rectangular box in her hand.

***

Maggie spent the next week working at the hat shop, mailing her parents' gifts back to Porters Glen, and shopping for Rees and Anne-Marie.

With the blast of winter upon them, Maggie bought a soft, warm flannelette nightdress for Anne-Marie that would keep her warm in bed. For Rees, she wanted a distinctive gift, yet practical. She finally decided on a woolen vest he could wear on the coldest days when he might be on a photography assignment outside. She bought an expensive herringbone one at B. Altman's and had them wrap it.

On Saturday, Rees came to the shop before closing. He brought with him three wrapped gifts.

"Merry Christmas, everyone!"

Maggie was touched; he had bought a tea towel for Anne-Marie. The second gift came from Macy's. The small box made Maggie think, just for a minute, that it might be jewelry. When she opened it, it contained a bottle of La Rose perfume by Coty.

The third gift perplexed her, but then he handed it to Isabelle. Maggie pursed her lips as if she had chewed on a lemon. Isabelle opened it to find a calendar for 1919. Nothing personal but thoughtful. Maggie wanted to spit.

"Miss Charbonneau, I'd like to take Maggie out to dinner to celebrate Christmas. Would that be permissible?"

"After you brought all of us gifts, how could I say no?"

Rees helped Maggie on with her coat. As they headed out, she picked up the wrapped box from B. Altman's. They walked the few blocks to West 4th Street and found the Hearthstone Restaurant.

Walking in, Maggie found herself in a large cozy room, filled with tables, and two large fireplaces that sufficiently warmed the entire place. Rees ordered the table d'hôte meal for both of them which turned out to be French onion soup, followed by Chicken Provençal, with simmered potatoes and tomatoes. Dessert was a delightful trifle cake.

"I brought you here, Maggie, knowing you like French food."

"Thank you. Now, open your gift." She handed him the box.

"No, Maggie, there's something I have to tell you first." His voice became more serious than usual. "I've accepted a photo assignment that will last several weeks—in Chicago."

"Chicago!"

He nodded. "It's a wonderful opportunity. I'll be on temporary assignment for the *Chicago Daily*, documenting city children during winter. It will be similar to my New York project that I never was able to sell to the papers here."

"How long will you be gone?"

At least until the beginning of February, perhaps a bit longer."

"And where will you stay?"

"At the YMCA."

Maggie remained pensive. "When do you leave?"

"That's the bad part. I start on January second, so I need to be in Chicago by December 30th."

"You won't be here for New Year's?"

"Unfortunately, no. This opportunity means a lot to me, Maggie. I hope you understand."

She bit her lip. "Of course, I do, and I'm happy for you, but January will be a dreary month without you."

"You'll fill it up; I'm sure."

Maggie nodded, trying not to show her disappointment. "Well, go ahead and open my gift. I guess I'm clairvoyant. You'll certainly be able to use it in Chicago."

When he lifted the box lid, a lopsided smile spread across his face. "It's a lovely vest, Maggie. Thank you."

They walked back in relative silence to her apartment. When they kissed goodnight, Maggie clung to him, not wanting to let go.

"The assignment is only until the end of January."

"Will I see you before you leave?"

"Of course." His kissed her, but not with the same intensity as before.

Maggie walked inside and shut the door. Had he already known about Chicago when they made love last week?

***

Christmas Day dawned bright and clear. Maggie and Anne-Marie walked over to St. Joseph's to attend Christmas Mass. Next, they trooped over to their favorite deli, which, being run by a Jewish family, was open on Christmas Day.

With church and brunch behind them, they went home to open their gifts.

The family had sent thoughtful presents. Maggie received a new sketch pad from Grand-papa, a warm winter scarf from her father, and a bound copy of many of Grand-papa's recipes from her mother.

When Maggie opened Anne-Marie's gift, she giggled. "Open yours now." When Anne-Marie lifted the lid off her present, both women dissolved into laughter. They had bought the same flannelette nightgown for each other!

"Well, we'll both be fashionably adorned for going to bed."

"Yes, and we'll look like twins!"

When Maggie opened her last gift, the small long box from Sean, she let out a tiny gasp. There, nestled next to each other were two sable hair art brushes, #2 and #6, the recommended ones for watercolor.

"What is it?"

"Watercolor brushes."

"From whom?"

"My friend at Greenwich House."

Maggie shook her head, picked up the brushes, and ran her fingers through the hairs of each brush.

Then she stared at their small Christmas tree. *Why couldn't Rees be more like Sean?*

TWENTY-TWO

Maggie had already explained she and Rees would be going out on Sunday since Greenwich House was closed till after New Year's.

Anne-Marie had countered with a gentle warning about not getting carried away—this would be the last time seeing Rees for a while.

Maggie had stashed the pessary equipment in her art satchel and said she would see Rees and then perhaps sketch Christmas decorations. Most of that was true.

Walking back to her room, she crossed her fingers out of habit.

Rees came to pick Maggie up at the apartment and stayed long enough to chat with Anne-Marie about his temporary assignment in Chicago. For today though, he wanted to show Maggie his finished project of *Faces of Innocence* which hung in a nearby gallery.

Once outside, Maggie linked her arm with his. "Are we going to see Jessie?"

"Of course. You don't think I'd lie to your aunt?"

They went directly to Jessie's art gallery. The plain walls held new photographs, and Maggie scanned the room to see where Rees's pictures were located. As she walked around the room, she detected the aroma of lavender, similar to the sachets Anne-Marie hung in the hat shop.

Then Maggie stopped. There in front of her was the photo of young girls slaving over a table filled with bottles of glue, pieces of artificial flowers, and green stems. She recognized it as the Fleiss Factory. Closing her eyes for an instant, she felt the suffocation of having been there.

Moving on, Maggie inspected each photo while Rees chatted with Jessie.

"No strawberry shortcake today, the berries are too expensive in winter and almost impossible to get." Jessie approached Maggie. "Do you see any photographs that interest you?"

"I know which ones were shot by Rees, so of course I'm partial to those."

After staying a while, they said good-bye to Jessie and headed to Rees's studio.

Maggie took a deep breath. "Rees, I bought a pessary for extra precaution."

"All right."

"Let me use the bathroom, and I'll be right back."

The bathroom was a shared room in the hallway, and Maggie prayed no one else would need it right away.

She unwrapped the equipment, but inserting the pessary took a few tries, bringing Maggie close to tears.

"I was afraid you might have left." He tried to get her to smile as she returned.

Maggie stood silent and then undid buttons and let her dress fall to the floor.

Rees took her in his arms and kissed her, then leaned his head against hers. "I've never known any girl like you, Maggie."

"Then don't forget me while you're in Chicago."

"How could I?"

She waited while Rees put on a condom. They ran their hands all over each other's body. Maggie's heart pounded, knowing she wanted him as much as he wanted her. He scooped her up into his arms and carried her to the couch where they consummated their desire for each other.

"I hope it didn't hurt…with the pessary in, I mean."

"No, it was all right. But I need to go back to the bathroom."

"So soon? You don't want to lay here for a while?"

"I do, but I need to follow the directions exactly."

Maggie redressed, picked up the satchel and went back to the bathroom where she removed the pessary and mixed the douche powder with water from the tiny sink. After swirling the rubber bulb, she used the douche solution to cleanse herself.

My goodness, that was a lot of work to prevent pregnancy.

However, the alternative would have been disastrous. Thank you, Maggie whispered to whoever had invented the Dutch Cap and Omega Spray.

They walked back home, arm in arm. When Rees kissed her goodnight, Maggie wanted to hold on to him, a bit longer. But he kissed her on the forehead and smiled, "Happy New Year, Maggie. I'll see you in 1919."

Then he stepped into the elevator, the door closed, and Maggie stood alone in the corridor.

***

January descended with a blanket of bitter cold. Maggie had survived twenty-two winters in the mountains of western Maryland, but those winters had been full of snow and family cheer. Here in New York, the wind whipped through the streets, the cold captured one's body, and everyone hurried to get inside.

With Rees gone, the cold of New York penetrated Maggie's spirits.

New Year's Eve came and went. Anne-Marie declined invitations and spent the night with Maggie. They dined at the Brevoort Hotel and stayed up till midnight to welcome in the new year.

Refusing to succumb to the blues, Maggie cleaned out her art satchel. In the process, she discovered the card from the artist she met in the park. *Vincent Fox, Artist, Greenwich Village, New York.* His phone number was listed on the back.

Maybe I could take art lessons with him? She walked over to her bureau and opened the top drawer. Inside a satin stocking bag, she pulled out her bank statement. Yes, she had saved enough to hopefully pay for at least a couple of lessons, maybe more. She could always sell the Flower Lady sketch if she had to.

***

The phone call had been relatively easy. Mr. Fox gave her his address, and they set a date for the first Monday in January.

"Maggie, how do you know this, Mr. Fox is on the up-and-up? He might be a shady character posing as an artist. I don't know if I'm comfortable with you going there alone."

"I called Jessie at the art gallery, and she vouched for him. Honestly, Aunt Anne-Marie, I'm not that naïve."

Not sure what to bring, Maggie gathered up her sketchbook and pencils. Then she included her colored drawings of Gladys and the Flower Lady as well. Dressed in a warm navy wool skirt and cream-colored shirtwaist, she headed to Mr. Fox's address, Seven Patchin Place.

Crystal Eastlake had warned her that the alley called Patchin Place was a bit tricky to find. Her instructions said to walk to the Jefferson Market and make a right onto Greenwich Avenue and continue walking. Then, look carefully to the right, and she would see the entrance to the small alley.

Maggie knew nothing about the alley but followed the directions. Once on Greenwich Avenue, she walked on a bit further and found the entrance. Stepping into the lane, she felt a few errant snowflakes whirl in the air, which made the alley appear as a snow globe and made Maggie feel like she was entering a secret destination.

The alley was a dead-end, and Maggie counted ten brick townhomes, five on each side of the lane, and each with three stories. She walked in further until she came to number seven. Ringing the bell, she was thrown off guard when a window opened on the third floor, and a man's head popped out; "Come in, the door's unlocked and I'm on the top floor."

Maggie opened the door and saw a set of stairs to the right. She climbed to the first landing and then the second landing and finally to the top floor. There were multiple doors, but one on the left hung open.

"Mr. Fox?"

"Yes, my dear and delighted to see you." He stood in the doorway and ushered her into his studio. Paintings took up every imaginable spot. Several sat on easels, others adorned the walls, many leaned precariously against the furniture, and the rest fought for a position in any nook or cranny. No space was wasted.

And art supplies lay everywhere. Piles of unpainted canvases competed with wooden frames leaning against the main wall. A variety of glass jars filled with multiple paintbrushes sat on former bookcases. Paint tubes of every color lay spread by the easel, on a worktable and nestled in shallow boxes by a stool. The cloying odor of pine sap permeated the room.

Turpentine, perhaps? That would explain the open window.

Then Maggie peered at Mr. Fox. A man of medium height and build, he had a shock of jet-black hair, sparkling brown eyes, and sported a goatee. Rumpled trousers, a shirt with the sleeves rolled up, and an apron splattered with innumerable streaks of paint completed his attire.

"Welcome to my studio."

"Thank you."

"Now, please sit down…here." He moved a painting off a chair to find space. "Tell me about yourself. All I know is that you sketch in Washington Park."

"Well, I have always enjoyed drawing, and I came to New York so I could take professional art lessons. I'm currently living with my aunt."

"What type of art do you enjoy doing?"

"I love to sketch, both fashion and people. I have hopes of becoming a fashion artist and sketch designs appropriate for working women."

"Well, let me see your sketches."

Maggie pulled out her sketchbook and handed it to him. Then she held her breath. She watched as he carefully paged through the sketches, smiling at one or two and cocking his head at others.

"I like the ones you've done of Gladys."

"You know her?"

"Everyone who spends time in the park knows Gladys." He studied the drawings of Gladys further. "It seems you do have talent. And that's good. I hate to invest energy in students who are lacking in either talent or ambition. You are serious about furthering your art?"

"Yes."

"Well, then, let's get started. Show me your drawing pencils."

Maggie reached back into the satchel and pulled out four pencils.

Mr. Fox smiled. "I am impressed that you have pencils of differing hardness."

"I attended an Edith Young lecture back in the fall. I took copious notes on her suggestions."

Mr. Fox smiled again. "And I'm impressed that you took my suggestions about hands. I can see your later sketches are much improved. But you also need help with people's faces. Yours are too stiff. Let me show you how sketching faces is a matter of creating either a circle, heart, rectangle, or square shaped visage. Like this…"

The two hours flew by as Mr. Fox coached Maggie on her production of faces.

"I see by the clock our time is over for today. Before you leave, I want to ask you two important questions."

"Yes?"

"What are the two best times of the day to paint or sketch, and, what type of light is the most preferable?"

"I know northern light is the best, but I don't know about the times of the day."

"Good. I like honesty in a person. The two best times are early morning or late afternoon. That is when the light is the gentlest. Do you have a north facing window in your apartment?"

"Yes, my bedroom windows face north, and I have already turned my bedroom into a studio of sorts."

"Excellent. Now, you have two assignments for next week. First, I want you to find a muse."

"A muse?"

"Here." He pointed to a painting of a young girl dressed in the old Dutch style and wearing one earring. "She is my muse. The great Dutch painter Vermeer captured both the light and her spirit. I salute her every day, and she inspires me."

Maggie nodded. *Where am I going to find a muse?*

"Assignment two is to go home and sketch during the mornings and afternoons, practicing faces."

"I work at my aunt's hat shop during the week."

"Then sketch before you go to work and late on the week-ends. If you are serious about becoming an artist, you'll make it a priority."

"Thank you, Mr. Fox. I enjoyed today. But you haven't told me the price for the lessons."

"Do you have savings, or is your aunt paying?"

"I'm using my own savings."

"How much do you make a week?"

Maggie frowned. That information was personal. "I make ten dollars a week."

"Then, shall we say two dollars per weekly lesson?"

"Yes." Maggie grinned and shook his hand.

***

When she returned the following Monday, she showed Mr. Fox her first poster for the Heterodoxy Club. It depicted three women standing in a row; a young mother, an office woman, and a factory girl. At the bottom, the message read: All of them deserve to vote.

"Maggie, the faces are better. But, for the poster to command attention, you need to place the women in a better focus."

"What you mean?"

"All of your artwork, including Gladys, has your subject right in the middle of the scene. You need to place it slightly off center."

"I don't think I follow."

"Think of your paper as a grid of nine blocks. Putting your subject in the direct center is not as pleasing to the eye as placing it slightly to the right."

"But I drew three women."

"And you can paint them in a circle fashion, or even a curved diagonal. But you want each woman's image to be commanding. As you paint, look at her through the eye of a needle."

"Mr. Fox, it's like you are talking in riddles."

"If you hold up a needle and look through its eye, your focus becomes narrowed. It is easier to paint each woman when you take the time to focus on them one by one. It is also a good lesson for life; learning to focus on one thing at a time."

"That's easier said than done."

"Then prioritize. Decide what is the most important; then concentrate on that."

Maggie went home and sketched a new rendition of the three women. When she finished, she smiled at the new perspective. Calculating that she could finish the poster within the next two weeks, she looked forward to giving it to the Heterodoxy Club for reproduction.

While she had understood Mr. Fox's decree about prioritizing her life, it did not seem possible right now to give anything up—she wanted it all.

TWENTY-THREE

January morphed into February with little news from Rees about his return. His last note said he might be back by Valentine's Day.

Today was Valentine's Day, and she thought he might surprise her at the shop. If not, then there was sure to be a letter.

After work, she and Anne-Marie took the El back up to 14th Street and dashed inside their lobby to escape the cold. Maggie inserted the key into the mailbox and squealed with delight when an envelope with Rees's unmistakable handwriting sat on top of the pile. She told herself to wait until they were in the apartment. The suspense would make his words all the more special.

She wrenched off her coat and quickly hung it in the closet, then ran to her room and plopped on the bed while her fingers tore open the envelope.

> Dear Maggie,
> This is not the kind of letter I know you wanted to receive, but you need to know that I am not coming back to New York.

What? She must have read this wrong. Her eyes darted back over the first two lines of print, at first confused, and then she held her breath as a feeling of dread emerged.

I have not been completely honest with you. Remember the family I took pictures of at the resort in the Catskill's last summer? I had been corresponding with them ever since. The father is an editor at the Chicago Daily News. He was the one who invited me to come to Chicago for a few weeks and interview at the paper.

I didn't tell you because I wasn't sure if I would be offered a job.

When I first arrived, the family's daughter, Jessica, introduced me to a group of local photographers. They have all been welcoming and helped me acclimate to the city.

As it turns out, I now have a permanent job with The News. You know this is what I have always wanted.

I hate to think that I have hurt you with my decision. That was never my intent. I will be forever grateful for our time together in the Village, and that it was me who introduced you to the joy of love in the afternoon.

Someday you'll be a famous artist, and I'll smile and say, 'I knew her when.' Best of luck, Maggie, you will always be special to me.

Love,

Rees

Maggie sat, stunned. *I hate to think that I have hurt you.* Tears tumbled down her cheeks.

Oh, God. How could I have been so stupid? How could I have believed that he loved me?

"What did Rees have to say?" Anne-Marie called out as she made her way to the back.

Maggie couldn't even speak; the words choked themselves in her mouth.

Anne-Marie opened the bedroom door. The sight of Maggie's face propelled Anne-Marie into the room.

"He's not coming back. He's gotten a photography position at a Chicago newspaper."

"Oh, honey." Anne-Marie flew to Maggie's side and wrapped her arms around her niece. "Perhaps it will be temporary."

Maggie shook her head as tears flooded her face. "Here, read the letter."

Anne-Marie took the pages and scanned them. The message was clear; he had gone to Chicago with every intent of procuring a newspaper job. Coming back to ask for Maggie's hand in marriage had never been a part of his plan.

Anne-Marie's eyes hardened. She returned to the lines about 'love in the afternoon.'

Taking a deep breath, she asked, "Maggie, are you carrying his child?"

Maggie shook her head, and Anne-Marie let out a sigh of relief.

"I am so sorry he broke your heart. But I promise you; you will find a man who will deserve you and love you back."

Maggie lay down on the bed. "I want to close my eyes and rest."

"Of course."

Anne-Marie padded back to the kitchen, swearing a curse at Rees Finch under her breath and listening to sobs from the back bedroom.

***

Meanwhile, across town in the East Village, Isabelle had returned home to the apartment she shared with her aunt and uncle.

Reaching into her coat pocket, she withdrew a square envelope addressed to Maggie at the hat shop. The return address read, Sean Murphy.

Intrigued, Isabelle opened the envelope and pulled out the Valentine. Opening the card, she read the chirpy Valentine and the handwritten line, which said, "I hope we will become more than just friends."

"Humph. She already has Rees Finch; she doesn't need this guy, too."

Walking into the tiny kitchen, she tossed the Valentine into the trash.

***

On Sunday, Maggie walked into the reading room at Greenwich House. A single yellow rose stood in a vase on top of the bookcase. She was perplexed. Did the entire staff receive a flower today?

She moved the vase out of the way from where the children might knock it over. Looking up, she saw Sean standing in the doorway.

"Did you see the rose?"

Maggie nodded. "Did you get one, too?"

A perplexed look crossed his face. "No, I only bought one for you. I supposed you would have gotten flowers from your beau, but I wanted you to have one from me, as well. The grocer told me that red roses are for sweethearts, but yellow roses show admiration."

He smiled at her and then averted his eyes.

"The yellow rose also reminded me of sunshine. February can be so dreary in New York. You've brought sunshine into my life, Maggie. You deserve a burst of it yourself."

Maggie forced a smile. *He has no idea of how badly I need sunshine in my life right now.* "Sean, I've never been given a rose before."

"I find that hard to believe."

Maggie walked over to the vase and inhaled. "It even smells like sunshine. Thank you."

"I'll check back with you after the children leave."

As Sean retreated, Maggie thought how lucky she was to have him in her life. But images of Rees would not let go. She fought with herself to banish those emotions. They would only bring back the hurt.

Once the reading hour was over, Sean appeared at the door. "Maggie, a few guys from the precinct are meeting at Central Park to go ice skating on Saturday. How about coming along? It will be a boisterous group, but we'll have fun."

"Ice skating? Sean, I don't own skates, and honestly, I've never been skating. Maybe another time."

"We can rent skates at the park, and I can teach you. It isn't too hard."

"Well, I guess it could be fun."

Sean's face brightened. "We'll take the subway up to 59th Street."

"I can meet you here. What time?"

"One o'clock." He beamed. "Dress warm; the park will be cold."

"Sean, I grew up where ice froze on the inside of the windows. I know cold."

***

The next day, before her art lesson with Mr. Fox, Maggie visited Jessie.

"I had to come to see you."

"Of course, dear. Come in, and I'll put on the kettle."

While Jessie fiddled with the kettle, Maggie poked around the gallery. Many of the photographs were new ones she had not seen before. Did any of them belong to Rees?

"There, sit down and let's catch up."

Maggie sat down, trying to ignore the presence of Rees all around her.

Jessie did not speak but studied Maggie's face. "It's about Rees, isn't it?"

"Partly."

"He's not coming back to New York, is he?"

"How did you know?"

"I haven't heard from him. But I know Rees, and I know other men like him. Surely, Maggie, you must have had some glimpse?"

"Of what?"

"I'm sure Rees made you feel like he loved you, and he probably did, at the time. But Rees will always be married to his photography."

"But I gave …myself to him."

Jessie nodded. "It can happen to the best of us. You're not pregnant, are you?"

"No." Maggie wiped away a stubborn tear.

"Believe me when I tell you, you'll emerge as a stronger woman. You'll be wiser the second time around."

"There won't be a second time."

"Of course, there will. Everyone gets a second go-round with love."

"Jessie, I thought it was love. Now there's this emptiness. I know he's not coming back, but I can't let go of my feelings for him." Maggie smudged the tears off her face.

"What you need is to jump full force into your art. Let it take over your mind and heart."

"I don't have the energy."

"Then get the energy. When you are ready, I will display your work here in the gallery, with a price agreeable to both of us. Nothing boosts the spirit of an artist better than having a piece of their work sell."

"Thank you. You've become a good friend."

"Bring me your best piece. Second rate art never sells."

Walking home, Maggie made a promise to herself.

I will survive this heartache. One day Rees will see my artwork and realize my life went on without him. She blew out a breath of steam and forced herself to march home with a semi-sense of bravado.

Entering her bedroom, she spied her favorite drawing of Gladys. Maggie blew out a forcible sigh. *Well, at least now I know who my muse is.* She smiled and gave Gladys a salute.

***

On Saturday morning, Maggie dug through the winter trunk her mother had sent from home. Out came her acorn brown wool skirt and matching sweater. Then she retrieved her black wool coat. Groping along the closet shelf, she located her plum-colored wool scarf. All she needed was a fashionable hat.

"Aunt Anne-Marie, what type of hat would go with this?"

"You'd look good in my new cloche. The material is a plum color, so, it would match your scarf. Let's see."

As usual, Anne-Marie had the eye and the knack for fashion. The hat set off the outfit.

Maggie worked the morning hours at the shop and then dressed for skating.

As she moved to the front door, Isabelle whispered, "Going to the consultation room?"

Ignoring Isabelle, Maggie left to meet Sean at Greenwich House.

The afternoon was cold, and snow still lay on the side streets, but Maggie walked briskly down the avenue. When she turned the corner on Barrow, a group of men and women in front of the settlement house nudged Sean.

"Maggie, you look great! These are my friends. We thought it would be easier to all meet here and take the subway together."

The jovial ride uptown with everyone jostled together on the subway train filled Maggie with delight. When they arrived at the 59th Street Station, all the passengers piled out.

Only a short walk over to Central Park, and then Maggie was surprised to see people of all ages lacing up skates and stepping out onto the icy pond. She watched as Sean rented their skates, marveling how the snow-encrusted landscape of the park made it look like a fairy wonderland.

He helped her adjust her pair and then nudged her out onto the ice.

All around her, she could hear people laughing and children shrieking in delight. Her breath left trails of steam as she concentrated on staying erect.

She immediately lost balance, but Sean grabbed her in time to prevent a fall. "Here, Maggie, let me guide you. Once you get the feel of your skates, you'll find your balance. Then, gliding over the ice is pure pleasure."

He was correct. It took a half hour, but Maggie caught on and became immersed in the merriment of the excursion. Sean skated by her side, holding her hand. Her flushed cheeks brought a glow to her face, from both the cold and the exhilaration of the outing.

After they skated for two hours, the group returned their skates and trooped together to a nearby restaurant where the women sipped hot toddies, and the policemen drank beers. Laughter filled the air.

Maggie stole a glimpse at Sean. He had managed to bring New York City magic back into her life, and she found herself enjoying it.

As they walked back to the subway, Sean hung back from the group. "Maggie, I want to ask you a question."

"All right."

"I hope I am not interfering in your life. Are you still seeing your beau?"

She hadn't realized Sean's perceptiveness. "No, I'm not. We've parted ways."

"What an incredible idiot to let you go." Then he linked her arm in his as they made their way down the subway steps.

GREENWICH VILLAGE, NEW YORK CITY

SPRING 1919

The early March winds gusted through New York with a force that blew men's hats off their heads and forced women to hold onto their bonnets.

On a relatively calm Monday, Maggie walked to her art lesson.

"I did all the exercises you suggested from last week, and I think I've mastered the technique about faces."

Mr. Fox said nothing; an enigmatic smile spread across his face. "Really? You mastered faces in just a few weeks?"

"Yes!"

"That's interesting. It took me two years of art school to achieve believable faces."

Maggie's enthusiasm plummeted.

"Let's see. Hmm, yes these are better than your first attempts. You will soon learn that to be a real artist takes a lot of patience and many, many attempts to capture on the paper what you see in your mind."

He saw her shoulders droop. "But today we're not concentrating on faces. Today we're taking a walking field trip."

"To a museum?"

"No."

Just when she thought she understood his intentions, he changed gears.

"You can leave your sketch pad here; you won't need it for where we're going. Come on; follow me."

Maggie had no other choice.

Out on the street, they both flipped up the collars of their coats as they walked east along Greenwich Avenue.

"Here we are."

"But this is the park. We met here."

"We did, indeed. Now, tell me what colors you see." Mr. Fox pointed in the vicinity of the bare trees scattered around the perimeter of the park."

"I see gray, black, and white."

"Are you sure?"

"Yes."

"Because I see pearl gray, dove gray, ebony, coal-black, bone white, oyster white, and of course, arctic white."

"I think I get your point."

"Do you? I'm not sure. You see, my dear, you need to start looking at the world with an artist's eye. You need to be discerning. When it comes to colors, there can be many shades of a hue. From what I have seen in your sketches, you are not using your watercolors to their full potential. With more flair, your art could soar."

"But I don't want to draw trees; I'm interested in fashion sketching."

"And do you think the fashion world only uses plain colors? No, my dear, you need to slow down and learn to look, really look, at the world in front of you."

Maggie tried not to be offended.

"We're not done. Next, we visit a friend of mine in Chinatown."

"Chinatown?"

"You'll be safe with me. We do have to ride the subway to get there, though."

Once they entered Chinatown, Maggie tried not to stare, but the sights were like nothing she had ever seen. Mott Street overflowed with Oriental men and women speaking in a language that was unfamiliar to Maggie. The storefronts flooded with colorful displays, and every other store presented itself as a restaurant.

"Don't stare, and don't make eye contact. Just walk next to me." They ventured two blocks, and Mr. Fox made an abrupt turn down a side street. Maggie spied dead ducks hanging in front of a store window.

Oh, dear Lord, do not let Mr. Fox suggest that we eat here.

When Mr. Fox did stop, Maggie was puzzled about the store in front of her. Through the open doorway, she saw a large table filled with piles of fabric.

"Ah, Mr. Fox, my friend, how good to see you." Maggie watched as Mr. Fox and a man bowed to each other.

"Mr. Wu, may I present my newest pupil, Miss Maggie Canavan."

Mr. Wu bowed to Maggie. Not knowing the expectations, Maggie gave a slight bow in return.

"Maggie, Mr. Wu is the best tailor in all of New York City. I brought you here to see his threads."

This day could not get any stranger.

"Look over here."

Maggie followed where Mr. Fox was pointing and saw a back wall covered with cones of thread in every hue imaginable.

"This is what I am talking about when I say you will need to learn about colors. Mr. Wu has hundreds of threads representing every color on Earth. These are the colors of the fashion industry, Maggie. And if you want to draw the garments, then you need to start seeing the colors."

Maggie could not think of anything to say; she was amazed at the stunning array in front of her.

"Thank you, Mr. Wu. We will return to visit on another day."

Then Mr. Fox bowed again, as did Mr. Wu, and Maggie as well. When they exited the shop, Mr. Fox was grinning. "Never saw anything like that back in Maryland, I bet."

"No. Do all New York tailors have that many threads in their shops?"

"The good ones do. Do you see what I mean now about colors?"

"I think so. This hat that I'm wearing is not just purple; it's…?"

"Eggplant, my dear. Eggplant."

***

The week before Easter demanded herculean energy at the shop. Anne-Marie had warned Maggie that March was an incredibly busy month. Shoppers tired of winter were already looking forward to new spring hats, and especially Easter bonnets. For the past several weeks, one person would act as the saleslady while the other two sat in the back, sewing trimmings onto hat bands. At half past five on Saturday, Anne-Marie closed the front shop door. "Whew! Well, this has been a whirlwind. Thank goodness tomorrow is Easter."

While they walked back home, Anne-Marie admitted, "I'm not as young as I used to be. It will be a vacation to stay home after Easter and rest."

***

Both Easter Mass and the Parade had been lovely. Maggie relished the experience of walking down Fifth Avenue with Anne-Marie, both of them decked out in their most elegant outfits and new hats. But afterward, Anne-Marie said she was too tired to go out for Easter dinner. She wanted to go home and sleep.

Maggie concocted leftovers for herself while Anne-Marie slept.

Anne-Marie did not rouse for the meal, and Maggie let her rest through the night.

On Monday, Anne-Marie claimed she had no appetite, and wanted to stay in bed. Maggie busied herself with her artwork and periodically checked on her aunt. Maggie made an easy midday meal of soup, but Anne-Marie still did not rouse for lunch.

At dinner time, Maggie knocked on the bedroom door but found Anne-Marie still asleep.

On Tuesday morning, Anne-Marie opened her eyes but remained in bed. While this behavior was out of the ordinary, Maggie chalked it up to exhaustion from the previous weeks of intense work at the shop.

"I'll make breakfast, Aunt Anne-Marie. You can sleep for another twenty minutes."

Maggie put the kettle on the burner and lit the gas. Then she rummaged in the icebox for an egg or two to scramble. Opening the bread box, she saw they were down to a few slices of bread, which meant she would have to stop at the grocery store after work.

The teakettle whistled, and Maggie made two cups of tea. Then she proceeded to whip the eggs gently and pour them in the skillet; as she had seen Grand-papa do so many times. She deftly tilted the skillet and with a fork pulled the eggs together, allowing them to cook to perfection but not being overdone.

Rummaging in the small panty, she found a tray and assembled Anne-Marie's breakfast.

She knocked again on Anne-Marie's door, but only heard a moan from the other side. Balancing the tray, she opened the door. "Time to rise and shine. I made scrambled eggs. We need to open the shop; remember."

Anne-Marie whimpered. "Take it away; the smell's making me nauseous."

Maggie had never known her aunt not to be hungry. "Oh, come on, Aunt Anne-Marie. You need to eat, and you love the way I cook eggs, just the way Grand-papa does."

But when Maggie approached the bed, she realized Anne-Marie was more than tired; she was sick. Under the covers, Anne-Marie's body shook. Maggie went over and gently put her hand on Anne-Marie's forehead. The skin was burning hot.

"You've got a fever. There's no way you can go to work today. Let me call Isabelle and ask her to open up for us. Then I'll go in once I know you are resting."

Anne-Marie didn't answer but nodded in the slightest.

Maggie picked up the phone book and dialed Isabelle's number. A woman answered and said she would knock on Isabelle's door. Not wanting to be an alarmist, Maggie left the message that her aunt had come down sick and could Isabelle please handle the opening of the hat shop for a few hours.

She hung up and thought about calling her mother, but then decided not to. Her mother couldn't help from so far away. Rummaging under the sink, Maggie searched for the aspirin bottle Anne-Marie used for headaches. She found it, empty.

She dialed Bigelow's.

"Hello? May I speak with Mr. Otis, please."

Maggie waited, hoping he would remember her. "Mr. Otis? This is Maggie Canavan...Yes, Anne-Marie Charbonneau's niece. I need your advice. My aunt awoke with a fever and extreme exhaustion...Other symptoms? Well, she's hot to the touch and shaking with body chills... Yes, she is complaining of a raging headache...Loose bowels? No."

There was a pause in the conversation.

"What do you mean, influenza? I thought that had died out. Is there still a threat? Yes, I understand...we're out of aspirin though, can you send a delivery boy to our address?... No aspirin?... All right, yes, I know how to brew willow tea. Can you send willow bark? Quarantine? Is that necessary...All right, he could leave the package in the lobby."

Mr. Otis' last words chilled her to the bone.

"Yes, I do understand, the next two days will be critical. I'll take care of her and pray that it's not influenza...Me? I would already have been exposed?"

She mumbled a soft thank you and hung up.

How could this even be possible? They had both been so careful for months. Then Maggie thought back to Easter Sunday. It was true they were both bone-tired, and the Easter Mass had packed the church. After the extended service, they had taken the bus uptown to 50th Street to stroll in the Easter Parade along Fifth Avenue.

Maggie remembered the bus, the streets, and the sidewalks thronged with people; and many of those people coughing and sneezing.

Opening the bedroom door, Maggie saw Anne-Marie sleeping. Hopefully, this was a good sign. She closed the door and then got down on her knees; *Dear God, please do not let this be influenza.*

The delivery boy from Bigelow's arrived within the hour. Maggie went to the kitchen and boiled a quart of water for the willow bark tea, grateful that she knew the technique of making the tonic. Once the water was ready, Maggie added two tablespoons of crushed willow bark and allowed the mixture to simmer on the stove for ten minutes. Then she removed the pan from the heat and let the liquid steep for half an hour. Finally, she strained the brew to remove any residue. Once it cooled, Anne-Marie would be able to drink it.

Maggie called the shop and told Isabelle to close for the rest of the day and not to reopen until she heard from Maggie. "Yes, Anne-Marie is quite sick."

Then, Maggie turned her full attention to Anne-Marie, waking her hourly for sips of the tea and laying cold rags on her forehead. Maggie wasn't even sure her aunt was aware of her surroundings. Her glazed eyes stared off into a corner.

By late afternoon when Maggie entered the bedroom, she detected the smell of urine that got stronger the closer she moved toward Anne-Marie's bed. Pulling back the covers, Maggie saw the soaked bottom sheet under her aunt's body.

At this moment, Maggie understood how ill Anne-Marie had to be. Her aunt would have been horrified to know she had soiled herself.

Maggie remembered the medical masks they wore in October. She rummaged in the bathroom cabinet until she found the meager supply and put one over her nose and mouth.

Anything was worth a try to escape flu germs.

She rolled Anne-Marie on her side and began the task of pulling the wet sheet off the bed. Gently grabbing Anne-Marie under her shoulders, Maggie pulled her to a sitting position. Then Maggie pulled off the soiled nightgown; tossing it on the floor, Maggie lay her aunt on the mattress. Then she took a large bath towel and covered her aunt.

Not knowing what else to do, she took the wet sheet to the bathtub. The stink of urine permeated the small room.

She rinsed out the sheet. *Thank God, there is an indoor bathroom!* How did her mother clean up such messes without indoor plumbing in the Canavan home?

Maggie returned to check on Anne-Marie and give her a sponge bath when dismay descended—the fever chills were once again, taking over Anne-Marie's body. Feeling her aunt's forehead, Maggie realized that the fever had come back with a renewed force.

She performed a quick rinse of Anne-Marie's lower body, then covered her with a blanket. Anne-Marie tossed and turned, while

Maggie tried to mop her aunt's brow.

Exhausted from the day's ordeal, Maggie forced one more drink of the willow tea down Anne-Marie's throat. She slipped a clean nightgown on Anne-Marie. Then she knelt and prayed again that God would spare her aunt. Quietly, Maggie closed the bedroom door. Tomorrow she would get Anne-Marie up, and put fresh sheets on the bed.

Too tired to even eat, Maggie took off the face mask and lay down on her bed. In less than a minute, she was fast asleep, still dressed in her day clothes.

***

Maggie woke with every part of her body aching from yesterday. She got up, slipped on the face mask, and walked to Anne-Marie's bedroom. There had been little change; the fever had not abated.

Bending over her aunt's body, Maggie whispered, "I'm going to do everything possible to pull you through this." Then she retrieved yet another blanket and tucked it around Anne-Marie's shoulders, which were still trembling with chills. Maggie walked out to the kitchen and boiled up the day's allotment of willow tea. While the tea cooled, she rolled Anne-Marie to one side while she negotiated to get fresh sheets on the bed.

Wednesday progressed as an exact duplicate of the day before, except that late in the day Maggie noticed a blueish coloring beginning to form around Anne-Marie's lips. The fever periodically lowered itself long enough for her aunt to stir to a semi-lucid state, but she groaned about how her head hurt, and every bone in her body ached. She wanted to die.

Maggie hushed her aunt. "You'll feel better by tomorrow, and then we can call Mama and tell her how sick you've been."

Anne-Marie dozed fitfully on and off all day, and Maggie kept herself occupied rinsing soiled sheets and night clothes as best she could in the tub, wiping Anne-Marie's hot brow, and forcing her to sip willow tea.

A few hours later, Maggie dragged the upholstered chair in from the living room and created a sleeping space right outside Anne-Marie's door. That way, Maggie would be alerted if Anne-Marie cried out in the night.

Exhausted, Maggie fell asleep in the chair.

When she woke stiff and sore on Thursday morning, she remembered a nightmare. In it, she was tending to her aunt, but then Anne-Marie morphed into Maggie's mother. She resolved to call her parents that day.

By the end of the day, Maggie became aware of Anne-Marie's futile attempts to catch her breath. The gasping sounded like a person drowning on dry land. By late afternoon, Anne-Marie had a bloody liquid seeping from her nose and mouth.

Maggie mustered her courage and picked up the phone. She dialed the operator and asked for a long-distance call be placed to 172 – R in Porters Glen, Maryland. The operated answered that the party line was busy.

"Please, this is an emergency."

A moment later the operator announced that the call was going through.

Annie answered.

"Mama?"

"Maggie, what's wrong? I can tell by the catch in your voice that there is a problem."

"Mama." Maggie began to cry. "Aunt Anne-Marie is sick, awful sick. I've been tending to her since Tuesday morning, but she's worse."

"Has the doctor been to see her?"

"Doctor? No, I called the chemist, and he sent willow bark strips. He said it might break the fever. He suggested we quarantine ourselves in case it's influenza."

"Oh, Dear God. Jonathan!"

Maggie heard her father coming to the room.

"Jonathan, Marie is sick. Very sick, apparently. Maggie's been tending her, alone. I need to take a train to New York as soon as possible."

Maggie couldn't quite hear what her father replied, but it sounded like he was coming to New York with her mother.

"All right, Maggie. Be strong. We'll get on the first train out of Riverton tomorrow morning. If we travel straight through, we can be in New York by nightfall."

"Please get here as fast as you can."

Maggie hung up. Perhaps she should have taken Anne-Marie to the hospital as soon as she had gotten sick. Maggie reassured herself that she had done everything, except the old miners' remedy of boiled onions wrapped in cheesecloth and placed on the chest to alleviate congested lungs.

In a last-ditch attempt, she took out every pot and pan in the kitchen and boiled water. Then she brought the pots into Anne-Marie's bedroom and placed them on towels covering the floor. The steam vapor escaped upward and hovered in the air. It was the only thing she could think of to help her aunt breathe.

Maggie wiped her eyes. She did not want Anne-Marie to know she had been crying. In her aunt's bedroom, Maggie detected a rattle in Marie's chest that sounded like her lungs were filling with liquid. Maggie propped up the bed pillows.

"Come on, Aunt Anne-Marie, Mama's coming. You've got to hang on."

Then Maggie got down on her knees and prayed for the third time that God would spare her aunt.

***

At two o'clock in the morning, while Maggie dozed in the bedroom doorway, Anne-Marie Charbonneau succumbed to influenza.

She was forty-one years old; one of the 675,000 Americans who died from the disease, and left 21,000 children as orphans in New York City alone.

TWENTY-FIVE

Maggie woke to find Anne-Marie's body cold in death.

Too numb to cry, Maggie knelt by the side of the bed, praying for Anne-Marie's soul. She fervently hoped that God would understand why no priest had been called to give her aunt the last rites.

As Friday morning wore on, the crushing weight of guilt descended. Why hadn't she called Mr. Otis sooner? Why didn't she recognize how sick Anne-Marie had been? Why hadn't she called a priest? And, why in God's name had she waited so long to call her parents?

Maggie continued to sit by Anne-Marie's bedside in defiance of death coming to claim the body. After an hour of silent grief, Maggie got up, kissed Anne-Marie's marble-cold cheek, and began the arduous task of sponge-bathing the corpse. She did not want her mother to see Anne-Marie in her present state.

Maggie cut off the soiled nightgown and disposed of it in a garbage bag. The limbs of the body had stiffened, so after Maggie cleaned her aunt, she had to cut open the back of Anne-Marie's favorite dress and slide it to fit up the arms and the front side of the body.

Her final task was to cover Anne-Marie. Having run out of linens, Maggie took the sheet off her bed and pulled it up to Anne-Marie's chest. She could not bear to pull the cloth over Anne-Marie's face.

Driven now to action rather than face her grief, Maggie donned rubber gloves and went to the bathroom and rinsed the sheets over and over. Then she poured bleach into the new water and swished the linen back and forth multiple times, trying to destroy any lingering germs.

Not knowing what else to do, she drained the tub and let the wet sheets stay there.

Next, she opened all the windows in an attempt for some fresh air.

Even though she had little appetite, she knew she needed strength. She opened a can of soup and dragged a spoon through the liquid, forcing herself to swallow. Then she set about cleaning the apartment, trying to erase the smell of death.

She forced herself to stay busy. But by late afternoon, she lay down on the bed and did not wake until the doorbell rang.

Drawing herself from the bed, and not caring at all about her appearance, she peered through the peephole. Her parents had arrived.

Opening the door, Maggie began to sob. "I tried my best to save her, but I couldn't. She died in the night."

Her parents stepped into the apartment, and Annie enveloped Maggie in her arms. "Hush, hush, we know you did your best. I'm so sorry you had to go through this alone." They held onto each other. "I need to see her."

Maggie led her parents down the hallway to the back bedroom. Upon seeing Marie, Annie fell to her knees next to the bed, sobbing. Jonathan bent down and held his wife's shoulder, offering words of plausible comfort while Maggie stood in the doorway, watching.

It seemed an eternity to Maggie, but her mother finally stopped crying. "Mama, we have to make arrangements."

Annie looked up; eyes rimmed red with tears. "Maggie, will you brew a pot of tea."

"Of course."

Maggie went to the kitchen while her parents sat at the dining room table, discussing the situation.

"Maggie, is there someone we can call to help us?"

"We can call Mr. Otis. He's the chemist she always used. I have his number, and I'm sure he'll help."

"Good, we'll call him in the morning. It's been a hard day. Can you make up the living room couch for Papa, and let me sleep in your bed with you?"

In this way, the three grief-stricken Canavan's dropped off to sleep.

***

No one had much of an appetite the next day, and the atmosphere vacillated between bouts of intense silent grief and periods of discussion about funeral plans. Her father called Mr. Otis, who had the name of an undertaker.

Periodically each of them ventured into the bedroom to sit by Anne-Marie's side. No one wanted her to be alone.

Maggie went through Anne-Marie's phone directory and found the name and number of her aunt's lawyer, Mr. MacKay. The third phone call was back home to Grand-papa. Maggie heard him crying on the other end of the line. Louis Charbonneau had now lost his wife, and two of his three grown children.

Within an hour, the undertaker arrived with an assistant. Her parents told Maggie they wanted Marie buried in St. Bridget's cemetery back home, alongside her mother and brother. Maggie, not knowing any other alternative, agreed.

All three Canavan's were silent as Anne-Marie's lifeless body, covered in a death blanket left the apartment. Maggie then rushed into her parents' arms, and the trio hugged each other and cried about the cruel disease that had stolen Anne-Marie's life.

Annie finally took charge. "I will take the train home with Marie's casket. Mr. Fisher, the undertaker from Mt. Pleasant, will meet me in Riverton and handle the burial plans. Papa can stay here with you till the end of the week, helping you get the hat shop ready for sale, and the apartment as well. Then you can come back home with him."

Maggie froze. "I don't want to sell the shop or the apartment."

"I don't see where you have a choice. You can't remain here

alone and run a shop by yourself. It wouldn't be feasible or proper."

Panic rose in Maggie's throat.

"Mama, please. I can get a roommate, and I've worked at the shop for ten months, so I know how it operates. Don't force me to sell anything right now."

"Maggie, you're emotional. You need to be practical."

"The shop was Anne-Marie's life! She never got the chance to have a family, as you did. She poured every ounce of her being into that shop. I can't sell it, at least not yet. It would be like erasing Anne-Marie's entire existence."

Annie looked to her husband for re-enforcement.

"Why don't we wait until we see the lawyer? He can tell us if she left any instructions as to her final wishes. In the meantime, can we order food? I'm finally hungry."

Maggie called Murray's Deli and asked if a delivery boy could bring over an order. As she hung up the phone, her father asked, "Did Marie have a will?"

***

To Maggie, the apartment felt like a crypt without Anne-Marie. Could Maggie live there alone? Self-doubt crept in, mocking her idea of living independently or running the hat shop without her aunt. The prospect of not having Anne-Marie to guide her was terrifying.

For the remainder of the weekend, the Canavan's cleaned the entire apartment with a solution of Lysol and hot water. They also disposed of Anne-Marie's mattress.

Maggie phoned Mrs. Simons at Greenwich House to explain her absence.

On Monday, Maggie donned a black dress. She went into Anne-Marie's closet and found her black silk sailor hat. Removing the trimmings, she turned the chapeau into a mourning hat.

The Canavan family took a cab to the train station, where the undertaker waited. Once Annie and the casket were on board,

Maggie managed a weak wave to her mother. The train pulled out of Penn Station, and Maggie could not help but remember the joy of ten months ago when she had met Anne-Marie here in New York. It had also been the day she met Rees.

Shaking off her melancholy, she followed her father up to street level. They had an appointment with Anne-Marie's lawyer near the Flat Iron building.

"First, may I offer my sincere condolences."

"Thank you, sir."

"In going over Miss Charbonneau's will, it seems she left specific instructions in the event of her death."

The lawyer turned to Maggie.

"She left everything to you."

"What do you mean?" Jonathan asked.

"Well, Mr. Canavan, Miss Charbonneau states:

'Being of sound mind and body, it is my express wish that my niece, Magdalena Ellen Canavan, inherit my place of business, and all of my accrued savings and possessions.'

Maggie sat stunned, as did her father.

"What this means, Maggie is that you have inherited a business, and money to continue living here in New York."

"Are you sure?"

"Quite sure."

"How much money is involved?"

"Well, Mr. Canavan, your sister-in-law invested wisely. Her assets amount to $12,000.00. I can facilitate the transfer of the money into a bank account."

"I think first, my daughter and I need to talk."

"Let's go to the Brevoort Hotel. It was one of Anne-Marie's favorites."

While they were finishing lunch, her father voiced his opinion. "This does not mean that you have to stay in New York."

"Papa, I want to stay. At least for a while. I want to continue with my art, and I want the shop to stay open until I can figure out what to do. Aunt Anne-Marie's gift to the Village was the hat shop."

"You could open a hat shop in western Maryland."

"Please don't pressure me into coming home."

"Can I assume, then, you never intended to return to teaching?"

She waited a moment and then shook her head. "I only taught because you and Mama wanted me to."

Her father leaned back in his chair. "I'm sorry. I had no idea. I thought you enjoyed teaching."

"Only when I could do art with the students."

"I see." He remained silent, then added, "Perhaps one day you'll open a business of teaching art to children."

Maggie smiled. It was an appealing idea and one she hadn't considered.

"I know Mama fears I'll never come back, but I will. I have to find out what I'm supposed to do with my life."

"You've matured so much in the last ten months."

"New York forced me to grow up."

They continued their meal. "Papa, there is an important question I want to ask you, and I want a truthful answer."

"All right."

"How did I get gray-green eyes?"

He put down his knife and fork. "Why are you asking that?"

"I need to know."

"They're most likely from your Irish great-grandfather, James Canavan. He died on the voyage from Ireland. My Grandmother Canavan always said his eyes were the color of the wild Irish Sea."

"Why didn't you ever tell me this before?"

"You've never asked me about your eyes. Are you unhappy with them? I've always thought your eyes were beautiful."

"You do?"

"Yes, in the same way that you are beautiful. You are the perfect combination of your mother and me."

Maggie sat back in her seat. For the first time in her life, she tried to see her parents as two parts of a completed whole — two people who genuinely loved each other and supported each other throughout the years.

"Now, I have a question for you. Did Marie ever say why she never came home to visit us? It has always hurt and bothered your mother."

Maggie ached to tell him the truth about Edward, but she swallowed and lied, "No. She was always too busy with the shop, I guess."

He nodded.

"Papa, how long can you stay here in the city with me?"

"I am on leave this week. If you need me to stay longer, I will."

"I want to show you the hat shop, and Greenwich House— where I volunteer on Sundays. Can you excuse me a moment? Let me call them right now."

Maggie found a pay phone in the hotel lobby and called Greenwich House, explaining to Mrs. Simons she would need an additional week before she came back to volunteering. She inserted another nickel and called Isabelle, and asked that the hat shop should remain closed all week for mourning the death of Anne-Marie.

Walking back to her father, Maggie sensed a difference; she was older somehow. Perhaps the responsibility of the hat shop's future resting on her shoulders had changed her. Rather than perceiving it as a burden, she reminded herself it would be a privilege, and what Anne-Marie would have wanted.

Their last stop of the day was to visit the Irving Trust and open a bank account. To Maggie's surprise, her father needed to be a guarantor for the record. Maggie, as an unmarried woman, required a male family member to vouch for her! Another reason that women needed the vote. How had Anne-Marie accomplished that on her own?

***

The next day Maggie took her father to the hat shop. She could tell he was impressed. Then they walked over to Greenwich House.

Mrs. Simons offered condolences once again and said she had taken the liberty of informing Sean Murphy as to the reason for Maggie's absence.

"Sean Murphy? Who's that?"

"A friend, Papa. A very good friend."

He glanced over to Mrs. Simons, who smiled in response.

As they left Greenwich House, Maggie linked arms with her father.

When the phone rang back at the apartment, Maggie was not surprised to hear Sean's voice.

"Hello, Sean…Thank you…Yes, it was sudden…no, I'm all right, my father is here with me…no, there's nothing you can do, but I do appreciate your call…yes, I'll be back at Greenwich House the Sunday after next…the funeral will be back home in western Maryland…I'll see you in a week."

Her father stood nearby, smiling.

"I told you, Papa. Just a friend."

"All right, a friend. But I want you to tell me about your art and what plans you have for the hat shop. Also, to lessen your mama's fears, please tell me you know a reliable person who can move in with you."

"I do; I just haven't asked her yet."

After a simple meal of baked chicken and vegetables, Maggie brought her father back to her studio/bedroom and showed him her various pieces of art, from the pencil sketches of Gladys to her watercolor painting of Anne-Marie.

"Maggie, I had no idea you were this good."

She beamed.

"What do you intend to do with the art?"

"I intend to sell it. I have a friend who owns an art gallery here in the Village. She has already asked for a few pieces to display and hopefully, sell. I had wanted to illustrate for magazines, but I am reconsidering that."

"And the hat shop?"

"Aunt Anne-Marie's money will be my cushion, but I want to

make my own money. I've already accepted a commission to paint posters that support the vote for women."

"The vote for women? When did this happen?"

"Being here in New York, I've met women who are passionate about women's rights. I find that I agree with them."

Her father smiled. "You are reminding me right now of your mama, when I first met her and how she wanted to help the miners' wives."

Maggie blushed from the compliment. "I'll be all right here, Papa. If for any reason the hat shop goes under, then I would come home right away."

"I still have concerns about leaving you alone in the city. Until you get a roommate, I will check in with you on Monday, Wednesday, and Friday nights at eight o'clock. It will be the one way I can convince your mother not to worry."

"What about Saturday and Sunday?" Maggie suppressed a grin.

"Mrs. Simons has already offered to check on you when you come to her settlement house."

"Honestly, Papa, I can't believe you asked her that!"

"Wait till you have children, Maggie, then you'll understand." He squeezed her hand. "Now, as to your art, may I be your first client and buy the water-color painting of Marie? I want to give it to your mama as a gift."

"Of, course. I feel honored."

***

By Friday, Maggie felt enough confidence that she told her father to return home. After kissing him good-bye at Penn Station and returning to the apartment, Maggie decided to spruce up the spare room.

Shaking off any sadness, Maggie ordered a new mattress and planned to buy new sheets and make the second bedroom readily available for a roommate. Other than that, she did not intend to change any décor. After a cup of tea, Maggie pulled over the notepad and compiled a list of things she needed to accomplish, sooner than later.

First on the list, was to fire Isabelle.

On the following Tuesday morning, Maggie went to the bank and picked up her new checks, then headed to the shop. She wrote out a check to Isabelle, paying her for the week the shop had been closed for mourning and also for the current week. It was more than fair in her estimation.

A few minutes after ten Isabelle walked into the shop. "I am so sorry about Anne-Marie."

"Thank you, but don't bother taking off your coat."

Isabelle's eyes narrowed. "Why not?"

"As of today, you are no longer employed here. I have taken the liberty to draw up a two-week salary check for you. There is no reason we should ever have to see each other again."

Isabelle put her right hand to her hip, tilted her head back and laughed.

"I see nothing funny."

"Oh, but it's hilarious. You can't fire me. You're stuck with me."

"What are you saying? I'm the owner of the shop now; of course, I can fire you."

"My uncle will never agree to it."

"Your uncle? What has he got to do with it?"

"My uncle is Samuel Steinberger! He and your aunt had a business agreement. As long as she employed me, he would sell her the artificial flowers from the Fleiss Factory at a good discount. That's how she made such a profit."

Maggie's face paled, and her body trembled.

"Ah, so you never knew about that?" Isabelle's eyes blazed in perceived victory.

"I don't believe you."

"Go call him."

"I will not, and I will not tolerate this gibberish. Take your check and leave the shop."

"You don't get it, do you? If you fire me, not only will he revoke your discount, he'll refuse to sell to you at all. Then he'll get you blacklisted so none of the jobbers will sell to you."

"Get out, Isabelle, before I call the police."

Isabelle grabbed the check and stalked to the front door, then turned on her heel. "You haven't heard the last from us. You'll regret this, Maggie Canavan. We'll bury you."

Then she strutted out the door.

Shaking, Maggie dropped into a chair. *Dear God, how can this be true? Samuel Steinberger, the manager of the Triangle Factory! And Anne-Marie had to have known.*

Then the image of her grandfather popped into her mind. *God helps those who help themselves.*

She closed the shop and left for the grocer. She had a plan, and if it was to work, she needed cinnamon.

TWENTY-SIX

Maggie wanted Tessa to work at the hat shop, in place of Isabelle. But for that to succeed, Maggie would have to convince Tessa's parents how this would benefit the entire family.

If they agreed, the next step would be to offer Tessa's mother a job where she worked sewing flowers for Maggie only—no more ties to the Fleiss Factory.

The third part of the plan was to ask Tessa to become Maggie's roommate.

Knowing that food is the universal gift, Maggie baked Grand-papa's famous Pigtail Cookies and set out on Wednesday morning to visit Tessa's mother.

Armed with the treats wrapped in a linen towel and nestled in a small basket, Maggie left her apartment and took the Seventh Avenue subway down to Sheridan Square. Then she turned east and walked down West 4th until she came to MacDougal.

Once she turned south, she entered the South Village. Never having been here alone before, and remembering Anne-Marie's caution about the area, she expected the streets to look like the Lower East Side.

Within a block, the scenery did change from old apartment buildings to sagging tenements connected by laundry lines strung across the alleys. Lopsided fire escapes crisscrossed buildings teeming with over-crowded families in substandard housing. A gang of boys, who should be in school, rushed passed her in the muddy road, and groups of young children tottered around out on the cracked sidewalks while old women swept front stoops.

Maggie sniffed the air. The unmistakable odor of cigar smoke assailed her nostrils. As she ventured further, she spied a group of old men sitting outside a corner shop, each smoking cigar stubs. Their conversation ceased as Maggie walked past, but she was certain they would be commenting on her as a stranger in the neighborhood.

The area reeked of poverty, by anyone's standards, but everyone probably knew everyone else on the block—similar to the neighborhoods of Porters Glen.

The aroma of freshly baked bread wafted on the breeze, and Maggie peered around, but no bakery was in sight. Walking past a dilapidated tenement; Maggie saw open cellar windows. The smells of yeast and sugar poured out.

My God, that basement is the local bakery!

She thought back to Rees's statement of how the pickle vendors brought their barrels to the tenement basements at night, and there would be rat bite marks in the pickles. If the rats bit into the pickles, then they must also chew on the bread.

Her stomach lurched.

She turned from that building, and almost tripped over a dead rat. Nausea rose in her throat, and she clamped her hand over her mouth.

After two long blocks on MacDougal Street, Maggie had passed many residents of the neighborhood, but she had still not found the Brunelli's place. The tenements here looked as if they would fall in a good-sized windstorm and Maggie doubted there were any housing codes to ensure safe habitation. She shook with a suppressed fear for Gabriella and Tessa.

Finally, she arrived at the right address. Entering the tenement, she discovered that the ground floor listed four separate apartments. She assumed the upper floors did as well. Choking back the smell of urine in the hallway, she knocked at the door labeled "Brunelli." A soft shuffle sounded, and the door opened a fraction.

"Mrs. Brunelli? I'm Maggie Canavan, a friend of Tessa's. May I come in?"

"Tessa. She is at work."

"I know that. I came to meet you and bring you cookies for your family."

Maggie saw suspicion cloud Mrs. Brunelli's eyes.

"I have no time to visit. I am working."

"I promise I won't stay longer than ten minutes." Maggie held up the basket. "These are special. I learned how to make them from my grandfather. He is a baker."

The door shut, a chain rattled, and the door opened. "Come in. Only ten minutes."

Maggie stepped directly into a sparse kitchen. Two young children sat at a table, both dressed in hand-me-down clothing and involved with sorting stems of silk flowers. The air, filled with the smell of bubbling tomato sauce, also held the odor of the wet laundry that hung on a line stretched over the sink. Maggie glanced at the closed side window. Fresh air would have been a blessing.

She blinked as she refocused her attention to the kitchen table; the only light came from a bare bulb hanging from the ceiling. The side window was too small to provide much illumination.

This room must double as their workroom.

Other than the table, there were four wooden chairs, a large sink, and a stove. Two pictures hung on the wall—one of Jesus and one of the Virgin Mary.

Maggie walked over and bent down next to the table. "Hello, I'm Maggie. I'm a friend of Tessa's. I also know Gabriella."

The two young girls stared at her from under thick black eyelashes. Instead of speaking, they turned to their mother for confirmation. Mrs. Brunelli nodded.

"Hello."

"Now, which sister are you?"

"I'm Alissa. She's Lucy."

"Well, I am pleased to meet you, Alissa and Lucy." Maggie smiled. "You're hard at work."

"We help Mama."

Mrs. Brunelli stood next to the table. "The girls, too young to go to school. They help me with the flowers."

Maggie smiled. "Of course."

"Why are you dressed all in black?"

"Shh!" Mrs. Brunelli silenced her young daughter.

"That's all right. Well, my aunt died last week, and so I'll wear black for a month to honor her."

Alyssa's eyes grew wide.

Mrs. Brunelli crossed herself. "I am sorry for your family."

"Thank you."

"Can we have a cookie, Mama?"

"These cookies, what makes them special?"

"Well, my grandfather would save left-over pie dough and make these as a treat for the neighborhood children."

Mrs. Brunelli picked up a pigtail and bit into it. A small smile emerged. "Good." She gave each of her daughters a cookie. "How do you make them?"

"You take left-over pie dough and roll it out into a large thin rectangle." Maggie slowed down. "Then spread melted butter over it. Sprinkle with cinnamon and sugar and roll the dough into a long fat log." She pantomimed the idea. "Then cut off pieces about a finger-size."

"Finger size?"

Maggie looked at the two little girls. Alissa giggled and spoke to her mother in Italian. Mrs. Brunelli laughed.

Alissa spoke up. "Momma thought you said cut fingers for the cookies."

Maggie laughed too. "I'm glad you like the treat." She took a deep breath. "But I came here to talk to you about your flower making. My aunt owned a hat shop on Christopher Street that I now own. She bought her silk flowers from the Fleiss Factory. I know they pay you to make these flowers." She pointed to the flowers in progress.

Mrs. Brunelli nodded.

"But the work season only lasts nine months. What if you worked for me instead, all twelve months?"

A skeptical look crossed Mrs. Brunelli's face.

"I'd buy the materials, and you'd still make the flowers here in your home. Instead of working for Mr. Steinberger, I would pay you."

Mrs. Brunelli stared at Maggie. "No. We cannot anger Mr. Steinberger. We need the five dollars eighty cents that Tessa makes each week. And my husband, he would have to go to the Pig Market."

"The Pig Market?"

"Where men who get in trouble have to go; and hope for a day job."

Maggie shook her head in disgust.

"But I would pay you steady wages for each of the twelve months, instead of by the piece."

A heavy silence draped itself over the room.

"How much do you get paid for this?" Maggie gestured to the flowers on the table.

"Ten cents per batch."

"How many flowers are a batch?"

"144"

"You mean you earn ten cents for making 144 silk flowers? How many batches can you make in a day?"

"On a good day, we make 3 - 4 batches. The girls help."

"How many hours?"

"Five hours, sometimes more."

Maggie tried not to show her outrage. Mrs. Brunelli was making about 33 cents a day. "How do you make the flowers?"

"We pull the ....", Mrs. Brunelli looked to Alissa.

"Petals."

Mrs. Brunelli nodded. "Then we...", She pretended to pinch the petals to a stem. Sometimes we use..." Again, she looked at her daughter.

"Paste."

Good lord, Mama would be horrified. Even the miners' wives don't live in this kind of poverty.

"Mrs. Brunelli, please talk this over with your husband. You would be working twelve months instead of nine with a steady paycheck."

Mrs. Brunelli remained silent.

"There is one more idea. I want to hire Tessa to work in my shop. I know she's been taking classes in bookkeeping at Greenwich House. I could use her expertise."

"My Tessa, she knows nothing about selling hats."

"But I could easily train her. She would work Tuesday through Saturday from ten in the morning until five-thirty in the evening. I can afford to pay her $2.00 per day. What do you say, Mrs. Brunelli?"

Mrs. Brunelli uttered not a word, but walked over to the framed picture of the Blessed Mother and offered a prayer in Italian. Tears streamed down her face.

Maggie stood quietly.

"Thank you. I will talk this over with my husband."

"Thank you for allowing me into your home, Mrs. Brunelli. I hope we'll be able to work together."

Mrs. Brunelli nodded. "I will save a few of the cookies for my husband, and tell him your grandfather is a baker."

Mrs. Brunelli's eyes sparkled. Then she lowered her lashes, and her face returned to its former visage.

"Come girls, cookie time over. We get back to work."

Maggie walked back up to West 4th Street, hoping this idea would work and that the fall out would not force Mr. Brunelli to the Pig Market.

***

Sean was already in the room, waiting when Maggie arrived. "Maggie, I'm so sorry about your aunt. And even sorrier that I couldn't be there to help you." He walked over and hugged her.

As Sean held her a bit longer, she inhaled his shaving cologne. Having his arms around her was a comfort.

"Is there anything I can do now?"

"Continue to be my friend."

"I will always be that, and more, if you would let me."

"Sean, I don't know what to say."

"Then, don't say anything. I'll know by your actions when you decide to be my girl."

She blushed. Standing on tiptoe, she kissed him and let the kiss linger. A flood of emotions enveloped her, and she felt her heartstrings flutter.

Children came running into the room. Sean grinned at her and then went off to work. Maggie peered around anxiously for Gabrielle and Tessa. They arrived last, with Tessa carrying Maggie's basket – filled with cookies from Mrs. Brunelli.

"I did it, Miss Maggie! I quit the factory!"

Maggie hugged Tessa, and Gabriella started clapping. Soon, all the children were clapping, even though they could not possibly understand what had just transpired.

Tessa announced that she would appear first thing Monday morning at the hat shop.

"Oh, the shop is closed on Mondays. You don't have to come until ten o'clock on Tuesday morning. Ten Christopher Street. I'll be there waiting for you."

At the end of the afternoon, Sean came back to the Reading Room.

"Maggie, how about going to a baseball game with me?"

"Now?"

"No, later."

"I've only been to local games back home."

"This will be at the Polo Grounds. I'll buy us tickets for the April 28th game against the Philadelphia Athletics."

"Are your friends going too?"

"Yes. Each of us is bringing our lady friend."

"Oh, and with my kiss, I became your lady friend?" She teased.

"I'm hoping so."

***

Tuesday morning, about a quarter to ten, Maggie turned the corner of Christopher Street and saw Tessa standing at the door to the shop.

"I wish you could have seen Mr. Steinberger when I announced I was quitting. His eyes almost popped out of his head. He roared at me to get to my station, but I turned, waved to the other girls, and headed for the door.

I've never been so scared in all my life. He shouted that he would fire my mother. I turned and yelled, 'She's not working for you anymore, either.' I didn't hear what else he said because I walked out."

"You were brave, Tessa."

"My knees were knocking the entire time."

"I'm proud of you, and your mother. Your father, too, for agreeing to let you quit. Now, let me give you a quick tour of the shop. You'll take today to get comfortable with the inventory and follow what I do if we get any customers. Then, in a day or so, you can wait on your first shopper."

The morning progressed at a leisurely rate. Right before noon, the bell tinkled. Maggie hoped to see a customer, but to her horror, Mr. Steinberger swept into the shop.

"Think you're pretty clever, don't you, first firing my niece and then stealing my workers from me."

"I own this shop now. Isabelle has never been a productive employee. I gave her two weeks' pay, which was much more generous than any gesture you would have made."

"Your aunt and I had an agreement. You have no grounds to undermine me."

"My aunt is dead! The shop is mine now, and I do not, I repeat, do not have to do business with you or with Isabelle."

Mr. Steinberger pushed in front of Maggie and wagged his finger in her face. "You'll be sorry about this, wait and see. When you least expect it, I'll pull the rug out, and there will be no one to help you." Spittle flew from his lips.

"Are you threatening me?"

"I'm giving you a warning."

He turned to Tessa. "Think you're getting a better deal? Your family will rue the day they turned their back on me. I curse the lot of you."

Fuming, he left the shop.

Maggie sat down and held Tessa's trembling hands. "He can't hurt you, Tessa. He is all bark and no bite."

"I think you may be wrong about that, Miss Maggie."

***

Monday, April 28th provided the perfect weather for a baseball game. The skies were clear, and the temperature hovered at a steady seventy degrees. According to the Catholic church, Maggie could now dress in light mourning, which meant no more black. She chose a navy skirt, white blouse, and brought along her new navy spring cape. Realizing that large women's hats would be frowned upon by spectators, she wore the modern cloche style of a simple navy silk-blend trimmed with a small bow on the side.

Their group of twelve arrived at the Polo Grounds in time to purchase popcorn and beers.

Maggie studied the program so she would be able to hold her own in a conversation about the game. Jack Quinn was pitching for the Yankees, but she had no idea what SO meant next to his statistics. Hopefully, no one would ask.

The score registered two to zero, Philadelphia ahead, in the seventh inning when everyone in the stands stood up and stretched their arms. Watching the spectators, Maggie stood up as well. Then she decided it was the perfect time to visit the bathroom.

Assuring Sean that she knew how to get back to their seats, Maggie walked the steps to the mezzanine and headed toward the concession stand.

She searched for the sign for the Ladies Room and moved in that direction. Suddenly, two little boys dashed out in front of her, almost causing her to fall. She bent down to retrieve her handbag.

As she straightened up, she found herself face to face with a small group of spectators.

"Rees!"

"Maggie? I certainly never expected to see you at a ball game." He switched on his most charming smile.

Maggie's eyes narrowed, then shifted to his companions.

"May I introduce Mr. and Mrs. Goldman, and their daughter Jessica. They are the family I met in the Catskills. Mr. and Mrs. Goldman, this is Maggie Canavan from Greenwich Village. We were good… friends when I lived in New York."

Maggie drew herself up to her full height, and before she could stop herself, she blurted out, "Is that all we were, Rees, good friends in the afternoons?"

Caught off guard, Rees seemed to fluster as he spoke. "Maggie, Mr. Goldman is now my boss at the *Chicago News*."

"How convenient."

Tension filled the air, and Mrs. Goldman coughed a delicate sound.

"It was nice to see you again, Maggie, but we need to get back to our seats." Rees had perspiration beading on his forehead.

As the Goldman party turned to leave, Jessica Goldman looked directly at Maggie with an inquisitive look on her face.

"I hope you have better luck with him than I did," Maggie announced and then turned and walked to the Ladies Room. It took all her will power not to look back.

Once inside the restroom's safety, she found an empty cubicle. When she sat down, she realized she was shaking. *How could Rees act so cavalier? I hope I made him uncomfortable.*

She gave herself time to settle her nerves. The emotions of anger and indignation zinged through her—but not tears. When the horn blared signaling the end of the stretch period, Maggie ventured out to rejoin her group.

"You were gone so long, I was afraid you'd gotten lost," grinned Sean.

"Lost? No. I think I found myself."

Sean looked puzzled, and Maggie linked her arm in his. Partly for reassurance and partly for support.

TWENTY-SEVEN

Maggie smiled at the azure blue New York sky with puffy white clouds sailing across it like ships.

Tomorrow, on Memorial Day, she and Sean would celebrate ten months of knowing each other. Sean had planned a ferry ride and picnic on Staten Island. Perhaps Jessie had been right. Everyone does get a second go-round with love. It wasn't the same type of love as with Rees, but her heart flip-flopped whenever Sean smiled at her, and she felt safe and desirable in his arms.

He had been patient, waiting for her feelings to match his. Even though Rees had left her gun-shy, she intended to tell Sean how much her feelings had grown. The picnic would be the perfect opportunity to let him know.

With Mass behind her and the volunteer hour not till two o'clock, there was time to visit Mr. and Mrs. Brunelli and celebrate Tessa's official designation as Maggie's new roommate.

They had agreed on a Tuesday through Friday night schedule. Then on Saturday through Monday, Tessa would stay with the family. It seemed to be the perfect solution, even Maggie's parents had been pleased—especially after Mrs. Simons had vouched for Tessa's character.

Maggie whistled as she walked the now familiar path through the Village to MacDougal Street. She was approaching her first anniversary of living in New York. Who could have ever predicted that she would become the owner of Hats by Anne-Marie?

Walking along the littered sidewalk, she came within a birds-eye view of the Brunelli's tenement when she saw two patrolmen dash into that building. She couldn't be sure, but one of them looked like Sean. Maggie called out his name, but the neighborhood noise drowned out her voice.

She hastened her walk, hoping to catch up with them.

In the next instant, her body was blown through the air and knocked to the ground with such force that she lay dazed in the street.

Minutes later, she opened her eyes. An incessant ringing hurt her ears, and her eyes stung from smoke. Attempts to sit up were fruitless; everything tilted. Her legs were twisted beneath her and blood dripped from her face.

Aware of a severe pounding in her head, she couldn't understand the eerie silence around her.

My God, what just happened?

She saw people running in different directions. All she remembered was that she had been going to visit the Brunelli family.

A New York City patrol car careened to a stop, and two policemen ran from their vehicle toward the massive cloud of smoke and fire.

With difficulty, Maggie managed to raise herself on one elbow. MacDougal Street was a nightmare come to life. The Brunelli's tenement had been reduced to charred mounds of burning wood and broken bricks. The bizarre elements that had survived, like a single kitchen sink, sat forlornly in the debris.

Then with a crash, the adjacent building's side wall collapsed. Shattered glass lay everywhere. With a few more minutes another wall toppled.

A fire truck arrived on the scene, and Maggie watched the men work to extinguish the flames. She could not hear the sirens, but the intense heat prickled her skin.

Oh, dear God, had she seen Sean? People were running everywhere, but she didn't see anyone she knew.

A policeman ran over and slid his hands under her armpits and dragged her farther away from the burning buildings. His mouth moved, but none of his words were audible.

She tried to ask him about the Brunelli family, but she could not tell if her words had been garbled or understood.

The policeman laid her on a debris-free spot and motioned to her to stay put.

Maggie started shaking in convulsions. The next thing she knew, someone covered her with a blanket. Moments later, an ambulance arrived, and volunteers lifted her body inside the vehicle.

With tears of frustration, she tried to talk, but the firemen shook their heads, indicating they did not understand her. The ambulance picked up speed, and when it stopped, Maggie saw they had brought her to St. Vincent's Hospital.

Inside, a nurse and doctor began jabbering, but the ambulance men intervened. The nurse disappeared and then returned with a piece of notebook paper. She wrote on it, "You were injured in the MacDougal Street explosion. It appears you've lost your hearing. We are going to give you a sedative and let you rest. You'll wake up here, in a hospital room. Do you understand?"

Maggie nodded feebly. The next thing she knew, the nurse administered a needle into her upper arm, and Maggie lapsed into a sedated sleep.

**

When she woke, confusion clouded her brain. *Where was she?* Her eyes adjusted to the dim light of the room and the bare walls. She remembered St. Vincent's. There had been a terrible explosion at the Brunelli's apartment building.

She struggled to recollect what had happened. The explosion occurred on Sunday, but Maggie didn't know what day it was now. The hands on the wall clock pointed to 9:00, but with the curtains drawn and the lights dimmed, Maggie couldn't tell the difference between day and night.

What about Sean? Hadn't she seen him enter the Brunelli's

tenement?

She called for a nurse, but her throat burned, and her voice cracked. The pounding in her head had not subsided and brought tears to her eyes.

A nurse appeared and smiled, seeing Maggie awake. She tried to communicate, but Maggie shook her head and pointed to her ears. The nurse checked Maggie's chart, then wrote out, *I'm glad to see you awake. You have two perforated eardrums. Your hearing will eventually return, but not for several days, or possibly weeks. For now, rest.*

Maggie put her hand to her forehead and made a pained expression.

The nurse wrote out, *do you need something for the headache?*

Maggie nodded. The nurse checked the chart once more and then gave Maggie a pill with a small glass of water.

Maggie wanted to ask about Sean, but the nurse left the room. The brief encounter left Maggie exhausted, and she slipped back into a deep sleep.

***

It took Maggie three more days before the intolerable headache gave way to a light ringing in her ears. *Be thankful you are alive. And that your hearing is beginning to return.*

Maggie had no idea what had happened to her purse or where she lost it. Without proper identification, no one would have known to call her parents back in Porters Glen.

But Sean would have known something was wrong when Maggie did not show up at Greenwich House. Why hadn't Sean tried to find her?

She winced. Anne-Marie, and now this? She prayed that both Sean and Tessa's family were safe.

The nurse checked in during afternoon rounds, and Maggie asked if there had been any information on two policemen she had seen enter the building on MacDougal.

The nurse looked down at the floor. "Are you related to a

policeman?"

"No."

"Perhaps you should talk to one of the doctors."

A few minutes later, a doctor entered her room. "Good afternoon, young lady. We are all delighted with the progress you're making."

"I want to know about the two policemen I saw right before the explosion."

The doctor's expression changed.

"I'm sorry. No one in the building survived."

Maggie's throat constricted. "No one?"

"Most families were out, enjoying the afternoon. Two elderly ladies were inside on the top floor. I understand the two policemen who entered the building were responding to a call. The sixth precinct can probably give you more information."

"Thank you."

Maggie lie back down on the bed. Sean couldn't be dead. Perhaps he was lying in a different hospital, or it had not really been him entering the tenement.

Anne-Marie's words came back to her. "Never underestimate the city. Just when you think you're on top of the world, the city yanks you back to Earth, and slams you up against a wall."

Was this part of what New York demanded? Wasn't it enough that the city had taken Anne-Marie? Did it need Sean, too?

Fear caused tears to stream down Maggie's face, and when the nurse came in, Maggie turned her face to the wall, pretending to have fallen back asleep.

***

"I'm sure, Mama. My hearing has come back, and I don't need you and Papa to come here. I'm being released today and can go back to work in a day or two."

From the other end, she heard her father. "We're coming to New York, no matter what. We'll be there tomorrow night."

Later in the afternoon, Maggie left St. Vincent's and took a cab back to the apartment.

The day may have been warm and gentle, but she didn't notice. She walked into her apartment, as if in a daze.

Sean had died in the explosion. Mrs. Simons had come to the hospital and painfully broken the news.

The one saving grace was the Brunelli's had not been home. They had taken the family to Coney Island to celebrate their freedom from the Fleiss Factory. For now, they would live in Brooklyn with an aunt until they could find new quarters. Tessa would stay as planned with Maggie.

Maggie made herself a cup of tea. Then she ventured to her easel and began a sketch which morphed into the face of Sean. Hours passed. As the picture neared completion, Maggie broke down in fierce sobs and cried until no tears were left.

***

Her parents arrived the next evening. Their haggard faces betrayed their emotional exhaustion.

"Oh, Maggie, I could not go on if anything had happened to you. Thank God, you weren't hurt. We called Mrs. Simons, and she told us about your friend, Sean. We are so sorry."

"Thank you, Papa."

The evening was a subdued one, with Annie fixing soup for dinner. They haphazardly stirred the soup but only sipped at the broth. After they gave up on eating, they talked about the explosion, although Maggie could not remember many details. The only thing that mattered was Sean's death.

Her parents stayed for two more days, visiting Mrs. Simons at Greenwich House and meeting the entire Brunelli family. They were more than pleased with Tessa as Maggie's soon-to-be roommate.

"Are you sure you are all right?"

"Yes, Papa. The store is doing well, and Tessa will move in with

me this week for four nights a week. I promise I will call home every Sunday after Mass."

"You can still change your plans and come home."

"Thank you, Mama, I know that. But I still want to stay here and live in New York for a while. Losing Aunt Anne-Marie and now Sean, are two of the hardest things I have ever had to bear."

Her father held her in his arms. "You're strong, Maggie. The blood of survival runs through your veins."

***

A memorial service for the two police officers had been set for the following Saturday afternoon. Maggie's parents had returned home, and she was ready to reopen the hat shop. She asked Tessa to go with her to the church service.

When they arrived at Our Lady of Pompeii, the church overflowed with people who came to pay their respects. Maggie did not cry until the entire sixth precinct walked down the center aisle and filed into the front pews.

The funeral Mass lasted an hour, but instead of bringing closure, it brought Maggie further sadness about the unfairness of losing Sean.

Tessa suggested that they stop and have a cup of tea on the way home.

"My parents wanted me to ask you about the rent. You did not discuss that with them."

"Instead of paying rent, I want you to enroll in bookkeeping classes at Katherine Gibbs. That way, you'll become my bookkeeper."

"Thank you, Miss Maggie. You are so generous."

"Tessa, if we are to be roommates, you will have to call me, Maggie."

"All right." Tessa smiled.

Once Tessa left for home, Maggie headed to Barrow Street. She no longer wanted to participate in the volunteer program at Greenwich

House. That would only bring reminders of Sean.

Maggie trudged inside the entry door and made her way to the office. Mrs. Simons had been to the memorial Mass and was now seated at her desk. She listened to Maggie's explanation. "We will miss you, Maggie. You can come back at any time, and always join me at a Heterodoxy luncheon."

"Thank you. I will still stay in touch, but I need time to sort things out. I hope you understand."

***

Maggie reopened the store the following Tuesday and threw herself into the work, letting Tessa wait on the customers while Maggie filled out orders for trimmings.

Late in the day, Maggie was paid a surprise visit by two of Sean's friends from the precinct.

"Hello, Maggie. We wondered if this would be a good time for us to see you."

"Certainly."

"We went to Sean's boarding room the day after the service to clean it out. He didn't have a lot of possessions, but we gathered up his clothes and donated them to St. Vincent de Paul Society."

"Sean would have approved of that."

"When we cleaned out his closet, we found this on the top shelf." They handed her a locked box approximately the size of a kitchen toaster. Taped to the top of the box was an envelope, "To be opened by Maggie Canavan in the event of my death."

This surprised her. Taped onto the box was a key.

"Thank you." She took the box and laid it aside. "Have there been any investigations into the blast?"

"The official report says it was an explosion caused by a gas leak."

"So, an accident."

"We assume so. The owner of the building will receive compensation from the insurance, though."

"Who is the owner?"

One of the patrolmen flipped open a notebook. "Says here the building's owned by the Fleiss Company."

Tessa's face went white. "*Mio Dio!*"

Maggie gasped, "Steinberger?"

***

That evening Maggie placed the locked box on the living room table. She hesitated to open it, but gingerly lifted the lid.

Inside were several documents and a bank book. Sean had written out a will. He stated that without any family, he wanted Maggie Canavan to inherit all his worldly possessions and to be the beneficiary of his bank account. He had signed the paper with his full legal signature, Sean Ward Murphy.

She opened the bank book next. Sean's savings account amounted to four hundred dollars.

Then she rifled through the remaining documents, his high school graduation diploma, his membership card in the Knights of Columbus, and a photo of two adults who she assumed were his parents.

At the bottom of the box lay a larger sealed envelope, yellowed with age.

She broke the seal and peered inside to find a piece of cloth. Tilting the envelope, she watched as a strip of fabric slid out onto the table.

Maggie gazed at it for a moment. Confused, she picked it up.

Holding the material, she saw blue embroidered sides, and the name Ward spelled out in the red thread, sewn diagonally from top to bottom. The fabric had been cut on the top bias, indicating that this was the bottom half of a larger piece.

She looked back in the envelope. With heart pounding, she stood up and walked over to the secretary and retrieved Anne-Marie's Bible. Opening it, she pulled out Edward's birth ribbon and sat back down at the dining table.

Her fingers trembled, but she held the ribbon with the name Ed embroidered at the bottom and matched it with Sean's fabric showing the name Ward at the top. When connected, the two ribbon halves formed a perfect whole—and the name, EDWARD.

Sean had been Anne-Marie's lost son.

Maggie stared at the birth ribbon. With no tears left in her body, she lowered her head to the table, her soul numb with shock and impenetrable grief.

GREENWICH VILLAGE, NEW YORK CITY

SUMMER 1919

TWENTY-EIGHT

As hard as Anne-Marie's death had been, Sean's death had taken away Maggie's spirit. She longed to confide in someone about the devastating sorrow but remained loyal to her promise to Anne-Marie.

She plodded through the days at the shop, went to bed early each evening, and did not even have the desire to pick up a paintbrush.

And then, slowly, she found that her art was her salvation. As the brush slid across the canvas, and a picture came to life, the dull ache in her heart began to ease. At first, she drew on her memories of Anne-Marie and Sean; then she turned to paint numerous posters for VOTES FOR WOMEN.

By the end of summer, many of Maggie's posters were strategically placed throughout the Village. They depicted various women, all of whom deserved the vote. Each poster was signed M C. The accomplishment brought her back to life.

In August, newsboys were harking papers telling of the 19th Amendment passing in the Senate, 56 – 25. Each state now had to vote to ratify the Amendment. The possibility of women getting the vote was close to fruition. Maggie wished that Anne-Marie were alive to witness the milestone.

***

On a mid-August Monday, she awoke and contemplated how

to spend her free day. She could stay home and paint, or visit an art museum.

Instead, she went looking for Gladys.

It only took a few minutes in Washington Square to locate her. As always, the pigeons hovering over a bench gave her away.

Maggie eased herself down next to Gladys, who did not stir or acknowledge Maggie's presence.

Not exactly sure what she even wanted to say, Maggie reached into Gladys's paper bag and tore bread cubes into smaller pieces, then threw them up in the air for the birds.

"Drop some on the ground for the others."

Maggie followed Gladys's directive.

"He's gone; isn't he?"

How had she learned about Sean's death? "Yes, he was killed in the MacDougal Street explosion."

Gladys did not reply but continued to feed the pigeons.

"I don't know if I can stay here. In the Village, I mean. Maybe I should go back home to Maryland."

Silence.

"You see, Sean was…very special. Losing him has made me question everything."

Gladys emptied the remaining crumbs on the ground. "You would not be the first to quit."

Maggie sat up, straighter. "I hardly think of it as quitting. I gave it a year."

"Then how would you know?"

"Know what?"

"If you had what it takes to live here."

Maggie swallowed her indignation.

"If you want to sketch, then sketch here. If you want to go back to your former life, then go back. The choice is yours."

In a small voice, Maggie said, "But I don't want to go home. I want to stay here."

Out of the blue, a group of boisterous crows landed on an

adjacent bench. All of Gladys's pigeons took flight.

Maggie stared at the birds, and in spite of herself, she began to count.

"You don't have to count; there are seven."

Maggie looked at Gladys. Did she know the rhyme?

The old woman continued. "One for sorrow, two for mirth. Three for a wedding, four for a birth. Five for silver, six for gold. Seven for a secret that can never be told."

Then Gladys stared at Maggie with a penetration that rattled Maggie's soul.

Maggie held the stare, although Gladys's clairvoyance was unmistakable.

"Your policeman is gone, but he was only one thread of your life here. Keep your secret, but stay and find the other threads."

Then Gladys stood up, brushed crumbs from her lap, and sauntered off.

Maggie sat in silence. So much had happened in a year. After a while, she stood up and walked to the eastern entrance of the park. From there, her footsteps took her to the corner of Washington Place and Greene Street. She peered up at the eighth and ninth floors of the Asch Building, feeling once again the enormity of the Triangle tragedy.

"I promise, you will not be forgotten," she whispered to the ghosts, to Anne-Marie, and to Sean.

Heading home, she passed a beauty shop. In the front window, a poster advertised the newest in women's haircuts, the bob. She hesitated for a moment, opened the door, and went inside.

An hour later, she emerged with the new hairstyle. Looking in the mirror, she saw a wiser girl peering back at her.

I'm no longer the young ingenue who came to New York expecting to glide into art school. From now on, I will use my art to promote the hat shop. One more year, then I'll know for sure.

After dinner, Maggie went to her easel and began to sketch. She tossed aside her first attempts. They would not catch anyone's attention. Then she hit upon the idea of designing ads for the shop to coincide with the women's rights movement. The message would be that all women deserved equality with one another.

The first newly redesigned ad showed a factory girl seated at a sewing machine. The words underneath said, "She deserves a hat by Anne-Marie." Then at the bottom of the ad was the name, address, and phone number of the shop.

The girl was dressed reminiscent of a Triangle girl, but the face in the ad was the face of Anne-Marie Charbonneau.

Maggie would pay for the advertisement to be placed in *The Ladies Home Journal* and also *The New York Herald*.

She designed the next ad to show an office woman standing by her desk. The words underneath stated, "She deserves a hat by Anne-Marie." Again, the pertinent information was placed at the bottom, and the woman's face was still Anne-Marie's.

The third ad showcased a housewife standing at the sink. She too deserved a hat by Anne-Marie.

As summer sped along, the old leather satchel became crammed with samples of Maggie's sketches for advertising the shop. Energized with the idea of designing the ads, Maggie sketched a different woman for each week's advertisement, always with the same slogan, and always with the face of Anne-Marie.

It did not take long before Maggie witnessed an uptick in sales. She called home to inform her parents about the success of the ad campaign.

"Maggie, I am so proud of you," her father said.

She had been waiting for those words her entire life.

***

On a sultry August morning, Maggie decided to rearrange the front window display and moved the small step ladder to the front. Climbing up and reaching in, she swapped hats from two mannequins and then elevated the central mannequin so it would be in a more prominent view from the sidewalk.

When she finished rearranging the window to her satisfaction, she stepped outside the shop. The street was already busy with New Yorkers going about their morning, but Maggie didn't pay attention. She scrutinized the new display and looked up at the freshly painted sign, Hats by Anne-Marie. Happy with both, she breathed a sigh of satisfaction mixed with a drop of perseverance.

She crossed the threshold and went back in when the shop bell tinkled behind her. Looking up, and thoroughly expecting Tessa, Maggie was surprised to see a tall, good looking man, perusing the merchandise.

"May I offer assistance?"

"Oh, hello. No, not really." He walked around the displays. "I think I'm struck by this purple hat, here. Can you tell me the price?"

"Actually, it's *aubergine*."

"Excuse me?"

"*Aubergine*. That's French for eggplant. The color of the hat is eggplant, not simply purple."

The stranger broke into a wide grin. "I shopped here once before, back in December to buy my kid sister a Christmas hat. But the young lady who waited on me didn't use any French words." He smiled.

Maggie wracked her brain, trying to remember him. Winter, when she and Rees were still…

The customer moseyed over to a different hat and picked it up off the mannequin's head. "And this one, I suppose is not orange?"

"No. It's tangerine." A stifled giggle escaped her lips, and she moved her hand to cover her mouth.

"I dare say, I had no idea that selecting a hat would be so complicated."

"Is this for your sister or a sweetheart?"

"Oh, no. It's for my Mum."

"Your mother?"

"Yes. You thought I came in here to purchase a hat for a lady friend?"

"Well, that does happen."

"I came in here because I was crossing the street when I saw you in the front window, rearranging the display."

"That's why you came in?"

"Yes. But then I remembered I'd shopped here before. It's my Mum's birthday in a week, and I know she would love one of your beautiful hats, especially since the names of the colors are so... descriptive. The eggplant hat, it is purple, isn't it?"

Maggie smiled. "No. It is eggplant. Do you want me to ring it up or the tangerine hat?"

"The tangerine." He followed Maggie back to the cash register. "This shop is Hats by Anne-Marie, so are you Anne-Marie?"

"No, Anne-Marie was my aunt. She owned the shop for years but died last spring from the flu. I took over. Do you work around here?"

"Not exactly, I'm a student at NYU."

Maggie studied him. He was tall with chiseled blue eyes like her father's. Older than the usual college boys, he carried himself with a no-nonsense air. "Are you starting your studies or finishing them?"

"I'm hoping to finish within the next two years. I work during the day at an accounting firm in Chelsea and take classes at night. I'm going for a degree in accounting."

"That's admirable."

"Thank you."

Maggie wrapped up the tangerine hat and tabulated the receipt.

"I know this might seem a bit bold, but would you like to go with me to an NYU outing at Coney Island next Sunday? It's a farewell to summer party."

"Coney Island? I think that's a bit of a commitment. We don't even know each other."

"All right. Let's remedy that." He checked his watch. "Can I take you for high tea today? We could talk and get acquainted."

"High tea? Isn't that formal?"

"Not in the least."

"I thought high tea was a dress-up affair."

He threw his head back and laughed. "Not in England it isn't. High tea means you sit at a high table, like a dining table and drink tea with real sandwiches. You're thinking of afternoon tea, which the upper class has served to them on a low table with fancy sandwiches."

"And how do you know all this?"

"Because I'm a Brit. Well, I do have my naturalization certificate, so I'm an American, too. My Mum, Dad, and sister live in Brooklyn. I'm here in the Village so I can finish my studies at NYU."

"What else do you know because you're a Brit?" She teased.

"I know that eggplant is also called aubergine in England." He laughed, and so did Maggie.

She checked the clock on the wall. "All right. I can leave at four for tea. Should we exchange names now, or when you come back to get me?"

He smiled. "I'm Will Yarrow."

"All right, Will Yarrow. I'm Maggie Canavan."

He looked at her with a quizzical expression on his face.

"Is something wrong?"

"No. It's just that you have the most unusual eyes. They're the color of wild English heather."

"No." She smiled. "They're the color of the wild Irish Sea."

***

Strong women weave threads of courage across the generations.
Linda Harris Sittig
Purcellville, Virginia
2019

Maggie stayed in New York.

She married Will Yarrow the following June at the Little Church Around the Corner on East 29th Street and wore an ivory colored tea-length dress and carried a nosegay of violets. Atop her head, perched a hat of her own design with silk flowers attached to the sides. The color was champagne, and no crows were present at the ceremony.

Maggie and Will moved into Maggie's apartment on West 13th Street so that Will could finish his degree at NYU and Maggie could continue running the hat shop. Within five years she and Will would start a family and move out to the New Jersey suburbs where their children would have a real backyard. The shop was sold to another woman, equally passionate about hats.

Tessa became a bookkeeper, married, and moved to Brooklyn.

On August 26th, 1920, the 19th Amendment to the United States Constitution was ratified in full, granting American women the right to vote.

Maggie's Irish ancestors, the Canavan family, had arrived in the 1850s at a dock in Philadelphia. Leaving the poverty of Ireland behind them, they hoped for a better life in America. The youngest daughter, Ellen, yearned for the right to vote.

Almost seventy years later, Maggie Canavan would fulfill that dream when she arrived at the polls to vote in the first Presidential election where American women counted.

RECIPES FROM COUNTING CROWS

Grand-papa's Pigtail Cookies

Here is the original recipe for Grand-papa's Pigtail Cookies, like the ones served at Charbonneau's Bakery in Porters Glen. This recipe has been passed down for four generations.

Make pastry for a one crust pie or buy a package of **refrigerated** pie dough. Use the amount of dough for one pie crust. Let it rest at room temperature for 15 minutes while you melt three tablespoons of butter. Then roll out the pie dough **THIN** into a rectangle of 12 x 8 inches. Brush the dough with two tablespoons of the melted butter. Then sprinkle three tablespoons sugar over all the dough. Go back and sprinkle one tablespoon of cinnamon. Starting with the long end, tightly roll up the dough in cigar-like fashion. Then cut the rolled dough into 3/4-inch portions. Place each cookie, cinnamon swirl-side up, on a parchment paper covered cookie sheet. Brush the tops with the remaining melted butter and sprinkle with additional sugar. Bake in a 350-degree oven for 10 – 12 minutes, allowing cookies to be slightly underdone when removed. Cool, then eat.

New York Egg Cream*

In a tall glass, squeeze two full squirts of Ubet Chocolate Syrup. Add in 1 and ½ tablespoons of milk. Then fill the glass with seltzer water almost to the top of the glass. Stir with a long spoon until the chocolate dissolves, and foam appears.

*In New York, each restaurant or deli had their own guarded recipe for making an egg cream. The recipe shared here is courtesy of Attman's Delicatessen, Baltimore, Maryland. Ubet Chocolate Syrup is available online from multiple websites.

AUTHOR'S NOTES

What led me to writing Counting Crows?

Like Maggie, I first read about the Triangle Shirtwaist Fire in an article. And like Maggie, I felt the mixed emotions of outrage and compassion. The story struck a personal note with me because I had spent the first five years of my life living in Greenwich Village, where the Triangle Factory had been located.

I felt compelled to write a story incorporating the Triangle tragedy.

Then there was my mother. My mother was drawn to New York City like a homeward bound honeybee, and once there, she experienced both excitement and heartbreak.

I based Maggie on my mother, Mildred Katherine Weikel, who did indeed leave home in her twenties and move to New York City. My mother was the granddaughter of James Nolan from Book #1, *Cut From Strong Cloth*.

My mother found housing in the Village, and both she and her roommate worked at a costume agency on Broadway, similar to Van Groot's. She loved New York, and she loved hats.

Anne-Marie's hat shop was modeled after my mother's favorite store, Jenny Banta's, whose hat boxes were pink and white striped.

Although my mother did not sketch, she wrote. She penned many short stories but never submitted any for publication. Like Maggie, she was rebellious and creative—yet insecure; independent, and strong-willed, but vulnerable. Having a strong Irish heritage, she was also very superstitious.

I based the character of Marie (Anne-Marie) Charbonneau (from Book Two, *Last Curtain Call*) on a relative from Eckart Mines,

Maryland who left the small coal mining village for a life in a big eastern city. For my novel, I made that city be New York.

Many of the characters in *Counting Crows* were formed from real people. Crystal Eastlake was inspired by feminist Crystal Eastman, a vital member of the real Heterodoxy Club. Jessie was Jessie Tarbox Beals, a famous Village photographer. Mrs. Simons was Mary Simkovitch, who ran the Greenwich House Settlement.

Samuel Steinberger was based on the manager of the Triangle Shirtwaist Company.

Vincent Fox came from Val Fox, an extremely talented painter who lived in the Village and became friends with my mother. In later years he and his wife moved to a small town in New Jersey to raise their two boys, Rich and Brian. A few years later, my parents left New York City and moved to that same small Jersey town, where the two families reconnected.

A print of Val Fox's Washington Square hangs on the wall of my writing office. It is my writing muse, and I look at it every day. The cover of this book shows his painting.

The character of Rees Finch was a must. So many readers wrote asking if Nash Finch from novel one (*Cut from Strong Cloth*) would ever appear in another one of my books, that I created his grandson, Rees, to carry on that legacy. The name Rees came from a gregarious bartender on St. Simons Island, Georgia.

As for Edward's birth ribbon, years ago I attended a museum exhibit entitled "Threads of Feeling." As I walked through the displays, I saw many birth ribbons from Foundling Hospitals. It was heartbreaking to see where a mother had relinquished her baby with only a birth ribbon pinned to the clothing for identification. In most cases, the mother believed when her life improved, she would be able to reclaim her child.

In reality, that hardly ever happened. Almost all the children who came to Foundling Hospitals were never reunited with their birth mothers.

The ribbons were often cut diagonally on the bias with the hospital retaining one half and the mother keeping the other half for later identification.

I stood in front of one particular ribbon with blue-sided embroidery and the name of a baby boy stitched in red thread, and I couldn't hold back the tears. The idea of having to give up a child was just too painful. I knew, then and there, I would eventually weave this part of history into one of my novels.

All the settings in *Counting Crows* were authentic, as were the historical events.

The sweatshop industry, once the backbone of the New York Garment Industry did eventually change faces. Instead of young Italian and Jewish women, it soon supported newly arrived immigrants from other countries who were willing to work for low pay, even in unsafe situations.

In 1938, President Franklin D. Roosevelt signed the Fair Labor Standards Act where underage children were finally protected from being brought into the factory system; in most cases.

Not until 1961, fifty years after the Triangle Fire, was a memorial plaque installed on the former Asch Building in commemoration of the 146 victims who died. In 1991, the building was designated a National Historic Landmark with a secondary plaque added. The Asch Building is now called the Brown Building, owned by New York University.

The first time I stood in front of the Asch Building, I imagined being transported back in time to the day of the fire. Goosebumps surfaced on my arms. Like Maggie and my mother, I too, am superstitious. It must be the Irish in us.

Many of the buildings in the story still exist in Greenwich Village, while others have sadly been demolished. The building that would have been Anne-Marie's hat shop is today a nail salon in the West Village.

Bigelow's Pharmacy still sits in its original location on Sixth

Avenue, selling its iconic lemon body cream.

The Cooper Union is still a prestigious university with an excellent art program.

The townhomes of Patchin Place are privately owned, but many famous artistic residents lived there over the years.

Coney Island is still a recreational mecca for city residents, although its former beauty has dimmed.

Mrs. Blanchard's Boarding House, nicknamed the House of Genius with so many resident writers and artists, was demolished. In its place is the new student center for NYU.

Jessie's art gallery is also gone. Its location would have been approximately where the Sheridan Square Garden is located today.

Maggie's apartment on West 13th Street survives. And it is where I spent the first few years of my life.

Washington Square Park is still the anchor of Greenwich Village. On my last visit in 2018, I saw an eccentric woman, like Gladys, feeding the pigeons.

And what of Will Yarrow?

He was my father.

CHARACTERS

IN THREADS OF COURAGE SERIES

CUT FROM STRONG CLOTH: Philadelphia, 1860 (Book #1)
Ellen Canavan – daughter of James and Cecilia Canavan, Philadelphia
Patrick Canavan – Ellen's brother
James Nolan – Irish immigrant now owning a Kensington textile factory
Mary Ready – James Nolan's sister
Ed Ready – Mary's husband
Michael Brady – an itinerant Irish laborer working in the Kensington area
Catherine Biddle – a Philadelphia Quaker woman who befriends Ellen Canavan
Magdalena Fox – a chemist, working in Savannah, Georgia
Dr. Fallon – a surgeon working in Savannah
Nash Finch – an entrepreneur living in Savannah

LAST CURTAIN CALL: western Maryland, 1894 (Book #2)
Louis Charbonneau – the owner of the bakery in Porters Glen, Maryland
Stephen Charbonneau – the son
Annie Charbonneau – the oldest daughter
Marie Charbonneau – younger daughter
Frankie Hennessey – a coal miner in love with Annie Charbonneau
Jonathan Canavan – a school administrator also in love with Annie Charbonneau
Josie Canavan – Jonathan's sister and a high school English teacher
Randall Meyers – coal company superintendent

Herman Schumn – paymaster of the coal company
Aunt Hulda – the Charbonneau's housekeeper

COUNTING CROWS: Greenwich Village, New York, 1918 (Book #3)
Maggie Canavan – daughter of Annie and Jonathan Canavan
Marie Charbonneau – Maggie's aunt and owner of a hat shop in the
    Village
Rees Finch – Maggie's first love in New York City
Sean Murphy – an Irish cop who takes a fancy to Maggie
The Brunelli's – an Italian family working in the sweatshop industry
Vincent Fox – an art teacher and mentor to Maggie
Isabelle Levine – sales girl in the hat shop
Mary Simons – manager of the Greenwich House Settlement
Gladys – the iconic eccentric woman of Washington Square
Jessie – the owner of an art gallery who befriends Maggie
Samuel Steinberger – a factory manager in the garment industry
Will Yarrow – Maggie's future husband

ACKNOWLEDGMENTS

Oh, where to begin?

I read extensively on the WWI Era of Greenwich Village, and a listing of many of those sources follows the Acknowledgements.

So many people graciously gave of their time and expertise in helping me recreate Maggie's experience in New York.

A hearty thank you goes to the Historical Society of New York City who allowed me access to viewing many of Jessie Tarbox Beals' photos of the Village, and whose tenement exhibits gave me the insight I needed to place Maggie in the right place at the right time.

I consulted the postings of the Greenwich Village Society for Historic Preservation on a weekly basis, and am indebted to them for all the valuable information they share.

The Tenement Museum on Orchard Street helped me recreate the Brunelli's apartment and helped me feel the aura of the family space.

Mr. Ronnie Jenkins, the concierge at the Washington Square Hotel, was my muse during the week I encamped, researching the Village. Mr. Jenkins has been with the hotel for over 40 years and knew the stories of the people who made the Village so well known. I am indebted to his sharing with me.

The sales staff at Bigelow's Pharmacy gave me the store's historical album so I could study photos of back-in-the-day and explained to me the tradition of colored water orbs in the front window. The globes were thankfully green on the week of my visit. While there, I did buy a jar of their famous lemon body cream and must admit, I am now a loyal customer.

Another thank-you goes to the staff at Greenwich House, now

used as a senior center and preschool. I was given access to the upstairs dining room and to stand in the hallway where the classrooms were located. Without visiting the settlement house, I would not have been able to accurately describe the scenes involving Maggie's volunteering and meetings with Sean.

Brian Fox, the son of artist Val Fox, read through the manuscript making sure the details I wrote about fictional character Vincent Fox lined up with his father's real history. Brian also photographed his father's painting of the Washington Arch for the cover of this book. And, I am also indebted to award-winning photographer Doug Graham, who photographed the cover.

Thank you to the Camera Club of Leesburg, Virginia, who helped me with the pertinent details of photography for Rees Finch. David Schwartz of The Camera Heritage Museum in Staunton, Virginia, spent time showing me the 1918 Graflex camera that Rees would have used as an up-and-coming press photographer.

A thank you also goes to artists Jill Perla and Alice Powers who allowed me to sit in on art lessons they were giving and showed me the appropriate paints and brushes so I could accurately write the scenes about Vincent Fox.

My Beta Readers, Harley Gamble, Diane Helentjaris, and John Rogers, read through the manuscript with eagle eyes, giving me feedback on the plot, characters, and emotional twists. Thank you. And to my fellow authors at the Round Hill Writers Group, thank you always for your continued support.

Thank you to my freelance editor, Jennifer Kay, who meticulously worked with me to make the final version polished before sending it to my publisher.

Eric Egger, my publisher at Freedom Forge Press, continues to believe in stories where people strive for the freedom to pursue noteworthy lives. Val Muller, my editor and art director at Freedom Forge Press, wins my undying gratitude for always making my books better than I could have envisioned.

My mother taught me to love New York City and took me

back to the Village throughout my impressionable years, pointing out the apartment house where we had lived on W. 13th Street, the church where I was baptized, and of course dragging me to Macy's for the Half Yearly Sale. Little did I know then that all those experiences would become fodder for my novel. If there are libraries in heaven, then I hope she is reading *Counting Crows*.

And yes, she did teach me to stand behind the stool of anyone in a New York luncheonette, so I could grab the seat as soon as it was empty.

The other person to whom I always owe so much is my husband, Jim. He is and continues to be, my true north star.

A SHORT LISTING OF SOURCES
FOR FURTHER READING

Bernstein, Leonard S. *Death by Pastrami*. Uno Press, 2014.

Barry, John M. *The Great Influenza*. Penguin Books, 2004.

Bial, Raymond. *Tenement*. Houghton Mifflin Books, 2002.

Carder, Mark E. and Andrew Sparber. *The Cumberland Electric Railway Company*. Privately published, 2017.

Dickhuth, Anita. *Images of America: Greenwich Village*. Arcadia Publishing, 2011.

Diehl, Lorraine B. *Subways*. Clarkson Potter Publishers, 2004.

Freedman, Russell. *Kids at Work*. Clarion Books, 1994.

Grippo, Robert M. *Macy's*. Square One Publishers, 2009.

Heyman, Therese Thau. *Posters American Style*. Harry N. Abrams, Inc., 1998.

Hoffman, Laura J. *Coney Island*. Arcadia Publishing, 2014.

Kisseloff, Jeff. *You Must Remember This: An Oral History of Manhattan*. Harcourt Brace Jovanovich, 1989.

Low, William. *Old Penn Station*. Henry Holt and Company, 20007.

McFarland, Gerald W. *Inside Greenwich Village: A New York City Neighbhorhood1898-1918*. University of Massachusetts Press, 2001.

Miller, Terry. *Greenwich Village and How it Got That Way*. Crown Publishers, 1990.

Alfred Pommer & Eleanor Winters. *Exploring the Original West Village*. The History Press, 2011.

Probert, Christina. *Hats in VOGUE*. Abbeville Press, 1981.

Sochen, June. *The New Woman: Feminism in Greenwich Village 1910-1920*. Quadrangle Books, 1972.

Soyer, Daniel, editor. *A Coat of Many Colors: Immigration, Globalism, and Reform in the New York City Garment Industry*. Fordham University Press, 2005.

Stonehill, Judith. *Greenwich Village: A Guide to America's Legendary Left Bank*. Universe Publishing, 2002.

Strausbaugh, John. *The Village.* HarperCollins Publisher, 2013.

Van Kleeck, Mary. *Artificial Flower Makers.* New York Survey Associates,
Inc., 1913.

Von Drehle, David. *Triangle.* Grove Press, 2003.

Young, Edith. Student's Manual of Fashion Drawing. John Wiley & Sons,
Inc., 1919.

Born in Greenwich Village, New York City, and raised in Northern New Jersey, Linda was lured into reading by *Lad, a Dog* and *Nancy Drew, Girl Detective*. Later her attraction to history and a bit of wanderlust led her to study in Switzerland, before returning stateside to earn a B.A. in History and a M.Ed. in Reading. Linda eventually chose to live in Loudoun County, Virginia, where the beauty of the Blue Ridge Mountains inspires her to write.

Combining her passion for history, stories, and the need for literacy, she began publishing commentaries on how parents could encourage the love of reading with their children. That led to a twenty-year weekly newspaper column, "KinderBooks" (*Loudoun Times-Mirror*); a non-fiction text, *New Kid in School* (Teachers College Press); and writing for a nationally syndicated educational newsletter, *The Connection* (PSK Associates).

Linda has been twice recognized by the Virginia Press Association with Certificates of Merit for her journalism. Her articles have appeared in *The Washington Post, The Reston Connection*, and *The Purcellville Gazette*, in addition to numerous professional journals and short story anthologies. Passionate about lesser known women in history who led extraordinary lives, Linda blogs monthly at www.strongwomeninhistory.wordpress.com, and has followers in over 64 countries.

From 1982 – 1994 Linda received three separate distinguished

educator awards from metropolitan, state, and international organizations. She continues to teach at Shenandoah University in Winchester, VA, where she works with educators on how to immerse literature into children's lives.

Contact email: Linda@LindaSittig.com
Website: www.LindaSittig.com
Blog: www.strongwomeninhistory.com
Twitter: @lhsittig

"Every woman deserves to have her story told."

FREEDOM FORGE PRESS

ABOUT US

Freedom Forge Press, LLC, was founded to celebrate freedom and the spirit of the individual. The founders of the press believe that when people are given freedom—of expression, of speech, of thought, of action—creativity and achievement will flourish.

Freedom Forge Press publishes general fiction, historical fiction, nonfiction, and genres like science fiction and fantasy. Freedom Forge Press's two imprints, Bellows Books and Apprentice Books, publish works for younger readers.

Find out more at www.FreedomForgePress.com.

Made in the USA
Coppell, TX
02 November 2020